MY GREATEST Mistake

T. GEPHART

Published by T Gephart

Copyright 2021 T Gephart
978-0-6487943-6-3

Discover other titles by T Gephart at the retailer of your
choice or on Facebook (https://www.facebook.com/pages/T-
Gephart/412456528830732), Twitter (https://twitter.com/
tinagephart), Goodreads, or tgephart.com

Cover by Hang Le
Editing by Insight Editing Services
Formatting by Elaine York, Allusion Publishing
www.allusionpublishing.com
Proofread by Rebecca, Fairest Reviews and Editing Services

MY GREATEST
GREATEST
Mistake

Dedication

*For Sally, who told me I could when I thought I couldn't,
and read each chapter as I wrote it.*

*And for the amazing Aerial and Pole Divas.
I was so mentally broken this year and
your passion, support, and community gave me wings.
#PDREZ #PADR I'm going to twirl and spin forever.*

Chapter 1

THEN - Zara

Coney Island, Brooklyn, New York

"**C**'mon, Zara, I want to go to the fortune teller lady and find out if Taylor is the man I'm going to marry. We can ride the rollercoaster later," Belle whined, her bright blue eyes full of wonder.

The smell of popcorn and cotton candy peppered the air as excited squeals and screams competed against the noise of music and motorized rides. It was sensory overload—lights, sounds and smells coming at you from every angle as you got jostled in the crowd.

It was summer, Belle's pale skin pinked from the afternoon's sun even though I reminded her a million times to reapply sunscreen. She was so much smaller than me, and not just because of the two-year age difference. Her pixie-like features were so little and dainty, she looked almost breakable. Unlike me, who was taller than some of the boys in my class. I wasn't dainty either, nor did I aspire to be, inheriting our dad's booming personality as well as his height, brown hair and brown eyes.

I sighed, shaking my head as I pulled her through the crowd. "Belle, we have one hour of freedom. Sixty-minutes. I don't want to waste them sitting in a chair while some crazy lady tells us stuff that isn't even true. And you're twelve, why are you even worried about getting married anyway?"

Mom and Dad had—begrudgingly—agreed to let us explore unsupervised for an hour. Oh, they were still around, probably tracking us via our cellphones from a safe distance, but that was as good as we were going to get when our dad was a criminal prosecutor. Honestly, it was a wonder he'd agreed, giving us the statistics on child abductions and warning us not to split up. He'd know if we even thought about it, somehow, he always did.

She pouted like she usually did when she didn't get her way, folding her arms across her chest in an exaggerated protest. "But I love him, Zara. He's the first boy I've ever *really* liked. And he likes me too. It's fate and I want to see if we end up together forever."

It was worse than I thought.

My sister had always been an idealist, believing in fairy tales, happily-ever-afters, and everyone's good intentions. If I wasn't so sure she'd probably end up heartbroken and jaded sometime later in life, it might've been endearing. But I was her older sister, and while there was a better-than-average chance she wasn't going to end up with her sixth-grade crush, I didn't want to be responsible for breaking her spirit any sooner than necessary.

"You need to stop stealing Mom's romance novels, Belle."

It wasn't a mystery where Belle got her whimsical, rosy outlook; our mom believing the glass was always half-full. Guess you kinda needed to be when you were a social worker in New York, while also being married to an attorney who was allergic to penicillin and injustice. Our parents were the perfect yin-yang, both hard and soft in all the right measures, and while they were probably more paranoid with us than most of the parents I knew, they loved us, and each other, fiercely.

Belle's lips hid her grin, plastering the doe-eyed *who-me?* look that constantly got her out of trouble. It was a talent for sure, her ability to get her way with virtually anything, something I couldn't help but admire. "I don't know what you're talking about, Zara. But, if I *did* read Mom's books, I'd know that you can take over the world, be a badass annnnnnnnnd still have the man of your dreams."

Well, at least there was that.

"Plllleeeeeeeeeeaseeeeeee." She blinked, doubling down on the charm as her clasped hands nestled under her chin. "We'll use my money, and I'll ride anything you want right after. I won't even complain that my hair is getting messed up."

It was a tempting offer, and a negotiation that was hard to walk away from. Five minutes listening to some woman spout bullshit for the remaining balance of time for me to spend totally however I see fit.

"Deal!" I held out my hand, our father drumming into us the importance of formalizing the closing of any agreement. "But it needs to be quick, and don't even think about dragging me into it. She tells you what you want to hear and then we go straight to the rollercoaster."

Belle waved me off, her smile at getting her way—again— widening as she led us to the tent. "Sure, sure, we won't ask about how you end up as the Attorney General or whatever."

"Supreme Court Justice, kid. Get it right." I laughed, following her against my better judgment.

It was no surprise there wasn't a wait, the faded canvas of the tent looking like it had seen better days as we stepped inside. Belle didn't even wait, barging in with enough energy and enthusiasm for the both of us.

"Hi!" Belle waved, the dark-haired woman sitting behind the table not looking old enough to fit the stereotypical description.

She was maybe a college kid? The painted-on wrinkles and cheap wig doing their best to make her look like "Madame Delia" even though I was fairly sure she wasn't.

"Come in, come in," Madame Delia beckoned, perking up at the sight of customers and possibly a payday. "Let's see what the magic stones have in store for you."

Belle clapped her hands in excitement, not even noticing my eyeroll as I sat down beside her.

Magic stones.

What kind of fake bullshit was this? She wasn't even going to flip over some Tarot cards or gaze into a crystal ball like all the other fraudsters? God, I hoped Belle was going to be satisfied even if her "experience" wasn't as advertised; regardless, it still counted, we had a deal.

"I want to know if me and Taylor are going to get married." She barely took a breath. "Also, if I'm going to be famous. I can sing and dance, I just haven't worked out which one I like better."

Madame Delia made a show of picking up the stones, waving her hands around like it would convince us—it didn't—like it was somehow more legitimate. "Let's see, little girl, the stones know all."

I was about to correct Madame Fake-ster that while Belle looked like she was eight, she was days away from her thirteenth birthday, when Belle threw out her hand and made me stop. She knew me as well as I knew her, and while there'd be a cold day in hell before I'd let a scam-artist call me a "little girl" she was fine with it if it meant she got her way.

"Don't ruin it," Belle whispered. "I need to know."

Inwardly I cringed, praying the stones and their magic didn't take long as my hands balled into fists by my sides. I'd be quiet, but only because Belle had been the one to ask, waiting not so patiently as non-remarkable colored rocks dropped onto the table in an uncoordinated heap.

"Ahhh, yes, I see your future," Madame Delia said, studying the rocks like they were actually spelling it out. "But love, love will be a long and difficult road for you. It will be a long time before you find your special someone. If at all."

"What?" Both Belle and I responded at the same time, not expecting such a harsh dose of reality.

I mean, sure, Taylor wasn't my sister's soulmate.

And relationships were hard work and if she eventually got married and had a family, it was going to have to be with a really special guy. Preferably someone with a backbone too or Belle was going to walk all over them.

But that wasn't what we were paying for, only putting up with the charade, because unlike me, my sister liked to hear stories that probably weren't true. She even believed in fortune cookies and horoscopes, and that hotdogs weren't filled with all kinds of extra bits no one would even consider eating if they weren't slathered in ketchup.

No one wanted to hear bad news. That was what the internet was for, not to be provided by a drama major with a superiority complex.

"No." Belle shook her head, tears welling in her eyes. "Check the stones again. There's been a mistake." Her emotions bubbled to the surface, always having been overly dramatic. "You can't tell me that I'm not going to find love ever. Take it back."

Even though I knew it was a scam, and that nothing the woman told us was true, I hated she'd upset Belle. And while, yes, my sister could give a daytime actress a run for an Emmy, intentionally making someone upset wasn't a good service model.

"Tell her," I insisted. "Tell her you made a mistake."

"I don't control the stones. I can only read them as they fall."

Madame Delia was playing the part until the end, refusing to budge or modify her so-called reading even if it meant making someone cry.

"The stones?" Irritation bit at my voice, annoyed we'd wasted precious time only to have Belle get upset. "These are nothing but colored rocks." My fingers reached down picking up the offending pebbles and tossing them aside.

It was childish, throwing rocks, but tossing Madame Delia wouldn't be acceptable and I wasn't sure I had the arm strength. She took a step back, anticipating she might be my next target before her eyes fell down to where they'd collected on the floor.

"You find love!" She pointed accusingly at the scattered stones. "You find love, and he's a good man, and you're together forever."

I turned, still irritated but glad that she'd finally given us what Belle had wanted. "See, Belle. She made a mistake and it's fine now. She said so herself. You find love, it's forever, he's a good man."

At no point had I bought into it, knowing the whole charade was horseshit. But if it meant my sister's happiness, then I'd play along. At least until we could get out of there and onto a rollercoaster.

Madame Delia cleared her throat, shaking her head as our gazes connected. "Not her. You. His name is . . ." She snapped her fingers, expanding on the theatrics. "Edwin. Edwin Carlisle. He's the one."

It was tempting to argue, to tell her she'd gotten the wrong sister. I didn't give a rat's ass about my potential true love, too worried about getting a solid GPA so I could get into a decent college and then law school.

And Edwin, really? She couldn't think of *any* other name? Possibly something popular from the last three decades? Or maybe it was her safety net, building in a clause so I couldn't come back later and accuse her of lying. The *"well, it's not my fault you didn't meet Edwin Carlisle. I just told you he was the man of your dreams and would love you forever, not where to find him."*

A loophole.

Which just made it worse.

"We're leaving," I announced to Belle, not willing to give Madame Delia any more attention than she had already received. And with a firm and definite tug, I pulled Belle from the tent, leaving the stones, the reading, and hopefully the bad memories as we left.

Belle was uncharacteristically quiet, her small hand grasping mine tightly as we silently navigated the crowd. I didn't need to see her face to know she was probably fighting back tears, worried that if she did cry, I'd yell at her for being silly and dramatic.

"Hey." I pulled us to a stop, angry at the stupid woman who'd upset my sister in the first place, and at myself for obviously being so hard on her. "I'm sorry."

"Why are you apologizing?" Belle hiccupped, her eyes glassy as her head tilted back.

"Because sometimes, I'm an asshole, and make fun of the fact you care about this stuff. It was insensitive of me. It's okay to want love and a relationship. And just because I think you're too young to worry about that or don't see that as important, I shouldn't make you feel like you can't want it."

Belle's head nodded, a single tear trailing down her cheek as she wiped it away. "You're right. It is silly."

"No, no it's not. And you know what, it's ridiculous what she said," I insisted, doubling down on my efforts to cheer her up. "Belle, everyone *loves* you. You've got more friends than I've ever had and anytime you meet someone, they can't help but smile at you. You're so talented and funny, and you constantly make people happy. Any guy would be lucky to have you. And if there's a reason that bitch couldn't see it, it's because there's going to be hundreds of them vying for your affection. You're going to have your pick. Like *The Bachelor*, but less sexist and with waaaaay better options."

Belle laughed, knowing that even her idealistic, romantic heart could see what a train wreck that show was. "Yeah, and they all have to bring me roses, not the other way around."

"Whatever you want," I agreed, glad to see the smile back on her face. "Whole bunches. The poor bastards are going to go broke."

She laughed again, sucking in a breath. "And I want to be your maid of honor when you marry Edwin."

God.

Really?

"Belle, there is *no* Edwin. He doesn't exist."

"If you're so sure, why don't you just agree then." Bell folded her arms across her chest, the sadness from earlier having disappeared and in its place smugness.

And she did have me on a technicality. If I was as convinced as I said, it would be a fairly easy promise to make, right? It was like promising if you became an astronaut and went to the moon, she could have my room. And I got airsick.

"Fine," I conceded. "If I marry a man named Edwin Carlisle, you can be the maid of honor." It might as well have been a trip to the moon, because they had the same probability.

"In *writing*," Belle insisted, pulling out a flyer she had advertising Madame Delia tucked away in her pocket.

For all her doe-eyed naivety, she wasn't an idiot. Then again, it had been drilled into us by our father that nothing was more ironclad than a contractual agreement. Hell, he'd even drawn one up for our allowance, stipulating the terms and conditions to guarantee our payout.

"Okay, okay. In writing." I looked around us, spying a small stall selling oversized novelty pens.

Begrudgingly, I parted with the few dollars it took to secure the ridiculous writing instrument, trying to balance it in my hand as I wrote very clearly on the back of the flyer.

*I, Zara Mathews, of sound mind and body, legally assure
that Belle Mathews will hereby be my maid of honor should I
marry Edwin Carlisle.*

It was signed, handing it over to Belle who inspected it and
put it in her pocket with a satisfied grin. "Now it's a done deal."
She threw her arms around me, looking at the pen still in my
hand. "Can I have that too?"

"Fine." I rolled my eyes, thinking it would not only be better
appreciated but it was more suited for her anyway. It was pink
with unicorns—enough said.

"Now can we go ride the coasters?" I asked, looking at the
time display on my phone and knowing it was going to be down
to the wire. Maybe we could ask Mom and Dad for an extra hour.
Surely once they'd seen we hadn't been kidnapped or gotten into
trouble—no one had to know about the Madame Delia mess—
they'd cave. Especially if Belle did the asking, everyone had a
really, *really* hard time saying no to her.

Belle nodded, the earlier shitshow obviously forgotten.
"Yep, we can go now. And when we're done, milkshakes!"

"Sounds good," I agreed, looping my arm around hers.
"Let's go scream until we lose our voices."

Her eyes brightened, always up for anything that was
extreme. "You're the best sister ever, Zara."

"You're not so bad yourself, Belle."

Chapter 2

NOW - Zara

"**S**ee, I told you this was a bad idea."

While I appreciated Belle's enthusiasm for celebrating my new promotion, a special dinner in my honor had been unnecessary. We could have easily ordered takeout, gotten it delivered to the apartment we shared, and toasted my success from the comfort of our living room in our pjs.

Instead, we had just finished appetizers at an overpriced Manhattan bistro when Belle had received the 9-1-1 call from Hayley, her best friend.

"We were not going to sit in our apartment on a Friday night like a pair of old ladies, Zara. They made you a senior associate and gave you an office, it's a big deal."

She was right, it was a big deal, and it was taking me a step closer to making partner. I knew at twenty-eight I was still a few years from sitting at the big boy table, but I was well on my way to eventually realizing my childhood dream of becoming a Supreme Court Justice. I was also getting the attention from all the right people for all the right reasons, and not just because I was a woman.

"Well, if we had been in our apartment when Hayley called, I would still be there instead of being in this cab on the way to the hospital. I still don't know why you're making me come. I'm not her birth partner." I sighed impatiently.

Hayley had recently decided my sister—who had the kindest heart of anyone I knew but wasn't exactly the most responsible person—needed to be with her when she brought her baby into the world. The baby daddy was out of the picture, and she didn't want a family member watching her deliver a watermelon from her vagina and then have to sit across from them at family dinners.

Honestly, I could understand that part. I loved my mom and my dad dearly, but it would be a cold day in hell before I'd let either of them see that. Assuming I had kids, which was a big *if*.

And of course Belle was only too thrilled at being selected, reveling in her appointed position like she'd been chosen for a lead role in a Broadway play. Which incidentally was her big dream, and where she met Hayley who up until getting herself in the family way had dazzled audiences as Christine in *Phantom of the Opera*. Belle had been one of the dancers, still working her way up the ranks.

"Zara!" she exclaimed dramatically. "You *know* I'll get lost looking for the right place to go. I can't read maps, and hospitals make me nervous. And Hayley needs me! I'll probably end up in the janitor's closet while she's all alone, bringing a miracle into the world, and I'll have let her down. I will hate myself forever for disappointing her. All you need to do is come with me, help me get to Hayley, and then you can leave. I'll even pay for your ride home annnnnnnnd I'll give you my undying, unending love and adoration."

"I thought I already had that?" I laughed, her ability to still get her way after all these years never failing to impress me. "And I'm here, aren't I? And you might want to dial down the drama. I've got a feeling there's going to be plenty of that in the room without you."

Belle nodded, her eyes shining with excitement as we got closer to the hospital. "Oh, shit! I almost forgot." She dug into her large Mary Poppins handbag and pulled out a beautifully wrapped box. "I was going to give this to you when we were having dessert, but I guess that won't happen now. Anyway, congrats!"

My heart swelled, feeling a little bad about being so cranky over being inconvenienced. "Belle, you didn't have to give me a present. Dinner would have been enough."

"Noooooooo. This is special, and you neeeeeeeeed it," she insisted, pushing the box closer. "Besides, I had so much fun buying it for you and I want to see your face when you open it."

The glint in her eye was slightly unsettling, the excitement replaced by mischief. My gaze flicked to the driver who was mostly ignoring us, the brightly colored box not giving me any clues as to what was housed inside. "Please tell me this isn't anything embarrassing. It's not from a sex shop, is it?" I groaned, knowing with Belle it could be anything. "And it better not be illegal either."

Belle laughed, nudging my shoulder with hers. "Come on, would I do that?" *Yeah, yeah she would.* "Just open it already."

Tentatively—because honestly it could be anything—I slipped off the red satin bow and lifted the glittery silver lid. Inside, nestled in a bed of crisp white tissue paper, was a beautiful wooden gavel, polished so evenly I could almost see my reflection in the lacquer. "Oh my God," I gasped, pulling it out of its wrapping and letting the box drop to the floor. "Belle!"

It was beautiful, expertly carved with such workmanship that it had to be handmade and custom. I couldn't stop looking at it, my vision getting blurry as I blinked furiously.

"Do you like it?" She grinned with expectation. "I know you're not a judge yet, but my drama teacher always told us it's good to have a visual cue. Something tangible to hang on to and remind you of your goal. I'm positive it's how I landed my gig for *Phantom*; I've been carrying around the stub from when we went to see it years ago. Now look at me! I just know my big break is coming, and this," she pointed to the gavel I'd cradled against my chest, "is coming for you."

I was such an asshole.

It was possibly one of the nicest, most thoughtful gifts I'd ever received, and Belle was the best sister anyone could ask for. Even if she was crazy impulsive and often dragged me into whatever shenanigans she got herself into.

"I love it, Belle. It's perfect." I stroked it, testing the weight in my hand and imagining myself sitting behind a bench wearing a black robe. "Thank you so much."

She nodded, thrilled I'd loved her present as much as she assumed. "I knew you would. Now we just need to find Hayley and you can go home and practice. You're out of order!" Her little fist smacked her thigh dramatically. "Sidebar immediately!"

I laughed, shaking my head at her little display. "You've been practicing."

"Always." Her hands knotted, shoving them under her chin as she grinned.

There wasn't any more time for conversation, the cab pulling up in front of Mount Sinai Hospital. "Here you go, ladies," the cab driver called over his shoulder, tapping his fingers impatiently while Belle counted out the money for the fare.

My feet hit the sidewalk as we shuffled out of the car, the bustle of the city still very much in full swing despite the sun having set an hour earlier.

It was my favorite time of the day, the early evening hours when the lights lit up the city and the night was filled with possibilities. There was an excitement that crackled in the air, the slight element of uncertainty because of the dark, while the busyness of New York City cradled you in familiarity all at the same time.

"Okay, let's get you up to labor and delivery." I looped an arm into hers, still holding the gavel with my other hand.

Unlike Belle, I'd brought a more elegant clutch purse instead of a huge handbag to dinner which meant I had nowhere to put it. I'd accidently left the box in the cab in all the excitement, leaving me holding my new prized possession.

It was probably for the best anyway, I didn't want anything happening to it and I would be on my way back home sooner than later. Besides, everyone in the hospital would be too busy to worry about me and my fancy accessory, so who cared.

We dashed through the main doors, our focus on finding Hayley before the baby crowned, laughing as we hustled our way to the site map.

"Edwin Carlisle, please report to the Nurses' station. Edwin Carlisle."

We both froze, the pop of the loudspeaker finishing its announcement as we turned to look at each other.

Belle gasped, pointing to the sky like she'd just heard the voice of God. "Did she just say—"

"No, we must have heard it wrong," I responded, convinced there was no way the announcement contained the name of my fictitious boyfriend who apparently was supposed to be my soulmate.

I mean, it had been *years* since that stupid visit to Coney Island, and I'd almost forgotten about it entirely. Obviously not totally, because the minute the name was mentioned, my heart did a weird summersault I knew wasn't healthy.

What the hell was that?

I didn't believe that shit, why did I even react at all?

"What?" Belle asked, incredulously. "We *both* heard it wrong? I don't think so."

Fine, I was willing to concede that the chances of both of us hearing the name—which didn't seem to fit in the current century—were remote, but that didn't mean anything. It was probably someone's grandfather or some crusty old man who'd wandered off confused. And regardless of what Madame Delia had said, I was not shacking up with some guy who was ready to pick out a headstone.

Nope.

Not happening.

"Okay, so we heard it, but we need to get you to Hayley and I'm almost positive that whoever *Edwin* is, he is not the guy for me." I tugged on Belle's arm forcefully, hoping to move her feet which were glued to the floor.

Last thing we needed was for Belle to get sidetracked. While I knew first-time moms could sometimes take a while to deliver, the sooner Belle was sitting safely beside Hayley, the happier I would be. It would lower the chances of trouble as well, which at the moment were rating fairly high.

Belle shook her head, staying rooted in her spot protesting like she was chained to a tree ready for condemnation at the hands of a logger. "Zara, you *have* to go see him."

"Belle," I huffed, half exasperated and half unnerved. "It was years ago, and you have to know that woman was full of shit, right? You had plenty of boyfriends. Some have even proposed. If she'd been right, you'd be by yourself, knitting tea cozies, surrounded by cats. She was wrong about you, and she was wrong about me."

Just as I'd predicted—without the aid of painted rocks—there'd been a long line of suitors who'd fallen under Belle's infectious charm. First boys, then men—all of them captivated, making heart-eyes at my sister while pledging their undying devotion. Some getting down on one knee with a shiny diamond ring. Belle had turned them all down because as much as she loved the attention and was still a hopeless romantic, she bored easily and lost interest even quicker.

"But was she wrong? I'm still single." Belle's eyes widened, her hand anchoring on her hip as she refused my continued tugs.

"By choice!" I pointed out. "You have been in love more times than I can count."

She waved her hand, dismissing me and the truth, and went with her own version of events. "Or maybe I wasn't. Maybe I was just infatuated and deep down I knew I wasn't in love which is why I broke up with them."

Great, of all the times for my sister to decide to find logic.

"Belle." I rolled my eyes. "What is it you expect me to do? Head to the nurses' desk and say, '*hi, you don't know me but you're the love of my life.*' We're in a hospital. They're going to think I've either escaped from the psych ward or they're going to put me in it."

Wouldn't do wonders for my career aspirations either.

"And," I continued, "he's probably gone now anyway."

"You *promised*. You made an agreement in writing. So whether or not he's gone, you need to at least go see," Belle insisted, pointing in the direction of the nurses' desk even though—apparently—she didn't know the layout of the hospital.

I scoffed, drawing in a sharp breath. "That stupid agreement was for you to be my maid of honor if I married him. It said nothing about me making a fool of myself in front of the medical staff at Mount Sinai."

"And how are you supposed to marry him—therefore fulfilling the agreement to me—if you don't meet him?"

She should've been a litigator.

Completely focused on finding whatever tiny loophole there was, even though to everyone else it was utterly unreasonable.

I was ready to continue my objection, prepared to argue like I was defending an innocent man on death row. But as ridiculous as the whole situation seemed, it was quicker to head to the nurses' station, confirm Edwin Carlisle had left, and get the hell on with delivering Belle to Hayley. And while I'd never admit it to Belle, part of me was slightly curious.

"Uhhhhhhhhh." I swore under my breath, my heels clicking on the tile as I almost jogged to our rerouted destination.

He wasn't even going to be there, I'd convinced myself. Going through the charade purely because, honestly, it would take less time and less effort than arguing.

Belle followed closely behind, her smaller strides moving into an animated skip in an effort to keep up.

And then.

Both of us stopped short.

We hadn't even made it all the way to the nurses' station, the desk still a couple feet away, but I needed a minute before going any further.

With his back to us stood a man.

Tall—over six-foot by my estimation—wearing a tailored suit so well it was impossible to miss how outstanding his body was. Broad shoulders took up all that expensive real estate in his jacket like it was paying Manhattan rent, his strong back tensing within the fabric as he twisted. It was mesmerizing to watch, the incredible ass that I found when my eyes dropped, our reward for their journey southward.

Shit, I whispered internally, slightly embarrassed I was obviously ogling a stranger. It wasn't my style, forcing my gaze back to his head where—I mistakenly thought—it was safe.

It wasn't.

Thick black hair flirted with the top of his collar, the short waves just long enough that it teased at what would have been a conservative cut.

If he was a grandpa or some older guy, he was obviously doing some black-market drugs that had stopped the hands of time. And maybe I'd been too hasty in my declaration of not being interested. Senior citizens needed love too, and if his front was half as attractive as his back, then I'd at the very least need to take a look.

To confirm it was drug use, of course.

Belle cleared her throat, biting back her grin as she pointed to him. "Go on, I'll wait here."

Her words jolted me, the kick of reality I needed to shake whatever bullshit hormone imbalance I'd been experiencing, and remind me I was in a hospital, about to approach a stranger. A seemingly attractive stranger, but a stranger, nonetheless.

Shooting her a stern sideways glance to warn her off any typical Belle shenanigans of interference—her assurance to *wait there* wasn't binding without a proper agreement—I took my first tentative step.

Only the first was tentative though, finding my confidence and straightening my back as I got closer. I wasn't some meek and delicate flower who crumbled into a pool of hormones at the sight of a good-looking man. I also knew that being attractive meant nothing, he could be rude, obnoxious, and conceited, all of which would have me losing interest almost instantly despite that incredible package.

My nerves still buzzed even if I didn't outwardly show it, my chin kicking up a little higher as I tapped him on the shoulder without hesitation. "Excuse me."

I wasn't the only one who hadn't hesitated, the handsome stranger turning as two dark blue eyes met mine, his incredibly handsome face lighting up with an amazing infectious smile.

He was too beautiful.

With the kind of face you found in expensive, thick and glossy magazines, both sexy, seductive, yet so goddamn compelling.

If that was the work of dark web pharmaceuticals, then I wanted in.

"Hi." I waved, having retrieved my hand from his shoulder before it did anything else more inappropriate. "I'm sorry to disturb you, have you got a minute?" My eyes darted to the nurse he was conversing with; the woman already having gone back to her computer screen. Whatever business they'd been discussing had either ended organically or I'd interrupted, and she was too busy to care either way. Good thing too, because I'd prefer not to have an audience.

"Surrrree." The word was unnecessarily elongated as his lips edged into a teasing grin.

His head tipped to the side, moving away from the desk. It was maybe three steps, both of us edging closer to the wall which gave us as much privacy as we were going to get.

"Hi," I said again. "I know this sounds really crazy," *it doesn't just sound it, Zara,* "but I was wondering, is your name Edwin Carlisle?"

There was no easy way to ask, no subtle way to segue into a conversation where I discovered his name. And considering Belle *still* had to get to Hayley *before* she had the baby, I didn't have the luxury of time to finesse it. Besides, the guy—whether he was Edwin or not—probably had a million things to do.

His eyes dropped down to the gavel I was still clutching, not having occurred to me to ask Belle to hold it. "Am I being subpoenaed, Your Honor?" The smile got wider.

There was a playful edge to his tone, like he was more intrigued by my sudden demand of his identity rather than annoyed. And if circumstances were different, I might've assumed he was flirting. But surely no one flirted with a strange woman in a hospital, did they?

"Ha!" I laughed, holding up the gavel and acknowledging it. "Actually, judges don't serve subpoenas. But nice try."

His beautiful dark blue eyes flicked over my body, studying me a little more closely than I thought was necessary. "A little young to be a judge, aren't you?" His hand waved, not waiting for my answer. "Unless you're some law prodigy. Is *that* what we're dealing with?"

Wait. Was he *flirting* with me?

While it was usually Belle who got the attention, I'd had the occasional guy try to pick me up in a bar or club. But not just randomly, in the middle of a hospital. And not by a man who was so . . . delicious. That *never* happened. At least not until they at least got to know me a little better.

And something must've been very wrong with me because for some stupid reason, I was enjoying it.

The corners of his smile edged wider as his brow lifted, like he knew, tipping his head to the side and waiting for me to answer.

"I'm Zara," I offered, sticking out my hand and attempting a proper introduction. "I'm a lawyer, but as much as I'd love to be a law prodigy, I'm not. This," I waved the gavel in my hand, "was a gift from my sister for my promotion."

"Pleased to meet you, Zara." He shook my hand, neglecting to add his name. "Congrats on the promotion. Now, why don't you tell me why you're so desperate to find Edwin Carlisle?"

There was a familiarity over the way he said the name, like he'd said it a million times before. And if he wasn't the guy we were looking for, surely he would've said.

The excitement bubbled inside of me, my own smile making an appearance. "It's too ridiculous to even repeat."

Instant attraction wasn't something that usually happened with me.

I could appreciate a guy who was good-looking, but then I needed a little more. Something beyond the window dressing to keep me interested.

He got closer, the familiarity and the proximity should've made me nervous, but it didn't. "I bet it isn't. And since it seems so important—finding *Edwin*—why don't you tell me."

My heart stopped, searching his face for confirmation even though he'd given me the answer. "I-I . . ." *there was no way I could tell him the truth*, "it was a stupid dare."

I wasn't sure what sounded more ridiculous, two grown women playing a game of dare or the idea that he could be my soulmate. I was usually better at thinking on my feet, the whole meeting-my-destiny-that-I-was-sure-was-bullshit throwing me off.

"Your sister?" His head tipped in the direction of Belle who was being completely obvious she was watching.

"Yeah." I nodded. "And since I've fulfilled the dare, I should go. So . . . thanks." I waved—ironically more the gavel than my hand—and turned to back away.

I mean, what else was there to say to the guy?

I'd met him, done whatever Belle had thought I was contractually obligated to do, and we still had to get my sister to the delivery ward.

So what if I was instantly attracted to him, and he had a nice smile. I knew nothing about him other than his name, which was just some weird coincidence.

It had to be.

Old-school names had made a comeback; it didn't mean anything.

Steady, measured strides took me away from Edwin, purposely not looking back as I moved toward my sister. Her face was filled with so much expectation, I almost felt worse for her than myself. Although, I wasn't sure I really could be disappointed in something that didn't happen.

There was a meeting, and it was over, what *more* did I expect?

A three-minute interaction was not long enough for me to form any kind of attachments, superficial or otherwise.

"Okay, now that's done, we need to get you to Hayley before this kid is born and has already celebrated his or hers first birthday." I didn't look back, keeping my voice unemotional so she wouldn't see I was slightly deflated.

Because as much as I knew it was ridiculous to even feel like that, if Belle sniffed it out, I'd have even bigger problems to deal with. Like her chasing the poor guy down and demanding he date me or something equally inappropriate.

"Oh, really?" Belle asked, her eyes widening.

Great.

Maybe I hadn't been as convincing as I'd thought.

"Belle, I said hello. What did you expect? A marriage proposal?" I huffed impatiently, tugging on her arm.

"Well, if I'd known there was a chance you might've proposed, I wouldn't have let you walk away."

The voice came from behind me.

His voice.

And suddenly Belle's excitement made sense.

It had nothing to do with me and what I'd said, but the fact he'd followed me back.

Chapter 3

Edwin

Meeting women wasn't usually a problem.

A bar, the grocery store—hell once I'd even gotten a phone number picking up my laundry from the dry cleaner. But a hospital, that was new even for me.

At first, I thought it was some kind of practical joke. I'd come to visit Nate, my old college roommate, since I was in town. Unlike me, he'd completed his medical degree and became an ER physician. I, instead, dropped out and decided to go into law.

It was still a bone of contention between us. Nate believed I should've followed him into the medical profession and saved lives. Instead, most of the time, I ended them. Not in the traditional way, I mean, they still got to be alive and breathe, but for most of them, they'd have preferred not to be. Not that most —if not all—of them didn't deserve it. And hey, I slept fine at night with my life choices.

But Zara—she wasn't a woman I was going to ignore whether it was a joke or not. Which was why when she said goodbye, I followed her.

She was beautiful. Her dark eyes were the color of a perfectly brewed espresso, with dark brown hair that hung loose in large waves, framing her gorgeous face. Her body was equally impressive, conservatively wrapped in a skirt and jacket that screamed corporate but was sexy all the same.

"Heeeeeyyyyy!" She twisted around suddenly, making me worried about where that gavel might land.

It was cute that she thought I didn't know how a subpoena was served, and I wasn't interested in correcting her.

"Zara." I liked saying her name and hoped I'd have the opportunity to say it a few more times. "So want to tell me more about this marriage proposal?"

Usually talk of marriage before you'd even dated someone was a huge red flag. And I'd been in enough bad relationships to run ten miles when it didn't feel right. But something about the situation told me Zara was different. And crazy or not, I wasn't running anywhere. Not at least until I got her phone number or a commitment I'd see her again.

She laughed nervously, shooting her sister a glare before turning back toward me. "It was nothing. Just a—"

"Dare?" I finished for her. "Well then, I don't want to be the one to stop you." I grinned, straightening as I waved a hand in front of me. "Go ahead, Zara, propose. I'll pretend to act surprised."

Unlike Zara—who had legs for days—her sibling resembled Tinker Belle. She was short and petite, with dirty blonde hair and light brown eyes, and would probably be carded until she was thirty. She was pretty, but wasn't even close to the level of heat Zara had simmering.

Her sister squealed, knotting her hands together and shoving them under her chin. "This is the best thing ever! Don't forget, I'm the maid of honor, we have an agreement."

"Would you stop!" Zara huffed, either embarrassed or frustrated. I had no idea how long their little game had been going on so couldn't guess either way. "I'm *not* proposing."

I wasn't sure who the statement was addressed to but claimed it all the same. "Oh? Shame." I tried to pull my mouth into an exaggerated frown, unable to keep from smiling. "I have my acceptance speech all worked out."

She rolled her beautiful eyes, nailing me with a look. "Even if I did propose, you weren't going to accept."

"We'll never know now, will we?" I shrugged, unable to help myself as I moved closer. "But I think at the very least we owe it to ourselves—and our almost trip to the altar—to have a coffee."

It was more direct than I usually was, and I'll admit, the strangest way I'd ever attempted a date. But regular or not, coffee would make a good start. Maybe dinner? I mean, if I had to be in town for the next week or two, I might as well take advantage of an opportunity that had landed in my lap.

Zara shifted on her feet, and I wasn't sure if she was uncomfortable with the indecision churning in her head or with me.

Before she had a chance to answer, her sister's phone erupted loudly. "Shiiiiitt," she swore. "It's Hayley. I've got to go. Better run. Have fun!"

Zara grabbed her sister's arm, stopping what looked to be a hasty escape. "I thought you said you didn't know where you were going? And that you needed me to personally escort you?"

She wasn't mad per se, more likely suspicious and if I'd been more of a gentleman, I might have been more interested. But the truth was that I was glad her sister was looking to leave, excited it meant that date or not, I'd get a few moments alone with Zara. But I wasn't going to leave any of that to chance, deciding to insert myself into the equation whether they wanted me there or not.

"You need an escort?" I asked, unsure of what I wanted the answer to be. "Because I know this place so well, I could probably give you a guided tour."

"No, I've got it!" The pixie clutched her phone against her chest. "You guys go plan your life together." She shot her sister a wicked grin. "I'll call you after the baby is born. Have fun."

And without giving either of us a chance to interject, she took off, leaving us behind to watch her leap and twirl like a ballet dancer in the direction of the elevator.

"So, Zara." I turned my attention back to where it wanted to be. "Seems like she has it covered."

She shook her head, sighing. "She does this. Pretends she isn't capable, only to have everyone else do it for her. But as you can see," she pointed to where her sister had run to, "she miraculously finds the ability when it suits her."

"Hmmm, and what about you?" I asked, not needing the confirmation to know she was probably the opposite. "You get people to do things for you too?"

She didn't even blink, meeting my eyes easily as the hint of a smile twitched at her lips. "When I need it."

Ooooooooohhh, maybe she wasn't as conservative as she looked, the hint of something naughty exciting me more than made sense.

"Something we have in common then," I offered, dancing the line between flirty and cocky. And as much as I wanted to believe I had her interest as much as she had mine, I wasn't so conceited to know she couldn't walk away.

"Edwin—"

"Zara." I cut off what started to sound like a goodbye and moved closer. "You were going to ask me to marry you, I think having a coffee is a good place to start."

Her eyes widened as she swore under her breath. "I wasn't going to ask you to marry me."

"Your Honor, I think the transcripts will show different." I smirked. "Should we review?"

She laughed, which was a good sign since I wasn't in the habit of begging women to go out with me. "You know, it's been a really strange night. Maybe coffee isn't such a bad idea."

I folded my arms across my chest, lifting a brow. "You want to give me just a little more enthusiasm there, Zara?"

"Well, that depends on where we go for coffee." Her manicured nail tapped against her pretty pink lips. "Cafeteria coffee isn't really worth getting excited over."

On that we could agree.

But there wasn't a chance I was going to be wasting the opportunity by heading to the cafeteria. "There's a coffee shop around the corner. And the coffee is so good, you'll be ruined for all future cups."

It wasn't a lie either.

Nate's schedule was ridiculous and nailing down a time to catch up like normal people was almost impossible. Which was why getting coffee at Cups was a solid reason for meeting him at the hospital.

It was in walking distance, so even when he was on-call—which seemed to be always—we could put some distance between him and the emergency room and pretend like it was old times. And the coffee was next level.

"That sounds promising." The smile on her lips edged wider. "I'll see if I can muster up a more appropriate response."

I loved that even though we were obviously flirting with each other, she wasn't telling me what I wanted to hear. That she wasn't batting her eyelashes, pursing her lips, and using that body of hers to get whatever she wanted. She had to know what a knockout she was, positive she'd brought men to their knees with little more than a smile. So it was surprising she hadn't used what I thought was an obvious arsenal, which just made her more attractive and intriguing.

Never had I been so glad that trucker had come in with multiple contusions. He might have different feelings about it, but Nate needing to go and play doctor instead of socializing with me meant I was in the exact right place at the exact right time.

"Shall we?" I gestured to the door, holding out my hand, palm up, and seeing if she'd take it. It wasn't going to bother me either way, but I'd be lying if I wasn't looking for an excuse to touch her. Even if it was just her hand.

Her delicate fingers wrapped around mine, the gavel held in the opposite one with her purse as she angled toward the exit. "If this coffee is as good as you say, I might very well end up proposing."

"Promises, promises, Your Honor." I laughed as I tightened my grip. "But I would never allow the caffeine to be responsible for my victory. If you want to marry me, it won't be for what's in your cup."

It was more suggestive than I'd intended, but honestly, I couldn't help myself. Pretending I wasn't attracted to her was impossible, and I was more than sure I could back up that statement.

She didn't even pretend to blush, raising a brow casually as her tongue slid against the seam of her lips. "Well, the night is still young, and I have a really good idea on where and how to get a marriage license."

Oh, I bet she did.

She probably had at least three judges on speed dial too, which would be handy. And even though I knew the situation— our fictitious future wedding—was complete bullshit, the possibility excited me. And I never even wanted to get married.

"Famous last words, sweetheart. Famous. Last. Words."

She was going to be mine before the night was out.

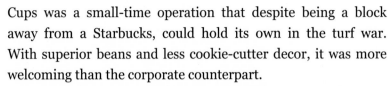

Cups was a small-time operation that despite being a block away from a Starbucks, could hold its own in the turf war. With superior beans and less cookie-cutter decor, it was more welcoming than the corporate counterpart.

It was also a lot smaller, most of the clientele preferring to pick up their order and leave rather than loiter in the few faded booths. But I liked the feeling of the old vinyl benches and resin tabletops, and the service was always polite without giving you a colonoscopy trying to earn extra tip money.

We walked together in comfortable silence, neither of us feeling the need to speak. For me I didn't want to waste the opportunity without the benefit of seeing her face. Those eyes held the promise of all kinds of trouble, and I was going to enjoy finding out if my hunch had been right.

Without waiting to be seated, I walked us to a table in back. It was counter service only, but I liked the idea of getting situated before ordering our coffee. She slid onto the faded red vinyl while I shuffled into the one opposite. It was a tight squeeze, management utilizing every square inch which meant I was actually closer to her than I'd been when we were walking.

"You have dessert with your dinner?" I asked, remembering she'd been out celebrating her promotion. "If not, they have some amazing cakes and pies."

She looked wistfully over at the glass counter, the rows of baked goods prominently displayed. "You want to split one?"

"Wow, not even married yet, and you're already splitting our assets, Zara. I'll share a lot of things, but dessert isn't one of them." I chuckled, unwilling to share what was probably the greatest apple pie in New York City.

"Ohhhhhh you're one of those," she mused, rolling her eyes. "Good to know."

"Know what?" I asked, not following her logic. "And one of *those* who?"

"You *know*." She raised her shoulder in a half shrug, pretending to be unimpressed. "The food police. 'Can't touch what's on my plate.' 'Order your own fries.' *That* guy."

"Who the hell shares french fries?" I reared back in horror. "Pleeeeeease don't tell me you're one of *those*," I added, equally impassioned.

It was her turn to act indignant. "One of those?"

"The *'I don't want any fries, I'll just eat a salad,'* people. Meanwhile I order a cheeseburger, and my fries miraculously disappear." I waved my hand across my imaginary plate.

She scoffed, folding her arms across her chest, which did great things for her cleavage. Hey, I wasn't trying to be a jerk, but we were literally inches away from each other. Not like I could ignore what was a superb pair of tits. "I don't order salad and then steal fries. And the women who do that mostly do it for their date's benefit. God forbid we look like we eat anything. Or enjoy food." She draped her hand across her forehead dramatically. "It's best I just have this one cherry tomato and slice of cucumber and faint from malnutrition rather than gain a pound or look like a healthy adult human in front of a guy who might see me naked."

"Trust me," I laughed, knowing it was without a doubt the weirdest first date conversation I'd ever had. "If a man has gotten to the point of seeing you naked, he's not thinking about what you ate for dinner."

She tilted her head in what seemed to be genuine interest. "Is that so?"

I leaned in closer, looking around cautiously, pretending I was about to divulge highly classified information. "Sweetheart, we're not *that* evolved. If there is a beautiful *naked* woman in front of you, it takes up all your mental bandwidth. I'd be lucky to remember what had been on *my* plate, let alone what had been on yours."

"Hmmmm." She drummed her fingers against her lips, her cheeks lacking any telltale signs of being embarrassed. "And you speak for *all* men? A little arrogant of you, don't you think?"

"Arrogant, or honest? You can take your pick. But those decisions you say women make—about what they eat or don't eat—aren't for our benefit, because we don't give a shit."

Her eyes darkened, her mouth dropping open slightly as she blew out a breath. And I wasn't imagining the heat between us. Whether it was because we'd been talking about being naked or just some crazy attraction, there was something definitely going on.

I liked it.

And her.

And the way her teeth discreetly gnashed against her pouty bottom lip.

"So . . . pie or cake?" she offered, her head tipping toward the display case.

"Pie. Apple. Vanilla ice cream." I rattled off my order like it was a list of demands in a hostage situation. "Is there really any other choice? It doesn't get any better than that."

"Well . . . I guess it's just as well we're not sharing. Key Lime. Cream *not* ice cream. And on the side instead of on the top." She added her own specific instructions. "And apple is a little boring, wouldn't you say?"

I drew in a breath, absolutely horrified, before lowering my voice to a whisper. "Wow, could you be any less patriotic? I realize that I basically know nothing about you and we just met, but I didn't take you for a communist."

"Where in the Constitution does it say anything about apple pie?" She raised a brow.

"Exactly what a communist would say," I sighed, unwedging myself from the booth. "Still, I feel like the least I can do is have this cup of coffee with you, let you eat your inferior pie before sending you back to the enemy. Be sure to tell them how humanely you were treated." And without waiting for her to respond, I headed to the counter to place our order.

It was only once I was there that I realized I hadn't asked her how she took her coffee. Or if she even drank coffee at all. She hadn't mentioned preferring tea when I'd first suggested it, so I had to assume she at least dabbled in the more caffeinated end of the pot. And as easy as it would've been to head back to the table and ask her, I decided to take a wild guess and see where it got me. Either way it would make things interesting, and if I totally got it wrong, I'd replace it with one of her choice.

The woman behind the counter gave me a warm smile as I got closer. She looked tired, the dark circles under her eyes the kind earned by five kids and maybe a husband who ignored her. But she wasn't letting the fatigue or her wedding band stop her eyes from traveling up and down my suit.

"Hi." I gave her a friendly—but not too friendly—smile of my own. "Can we have a slice of Apple à la mode, a slice of the Key Lime, whipped cream on the side, a latte and a brewed dark roast."

Molly—or at least that was the name tag on her uniform—glanced over at Zara, her eyebrow arching in curiosity. "Sure thing. I'll bring it over for you if you like. For you and your date?"

I don't think she'd meant to ask it as a question, but the inflection was definitely there. Then I guess she'd seen me with Nate a bunch of times and had probably assumed we'd been a couple. Unlike me, Nate actually *was* gay. But as close as we were, and I'd probably do anything for him, I drew the line at sucking his dick.

"Fiancée." I grinned pulling out my wallet, the possibility of regretting it later not enough to stop me. "She proposed tonight. We're very happy."

Molly's mouth dropped open, either shocked I was heterosexual or engaged but did her best to recover quickly. "Wow, congratulations. You look like a great couple."

And I had to hand it to poor Molly, because I actually agreed with her.

We did look like a great couple.

"Thanks." I turned, looking back at Zara who'd been watching on with interest. "She's one in a million."

Chapter 4

Edwin

She was still looking at me curiously when I made my way back to the table, her eyes darting to Molly with unanswered questions.

"Relax, I ordered your inferior pie with cream on the side," I assured her, easing back into the booth.

Her smile twitched at the edges. "And what coffee did you get since you didn't ask?"

"Latte."

Her eyes widened, seeming to be surprised. "How did you know that was what I wanted?"

"Oh, it was a total guess." I laughed, happier than I should be that I'd gotten it right. "I just tried to imagine what I *wouldn't* drink, and there you have it."

"You have something against lattes as well?"

I cleared my throat. "Not as an entity, no. All coffees should be loved equally without persecution. But I'm particular about what I put in my mouth. And a latte isn't it."

"Let me guess," she rolled her eyes, "black. No sweetener."

"Wow, we really *are* soulmates." I chuckled.

Her eyes widened, my flippant use of the word seeming to catch her off guard. And even though it had been a joke, there was no denying something was definitely happening between us.

It was weird that even though we'd just met, everything felt so *comfortable*. And not in a stale we've-been-dating-for-three-years kind of way, but where it just felt like I could be myself. I wanted to impress her, but I didn't feel like I had to try, the ease of the conversation between us, surprising.

"So, Zara." I rubbed my hands together, wanting to know more. "Since we've established we're obviously meant to be together, why don't you tell me a little bit more about yourself. Hopes. Dreams. The ten-year plan I bet you have drawn out in a notepad somewhere."

The last part was a guess, but I had a hunch I wasn't too far off the mark.

She was beautiful. Her face and body, lethal weapons that could bring any man to his knees. But there was something else about her, a smoldering sense of assurance that was sexy as hell. Just thinking about her in a courtroom was turning me on, and I couldn't help but wonder what other rooms she liked to dominate.

Her brow arched while her widening grin told me how right I'd been. "You already know I'm a lawyer." I nodded my head, waiting for her to continue. "I'm a senior associate at Bally and Cobb. We do family and corporate, but specialize in criminal law. And," she paused as she rolled her bottom lip with her teeth, "I can't believe I'm telling you this, but the ultimate goal is a judicial appointment."

"Ahhhhhhh. The gavel." I chuckled, tilting my head to where it was sitting on the table not far from her hand. "Well, that makes a lot more sense. Here I was thinking you were just some *regular* freak show, when really I was being hit on by a future Justice." I folded my arms across my chest, not needing to manufacture my interest. "Supreme Court?"

She hit me with the full weight of those beautiful brown eyes. "Wouldn't settle for anything less. And, I was *not* hitting on you. In fact, if that is what you think flirting is, then you seriously need to get out more."

"Oh, I know what flirting looks like, Zara." I laughed. "And unlike some guys, I don't need the road map. For that . . . or anything else."

So maybe I was flirting too, and maybe I really enjoyed it. Maybe I liked the way excitement lit up her eyes, warming those beautiful brown irises to the color of dark melted chocolate. Or maybe it was the subtle lifting of those stunning pouty lips, the way she fought her grin, not giving me a proper smile unless it was well earned. I liked that I had to work at it, that she wasn't just some girl I could flash my usual charm for and have her number in my pocket while her hand was already undoing my pants.

Her chin dropped, meeting my gaze without even a hint of embarrassment. "Now who's flirting."

I nodded not even trying to deny it. "And if that surprises you, then it's not me who needs to get out more."

"Here you go." Molly placed two cups on the table, interrupting the moment. "I'll just go grab your pie." She smiled, giving Zara her full attention. "And by the way, congratulations."

Zara's brows knitted, her confusion obvious. "Thanks," she responded cautiously, like she wasn't sure if she *should* be thankful, Molly giving her a curt nod before disappearing to get the pie.

"What was that?" Zara asked, keeping her voice low.

I shrugged, enjoying myself a little too much. "I might've mentioned your proposal."

"I didn't!"

"Semantics. We both know given half a chance, you will."
I grinned. "Anyway, she usually sees me in here with Nate so
assumed I was gay. I figured I'd give her some juicy gossip to
liven up her night. See, you don't know me, Zara, but I'm very
much a giver."

Zara looked back over her shoulder at Molly before turning
back to me. "Who's Nate and why would she assume you were
gay? Wait. . . *are* you gay? Your boyfriend isn't going to come
storming in all jealous, is he?"

"Wow, you accepted the date without being sure I was
single? Tsk, tsk, sweetheart. I never took you as a homewrecker."
I mock gasped, pretending to be shocked. "But if you must know,
Nate is one of my best friends and an ER attending at Sinai. He
is gay, and good-looking so I understand how she made the
mistake. Handsome *and* a doctor, there's a combo that's hard to
resist." I leaned in, lowering my voice to a whisper. "But I'm not
into dudes. Not even a little."

"Is that why you were there?" she asked, at that moment
realizing that while I knew her reason for being at the hospital,
she had no idea of mine. "Seeing Nate?"

I nodded, watching as Molly returned with two plates of pie.

"Here you go." Molly slid the plates onto the table before
pulling out napkins and silverware from the front pocket of her
apron. "If you need anything else, just come up to the counter."

She hesitated a little, giving us both a once-over before
heading back to the front of the store.

"Nate." Zara's hand reached out, stopping me from grabbing
my spoon.

My eyes dropped down to where her fingers were lingering,
the touch barely there, but very pleasing. "See, you hear he's a
good-looking doctor and suddenly you're interested. Did you
miss the part where I said he was gay?"

"You know, considering you asked me out, you haven't been very forthcoming with information. You know my name, my sister, my job, where I work and my aspirations. And you've given me nothing. So spill, because I'm not saying another word until you give me something too."

I wasn't denying that I was asking more questions than giving her answers, but honestly, who could blame me. I wanted to know everything there was about her, so talking about myself wasn't a priority. But I didn't want her to think I had something to hide, or was deliberately being cagey. Which is why I decided to go the expedited route, and give her the whole grand tour.

"Fine, let's see. I'm the middle child of three kids, a brother and sister—in that order—and my parents are still married living in upstate New York." I took a breath before continuing, "Nate and I met in medical school at Columbia, we were roommates."

"You're a doctor?" Her eyes widened, interjecting before I could continue.

I sighed heavily, shaking my head. "How disappointed are you going to be when I tell you no? I transferred out my first year, decided it wasn't for me. Besides," I held up one of my hands, "these babies were destined for more important things than being in someone's abdomen removing a spleen."

Her fingers trailed down my arm where it had been resting on the other hand still on the table. She took it into hers, turning it over to inspect it. "Hmmm, no callouses so no manual labor. Let me guess, hand model." She strummed my palm seductively. "They are *really* nice hands."

I didn't even care if she was joking, loving the contact and the sultry tone of her voice. "You mock me," I coughed out, pretending to be offended. Warmth traveling up my arm and across my chest as I stared into her eyes. "But you are wrong again. You want to keep going? Or should I just give you the plot twist right now?"

She leaned closer, keeping her hands on me. "Tell me. I want to know it all."

Jesus she was hot.

And while I had no doubt the exaggerated interest was part of a game we were playing, I had zero interest in making it stop. "Lawyer. Corporate law. Mergers, acquisitions, takeovers—I'm the asshole they call when they need a company dismembered with its head on a platter."

It was far from a noble pursuit, with my firm's biggest motivator being billable hours. Her hands lifted, my skin tingling from the ghosted contact. And I could see from the change of her expression, her opinion of me had taken a nosedive. "Ahhhhhh, so judgmental." I shook my head, expecting her response.

After all, she wanted to ascend to the Supreme Court, fight for good, equality, and the protection of the Constitution. And there I was, using Lady Justice to scale and gut corporations like it was open season.

"Go on, tell me how much more honorable I could be. If I used my power for good instead of evil. I assure you, there isn't an argument I haven't heard. My dad and mom are still wondering what happened to their 'dear sweet boy.' But the difference between me and all the other assholes, is I give a shit what happens to the workers. The people who don't have a choice. I make sure their pensions are taken care of. Their entitlements are honored. And yeah, if some CEO who's been holidaying in the Caymans, switching out his Benz for the newest model every year, ends up in a cardboard box under a bridge, then that's the kind of collateral damage I can live with."

She blinked, either not expecting the fully-loaded response or looking for a way to make a hasty exit. "You're a lawyer too."

"Indeed." I nodded.

"And yet, you let me explain how a subpoena is served?" Her brow arched, proving there was nothing wrong with her memory from earlier when we'd met.

"I was trying to work out what would be the bigger dick move. Cut you off and be all 'I know,' or play dumb and get a refresher. I can live with you calling me a jerk rather than have you believe I was trying to mansplain shit I'm positive you know more about than me."

And she'd been adorable. But I left that part out because while I could handle "jerk," "sexist jerk" wasn't happening.

"Hold up a minute." I recentered my thoughts, my brain still having some neurons firing even though most of the blood had been flowing southward. "Why are we talking about subpoenas, aren't you going to rail me for using the law for death and destruction?"

Her shoulder lifted in a shrug, glancing down at our cooling coffees and uneaten pies. "Someone has to do it, right? Might as well be you. It's not like you eat the souls of children."

"Well . . ." I trailed off, rubbing the center of my chest, "I am trying to cut down. Children's souls give me wicked heartburn."

She laughed, the sound of it crackling in the air as she threw her head back. "So why did you leave medical school?"

It was what most people wanted to know whenever they found out my original career path. "My dad is a doctor—GP—and my mom, a physician's assistant. So I guess it was sort of expected. Out of the three of us, I was the only one that really showed an interest in the "family business." Joe, my brother, likes to work with his hands. He makes handmade furniture. And my younger sister, Maddy, is a makeup artist. She does the pretty stuff, but her real passion is special effects, movie makeup. She's over on the west coast. Anyway, I thought it was what I wanted to do," I explained, remembering how I'd planned out college, then medical school, assuming I'd stay in New York for my residency. "But when it got down to it, there was no passion. I was going through the motions, making the grades, doing the assignments but there was no spark. And since it's the kind of job you really can't half-ass, I decided to go find something else that would light a fire under my ass."

"Law." The smile both on her face and in her voice told me she felt the same way I did about it. And even though we might be on different ends of the spectrum, excitement for the law was something you couldn't fake.

I nodded, picking up my coffee and taking the first sip. "Yeah. Finished my law degree at Columbia and then moved to Boston. Have been with Locke and Collins since I graduated."

She was about to start on her own coffee when she stopped suddenly and lowered the cup. "Boston? You live in *Boston*?"

"Yeah, I'm here on assignment. A week or two, and then I head back."

Her smile dropped, the latte forgotten as disappointment clouded her eyes. "I just assumed." She stopped, shaking her head like she was discounting the thought. "Well, I guess it makes sense."

"Make sense?" I asked, wondering what she was talking about. I hadn't suddenly developed a Bostonian accent despite having lived there for a few years. And as far as I knew, I still looked like a New York native.

"This is so crazy," she whispered under her breath before looking at me. "But I was hoping." She swallowed. "I was really looking forward to getting to know you."

It sounded so final, like whatever this was, was already over before things even started.

"You *wanted* to get to know me?" I reached across and ran my fingers over her knuckles. "Get to know me *how*, Zara?"

Her eyes heated, telling me that for all the honorable thoughts she had, she had plenty of naughty ones too. "Are you staying in a hotel or with Nate?"

"Hotel." I tamped down the significance of the question, assuming nothing and hoping for everything.

It had been a while since I'd had a one-night stand and none of them had started like that. But given the choice between one night or nothing with her, I knew exactly what my choice was. Even though I could already tell, one night would not be enough.

"We should finish our pie and coffee," she said suddenly, her tongue lightly darting across her bottom lip.

"And then what?" I asked, because Jesus, I really wanted to know. "You want me to give you a ride home?" I leaned across the table, wanting nothing more than to just kiss her one time. "I can call my car service, take you anywhere you want to go."

Please don't say home.

Please do not say you want to go home.

She didn't answer, the mental to-and-fro taking place in front of me as she weighed her options.

Everything about her screamed she wasn't the kind of woman who had random hook-ups, but there was an undeniable spark between us that couldn't be ignored.

"You could still get to know me, Zara," I whispered, my lips dying to get on hers. "I'll tell you anything you want to know. Either here or . . . at my hotel."

I was giving her the choice, because as far as I was concerned, my mind was already made up.

I wanted her.

Wanted to take her back to my suite and kiss her slowly.

We didn't even have to have sex, the chance to touch her and spend the night with her worth any discomfort from the perpetual hard-on I knew it would cause.

"Your hotel."

My muscles tightened, the heat pooling in my balls as my pants got tighter in the crotch. I knew it meant nothing, that we could get there, and she could change her mind. Or she might not even let me touch her at all. But she was giving me a chance, and since the whole thing had started on circumstance, I wasn't leaving anything on the table.

"As you wish, Your Honor."

Chapter 5

Zara

I had no idea what I was thinking.

I knew almost nothing about Edwin except there was some crazy sexual chemistry between us and I hadn't been *that* attracted to a guy in a long time.

Maybe it was stress hormones messing with my biology. The excitement of my promotion, the dash to the hospital, meeting some random guy who coincidentally had the same name of my supposed soulmate had worked me into a state. Heightened arousal from "pressured" situations was a real thing. And while it had been a while since I'd been reckless with a guy, I still knew how it all worked.

The car ride was almost unbearable.

As promised, he called a town car, which was so much nicer than a cab. It didn't have a fancy privacy screen, but it smelled of freshly cleaned upholstery and forest pine. Pity all I could think of was sliding across that leather seat, straddling him and making out like a fiend.

Instead, I stayed on my side of the car, my fingers white-knuckling my gavel while they stayed respectably in my lap.

If he was having the same predicament, he wasn't showing it, his body relaxed with his arm draped casually across the seat.

Who even was I? And why the hell was I so attracted to him? Was he as good-looking as I thought, or had I been spending too much time with Belle and was starting to believe in fantasies.

"So your family all live in New York?" I asked, trying to make conversation while heat pooled low in my gut.

"Maddy is in L.A. but the rest of them are here. Well, not *here*—in the city—but Rochester. You?"

"Belle and I share an apartment in Greenwich. But my parents live in Queens. A little closer than yours," I added lamely, not needing to point out that across the bridge wasn't nearly as far as upstate.

"Yeah, just a little." He grinned. "But I make it back enough times through the year they don't miss me too much."

Oh, now that was interesting information.

Did he add it to suggest that we could potentially see each other again? Or was he just making idle small talk? And why the hell was I analyzing it anyway? I'd just met the guy, and all of a sudden I was weighing up whether I'd dive headfirst into a long-distance relationship with him. It was unlike me, and more to the point, not helpful. Because regardless of whatever *destiny* was at play, life didn't work like that and I should've known better.

At least I used to.

I still did, right?

That stupid prediction was really messing with my head.

Determined not to get hung up on the details, I refocused on why I was in the car in the first place. And it wasn't to form some weird arrangement where he stopped by and saw me whenever he was in town.

"And there's Nate," I pointed out, remembering his friend had been why he'd been at the hospital in the first place.

He nodded, his fingers lifting to rub the gentle stubble on his jaw. "Ahh, yes, Nate. How boring his life would be without me in it." He playfully chuckled, the last bit added like it was some kind of inside joke.

I was about to ask him about it when the car stopped in front of the Four Seasons Hotel.

It was exactly the kind of hotel I'd expected. Expensive, luxurious and far enough away from Time Square he didn't have to deal with too many tourists.

"Here we are, sir." The driver slid out of the car, opening the door.

Edwin slid out first, stepping out onto the sidewalk with his hand outstretched. "Zara." He said my name like an invitation, my mouth watering as I looked up at him against the illumination of the star-lit sky.

He was beautiful.

Too good-looking to even seem real and I was about to go up to his hotel room with him.

While it might have been out of character—more so that I hadn't dated anyone the last few months—I had no issue with sleeping with him.

Sure, I could hear the collective gasps from the peanut gallery, shocked that someone with my level of professional standing would dabble with a one-night stand. But while I hadn't done it before, it wasn't something I was adverse to.

I'd had opportunities in the past, but none presented so . . .well, deliciously. And if I were ever going to do it, surely there wasn't a better candidate than Edwin . . . my supposed *soulmate* . . .

My body relaxed into his touch as I joined him on the sidewalk, his hand pressed against the small of my back with just enough pressure to let me know he liked control. And while I didn't usually get off on the whole alpha-dominating male thing, there was something about him—and his hand—that I really *really* liked.

"You want to go to the bar?" he offered, the heat in his eyes hinting that wasn't what was on his mind. But to his credit, he was a gentleman, giving me the option to slow it down a little—or a lot—if I'd had second thoughts on the ride over.

I had not.

"You have a mini bar in your room?" I asked, knowing that even the lowest priced rooms in a place like the Four Seasons would have a fully stocked selection of alcohol and overpriced nuts.

"I do, and if there's something else you want, we could always order room service." He didn't break his stride, leading me to the elevator.

Ironically it made me feel empowered. Loving the attention I usually didn't receive, but also being completely in the driver's seat. He was letting me call the shots, and that was one hell of a turn on.

"Guess we're going to your room then." I turned to face him, watching as his eyes swept over my body and he licked his lips.

The metal doors opened before he got a chance to respond, pressing the button for one of the higher levels as they closed behind us. We were the only two in there, the temptation to start kissing him almost unbearable as we rapidly climbed the floors.

His hand dropped from my back to my waist, bringing me closer to him. "Zara, I—"

I cut him off, understanding what we were doing was slightly crazy but not wanting to stop. "I'm here because I want to be," I assured him. "And I want to kiss you."

His mouth was on mine before I realized what was happening, moving us back against the wall and pressing against me as he took what I was offering.

My body arched into him, feeling his erection as he took my lips with no hesitation. Whatever he'd been about to say, he was no longer thinking it, the hot, deep kisses increasing in intensity and intention until the elevator finally stopped.

The doors opened, flooding the closed space with the bright light of the hallway and some much-needed air. My body felt hot, parts of me tingling with anticipation since it was clear where it was leading.

"Jesus, you're beautiful." He kissed my neck as his hand dropped to my hip. "You're making it hard for me to think straight."

He wasn't the only one having a hard time maintaining his intelligence, all and any reasons on why going into his room was a bad idea just seemed to no longer exist.

"Which one is yours?" I pulled him out of the elevator, wanting privacy to continue what we were doing. As much as I enjoyed being reckless with him, I wasn't ready to completely torch my career. And being caught on surveillance footage acting indecent was the kind of thing that would haunt you when you were trialing an important case. Or being ratified by the senate.

He nodded to a door not far on the right, leading us there and making quick work of unlocking it with the swipe card. We were met with a soft glow of ambient lighting, the lock behind us reengaging as he tossed the keycard onto the sideboard.

I didn't move, my body pressed against the door, feeling like I was in some weird dream.

It wasn't hesitation, more disbelief that I was actually in the room, about to be reckless like my sister, Belle, had been begging me to be. And to think I'd been ready to walk away from him only a few hours earlier, not even bothering to go to that nurses' station. I could already hear Belle's smug "I told you so," never being so glad to have been proven wrong in my life.

He stalked closer, keeping mere inches between us as his eyes steamrolled hungrily down my body. Everything hummed, feeling tight and needy as I watched him shuck his jacket.

My hand reached out, placing my gavel and handbag on the sideboard to join the key as he pulled at his tie. He was going slow, either because he liked to tease or was giving me the chance to back out. It was such a lawyer thing to do, making sure there were numerous opportunities to confirm consent so I couldn't argue later I had no idea what he was doing. The idea he was being careful just turned me on more.

"Take it off." I nodded to his shirt, anticipating what was underneath.

It was clear he had an amazing body, the evidence of those well-trained muscles barely contained by the suit. But since removing the jacket, I was positive the *preview* wasn't even close to how incredible reality was.

His shoulders rolled as he tossed his tie to the floor and pressed against me. He hadn't removed his shirt like I'd ask, but my protest was silenced by his mouth on mine.

What had I asked him to do again? I really didn't care, one hand hooking onto my waist while the other moved up my side.

"Yes," I breathed out, wanting to be touched so badly I was almost tempted to beg. I didn't though, not willing to waste the time or the energy while he was kissing me like that.

God, it had been a while.

Not since I'd been kissed, I'd dated a guy a couple of months ago.

But kissed *properly*, by a man who knew what the hell he was doing and how to make it feel good.

It wasn't a negotiation. It was a closing argument that no jury in their right mind would ever be able to ignore. And wow. . . I could only imagine how well he'd be able to command other parts of my body, the sweet pressure of his mouth making me whimper as I kissed him right back.

My hands—which had been pressed against his chest—were no longer content to just stay idle. Instead they decided to explore, confirming he was essentially a god—or at least built like one—as I mumbled my appreciation against his mouth.

"Zara," he groaned, his mouth moving to my neck as he palmed my breast. "You're making me crazy."

I liked that.

That he felt as out of control as I did.

"Edwin," I gasped, feeling the tug low in my gut. "I know you're going back to Boston. And I have no expectations. But I really, really want to sleep with you."

It wasn't going to be like one of Belle's fairy tales. We were not going to fall into some magical romance destined to be together forever, but holy hell did I want to have one night with him.

One night I knew would be mind-blowing in all the right ways, and something I knew I'd never forget.

"Fuck," he cursed, breathing heavily as he peeled himself off me. "Zara, I want you. Please know that I am so insanely attracted to you, I can't think straight."

My eyes widened, feeling the inevitable "but" that sounded like it was coming.

He was trying to save my feelings. Worried I was probably going to regret it in the morning, or worse, try and demand a relationship.

"No, it's okay. I want this too." I did my best to make my position clear, willing to sign an agreement—much like the one that had engineered our meeting—if it made any difference.

He huffed out a breath, shaking his head. "No, no you don't. Or at least you're not going to want to once I tell you the truth."

The truth?

The words rattled around in my head as the air expelled from my lungs. I had no idea what he was about to say but none of it felt promising.

"You're not a lawyer?" I asked, wondering if he thought it would get me into bed faster if he thought we shared some common ground. Maybe the whole story about leaving medical school had been bullshit, worried I'd fallen for the oldest con in the world.

"I'm a lawyer, Zara. I was honest about everything I told you about me and my family." His chest rose and fell, holding me steady before he locked his eyes with mine. "But I'm not Edwin Carlisle. My name is Lincoln Archer."

Chapter 6

Lincoln

It had gone way further than it was supposed to.

I'd meant to tell her at the coffee shop.

And then in the car.

Hell, even the elevator would've been okay, knowing it was really my last chance. There was no denying the longer I left it, the shadier I felt, letting her believe I was actually someone else.

But then there was that kiss. And whatever I'd meant to say got sidelined while I owned that sweet mouth of hers.

Jesus, she was hot.

So sweet and sexy, with a sense of humor that turned me on as much as her gorgeous body.

"What the hell?" She pushed me away, her mouth and eyes wide. "You are *not* Edwin Carlisle? What kind of sick, twisted joke is this?"

Her hands flew out at me, smacking my chest wildly as I tried to grab them. "It's not a joke. My name is Lincoln."

She was seething, her body visibly shaking from anger as her eyes narrowed. "Is this how you get off? Lying to women? Taking them to your hotel room under false pretenses?"

"Hey, I never lied to you. I never said my name was Edwin, or even confirmed that it was. You assumed. And I didn't lure you here pretending to be something that I wasn't. The guy in the hospital and at the coffee shop—that's me. It wasn't some act to get you into bed. I am not *that* guy."

I understood she was mad, and I absolutely deserved to be chewed out. But taking her to my hotel room hadn't been part of the plan. Hell, I'd assumed we have a coffee, I'd come clean and then either we'd laugh about it or she'd storm off. In both cases, we'd probably never see each other again. New York was a big city, and I didn't even permanently live in it. But orchestrating all of that to trick her into sleeping with me . . . yeah, that was something I'd *never* do.

Her nostrils flared, the rise and fall of her chest pushing out rapid, hard breaths. And not the sexy kind like she'd been doing a few minutes before. "Ohhhhhhhh you *really* are a lawyer." She choked out a humorless laugh. "Wow, glad you cleared up the technicality. But we both know, that even if you didn't say the words, you let me believe it."

"Look, I might not have been honest about my name but that was the *only* thing. Do you mean to tell me that the only reason you're here is because you thought my name was Edwin Carlisle?" It couldn't *just* be the name, right? That crazy attraction, the chemistry . . . that was with me. Not some random guy she'd never met and assumed I was.

Her hands anchored on her hips, her voice lowered in what I could only describe as both calm and unsettling. "Oh, so this is my fault? That I was so dumb, that because I took you at face value, I shouldn't be irate? Please tell me that isn't what you're saying."

I might not be an expert on women, but I knew when I'd fucked up. She might be smaller and lighter, but I didn't have any doubts she could do serious damage if she wanted to.

And she was right. No matter how I wanted to dress it up, it was a jerk-off thing to do. "No, no. It's not your fault. I just meant . . ." I stopped, trying to think of anything I could say that would make the situation better. "I wasn't intentionally trying to deceive you, okay. When I walked back over to you at the hospital, I'd meant to correct you. But you were so—" *beautiful, animated, funny, captivating* "—well, I hadn't expected us to hit it off."

The physical attraction had been there from the moment we'd met—she was stunning in ways I couldn't even begin to explain. But after talking to her some more, there was something else. An attraction of a different kind. "So yeah, I might've withheld setting the record straight because I wanted to spend more time with you."

"Is that your apology? Because I didn't hear the word *sorry* one time during all of that," she deadpanned, the anger level only slightly ratcheted down.

Great.

She wanted me to say *sorry*. Which was expected, I guess, but difficult when I wasn't completely apologetic about it. And I didn't want to risk having my balls ripped off with her bare hands by lying to her. Even if technically, it was for the first time.

I took a breath, meeting her gaze without hesitation. "I'm sorry I didn't tell you my name was Lincoln."

It was the best I could do, because honestly, it was the only part of the situation I was sorry about. "But spending time with you, getting to know you—however brief—and not wanting the night to end is something I'd never experience regret over. And whether you think that is wrong or not wouldn't change my opinion."

"Wow, you're really good at this," she chuckled, but I was positive the laugh was more ironic than amused. "I'd be impressed if this was a court room."

And while I knew it wouldn't help my cause, and would probably make her angrier, my lips edged into a smile. "You're impressed?"

"God!" She threw her hands up, rolling her eyes. "Only *you* would take that as a compliment."

"Hold on a second." I held up my hand, wanting the clarification. "What do you mean, only *I* would take that as a compliment? You barely know me. Now you're an expert?"

While I was glad I was no longer at risk of being pummeled by her fists or her gavel, I wasn't willing to let her latest series of misconceptions stand.

"Lincoln," she breathed out. "If that is even your real name," she added with the lift of her brow. "It doesn't take an expert to work out what kind of man you are. I see them every single day at work. Cocky, arrogant, and mostly delusional."

The insults should've offended me, but they didn't.

Because as much as I could be cocky and sometimes arrogant, I was *never* delusional. I also recognized an opening when I saw one, and if she'd wanted to leave, she'd have done that already.

I reached into my back pocket, her eyes tracking my movements carefully as I pulled out my wallet. She didn't seem convinced but was curious. And if there was one thing I knew about *her*, it was that curiosity was like foreplay.

"My driver's license." I held up my ID, letting her see it clearly. "And unless you think I've defrauded the Commonwealth of Massachusetts, you will see that Lincoln is my real and legal name."

She snatched it out of my hands, studying it for irregularities or signs of tampering.

"You want to search my registration with the bar?" I offered, irrationally jealous my ID was still getting so much attention. "I passed it in Mass and New York, so it won't be hard to find."

"Overachiever," she huffed under her breath, handing me back my license.

My smile got wider, no longer attempting to hide it. "Did I just impress you again?"

"No, no you didn't." She folded her arms across her chest which unfortunately drew my attention to her cleavage.

She had a beautiful body, soft feminine curves that were the perfect fit for my hands. I'd liked touching them, and wanted the opportunity to touch them again.

Kissing her again was out of the question.

Not unless I wanted to be gargling my testicles.

But even though the possibility was remote and unlikely, I couldn't stop staring at her mouth.

"I'm still mad at you." She licked her lips, hopefully having the same thoughts I did.

"I know. Rightly so." I moved closer.

"I'm not sleeping with you."

"Again, not news, Zara."

She had a point to prove, and no matter how badly she might have wanted it—wanted me—she wouldn't give either of us the pleasure.

And fuck me, did it just make me like her even more.

"Here's what I'm proposing." I cleared my throat, my voice a little lower and huskier than I'd intended. "Why don't you tell me why you need to find this guy so badly, and I will locate him for you."

She coughed out a laugh, putting her hand in front of her mouth when she saw I was serious. "There's over eighteen million people in New York City."

"True, but he's not exactly John Smith. So, tell me why and I'll give you something to really be impressed about."

She wanted cocky, she'd get cocky. And it wasn't just posturing either, I *knew* I could back it up. I wouldn't even need

Nate who, bound by HIPPA, probably couldn't tell me shit even if he did know. Lots of public information out there, and I was more than just a little cozy with most of the department clerks in Manhattan. It was why Locke and Collins continued to send me instead of one of the other senior associates, my track record for results speaking for itself.

Besides, part of me was curious why she was so compelled to see this guy. Who was he? And why did he matter? And more importantly, was she intending on kissing him like she had me.

And yes, maybe it gave me the excuse to stay in the picture, let her see I wasn't some desperate deviant who needed to trick women to get them into bed.

It seemed we both had a point to prove, and if I was to hedge a guess, I'd say neither of us were willing to concede.

"No." Her mouth moved slowly, extending the word a little more than was necessary.

"No?" I asked, wondering which part she was objecting to.

"Look, whatever you think you are trying to do, don't. If I wanted to find someone, I would." Her words were measured, and if she was worried about showing weakness, she didn't have to.

Five minutes with her and I could tell she was a force to be reckoned with, which was part of the reason why I just couldn't walk away. And even though I knew it would probably be the smart thing to do, I was seeing it through for as long as I could.

"Zara, I have no doubt that you could and would. But since I was the reason you missed your first opportunity, it will be my way of making a mends."

That was partially true.

I *was* the reason she hadn't had her rendezvous with the real Edwin Carlisle. But getting them together so I could get back into her good graces wasn't my motivation.

Nope.

Altruism was a nice trait but sadly not one I possessed. Neither was just being "a nice guy." But what I did want—and the reason I suggested the crazy idea—was to find out what exactly made that beautiful mind tick. And if her icy feelings thawed and we got back to the place where I was kissing her, then that was even better.

She blinked slowly, hopefully considering my offer. "I'll take it under advisement, but now, I'm going home."

Okay, again, not unexpected.

I wasn't so conceited to think we were just going to pick up where we left off, although I expected some additional questions.

"Sure." I didn't bother trying to argue. "Let me call my driver, he can give you a ride home."

"That won't be necessary. I can just call a cab." She straightened, adjusting her clothing.

There was a very real chance that if she walked out of my hotel room, I'd never see her again. I didn't have her number, or know where she lived, so other than going to her place of employment, my options would be limited. And while I was positive I could find a plausible and legitimate excuse for walking into the law offices of Bally and Cobb, it wasn't the move I wanted to make.

"It's just a ride, Zara. No strings."

"No strings?" she asked, almost not believing it was a genuine offer.

I nodded, accepting whatever opening she was giving me. "Yep, he'll take you either back to the hospital to be with your sister or to your apartment in Greenwich, whichever you prefer."

"And what . . . then he'll run back to you and tell you where I live?"

"You think I need my driver to find out where you live?" I laughed. "Zara, I just told you I could locate a guy with nothing but a name, give me a little more credit."

She rolled her eyes, grabbing her bag and her gavel. "If that was supposed to convince me you *aren't* a stalker, you failed."

"I figured you'd appreciate my honesty." I watched as she shifted on her feet but didn't move toward the door. "But it doesn't make it any less true."

"Fine, call your driver. But I'm leaving alone." She held up her hand, pressing it against my chest.

It was the first time she'd touched me since she'd found out I was Lincoln, and it wasn't to inflict grievous bodily harm.

"Whatever you want." I looked down at her hand, the attention I'd paid it causing her to pull it away. "Give some thought to my offer." I reached back into my wallet and pulled out a business card. "I'll call my driver."

It wasn't my smoothest move, but I had to work with what I had. And while I had no doubt she would be capable of tracking me down, I wanted to make it as easy as possible. After all, I was planning on seeing her again. And unless I wanted to be on the wrong side of the courtroom, defending a stalking charge, our next interaction would be initiated by her.

Was I worried she'd toss the number and forget about me?

Not a chance.

We'd be seeing each other sooner or later, and for both our sakes, I hoped it was sooner.

She took the card, tossing it into her clutch with little interest. But she'd taken it, and at that moment, that was all that mattered.

"Thanks, I'll go wait in the lobby." Her hand reached for the door handle, looking over her shoulder at me one last time. "Bye."

I nodded, knowing it wasn't where the story ended for either of us.

"Bye, Zara."

Chapter 7

Zara

I'd never thought I'd be one of those idiots.

You know, the kind you see on a daytime talk show, who believed they were in relationships with famous people. Or the ones who got catfished, thinking they had met their soulmate through an email. And if only their betrothed could pay off the pesky estate charges for their dead uncle, you could live happily ever after in millionaire bliss for all time.

But no, it turns out, I wasn't that smart.

Because as much as I wanted to blame the "miscommunication" on him, he was right in that he never actually confirmed who he was. And as an attorney, I knew better than to accept anything at face value. Not that I'd be confessing to any of that, happy to live in indignation, letting him believe that I did think he was wholly responsible.

And let's face it, a man like that could probably use a shot of humility.

Uhhhhhhhh, I was so mad.

Mad that I'd let myself believe in what was nothing more than some stupid carnival bullshit.

I should've known better.

Lincoln's driver had met me in the lobby, and with very little small talk—something I appreciated—led me to the car and drove me home.

There were no judgmental stares through the rearview mirror.

No asking me about my evening.

No rudeness of any kind.

He was the perfect gentleman and when we arrived at my Greenwich apartment, he hopped out of the car, opened my door and told me to have a good evening.

I wasn't sure exactly what I'd been expecting. Part of me assumed he'd treat me like some cheap whore who had been Lincoln's booty call. Or there was always the possibility Lincoln had told him I was some uptight cock-tease and I wanted to go home.

But whatever conversation had transpired between the two of them, it had either not been derogatory toward me, not painting me in a bad light, or the driver was the best actor in NYC.

Thanking him—because I saw no need for rudeness on my part either—I said my goodbyes and let myself into the main doors of our apartment building. It was quiet, my footsteps creaking against the old, carpeted stairs as I climbed to our first-story apartment.

Belle was at the hospital, the birth of the baby taking a little longer than expected, leaving me an exclamation mark heavy text demanding a status update. I shot back a quick reply telling her I was home, alone and I'd fill her in later. Secretly, I was relieved I didn't have to go through it all again so soon, knowing Belle would want every single insignificant detail to analyze. And while I was a fan of postmortems—watching the game-day footage and seeing where it all went wrong—my heart and my head wasn't in it.

Why couldn't I hate him, damn it?

Everything told me I should not only be seething mad, but should tear up his business card and never give him a second thought. Was I that hard up for affection and attention that I'd entertain getting to know a conman? And semantics or not, he let me go for hours calling him Edwin without correcting me.

But for all the logical, reasonable debate as to why he was the Devil's spawn of which I wanted no part of, there was an equal rationalization that he was sweet, and funny, and so goddamn good-looking.

No.

No, no, no, no, and no.

I didn't care how funny, sweet, good-looking and charming he was, it had bad idea written all over it. I had more important things to worry about. Like impressing the partners. Being a badass in the courtroom. And when the time was right, ascending to the highest court in the country. I didn't have time for stupid, complicated relationships that started with lies.

Then why was I so disappointed?

Ignoring my mood, I decided the best thing to do was to have a soak in the tub, listen to the serial killer podcast I was currently bingeing, and have a big glass of wine. Which is exactly what I did, leaving my clutch and gavel, peeling off my clothes as I moved to the bathroom. I'd forgotten the glass of wine, deciding I could get it later as I turned on the faucet and let the tub fill with warm water.

Steam rose in the small, confined space, my body breaking the water's surface as I slid in, and I felt my body let out a long, exaggerated breath. It had been a long hard week, and I was happy, so I wasn't going to let an unfortunate hiccup ruin what had otherwise been a monumental time in my life.

So with talk of murder and mystery coming out my Bluetooth speakers, I relaxed and closed my eyes. In the morning all thought of Lincoln Archer would be long gone, and I was never going to even mention the name Edwin Carlisle ever again.

"Jesus!" I woke up to find Belle perched on the edge of my bed, looking at me like a deviant. "You scared the hell out of me."

"Serial killers before bed?" Belle asked, noticing one of my headphones still tangled in my hair. "When I saw the trail of clothes out in the living room, I assumed you got lucky."

"So you came in here to confirm?" I asked, mildly horrified. I say mildly because it was Belle and it was on-brand for her to be nosey even if slightly inappropriate. "And I'm not going to bring some guy I just met to the apartment I share with my sister. If it's one thing those serial killers all have in common, is they like nothing more than hacking people up in their own beds." Well, not *all* of them, but there was overwhelming evidence to suggest it was a thing.

Belle rolled her eyes. "I can't believe you didn't wait up for me. I came home, all excited to hear about your big adventure and you were already asleep. I want details. All of them. And don't leave out any of the good parts."

I knew it was coming, the inevitable info dump Belle would require, but honestly it was too early, and I wasn't caffeinated enough.

"Ummmm, don't you have some of your own big news to share? Did Hayley have the baby? Or did you tap out and leave the poor girl to deliver by herself," I scoffed, knowing the chances Belle would leave anyone high-and-dry were remote.

"Fiiiiiiinnnnnnne. But then I want all the details," she sing-songed with a smile. "Hayley delivered a beautiful—well, it actually wasn't but I didn't have the heart to tell her—baby girl at three this morning. She was all squished and loud, but super healthy and we both cried. Me, because I can't believe something that big could come out of your vagina and her, because her little daughter finally made it into the world. Her family are with her now so I decided to come home and change. And of course to check on my big sister who hopefully got oodles of orgasms last night from her soulmate."

Uhhhhhh, poor Belle.

She was going to be even more disappointed than I was.

"Well, it turns out that he wasn't Edwin Carlisle. He was just some jerk who clearly was having a slow night and decided to use me as entertainment." There was no easy way to put it, and telling her I'd dumbly fallen under his spell was just adding insult to injury.

"What?" she coughed out, her face displaying the same wide-eyed expression she'd had when she found out Santa Claus wasn't real. "No, he's the guy. They said his name over the speaker."

"Belle, he played me. It wasn't him. I don't know who Edwin is or if he was even there. In any case, the guy we met last night was Lincoln Archer. A shark lawyer from Boston who is probably allergic to the truth."

My assessment was probably harsher than what was needed but I was still feeling like a dumbass. Besides, it was *mostly* true.

"He's a lawyer from Boston? He didn't sound like he was from Mass." She looked confused, rubbing her chin and ignoring the more important parts of my conversation.

Like him being a fraud and a liar.

I blew out a breath, rolling my eyes as I filled in the blanks. "That's because he's originally from New York. He just lives there for work. Or at least that's what he says. He could have ten wives all in different states for all I know, and Boston is just his address of record."

I didn't really believe that.

Mainly because as much as I hated feeling deceived, he had stopped and come clean before we'd had sex. And let me be clear, I was soooooo ready to have sex with him last night. It might not have been typical Zara behavior but that didn't make it any less true.

So had he been a complete jerk, con-artist, hustler—choose your favorite category of lowlife—he'd have let me make that mistake and then told me who he was. Not like I'd asked to see his ID before he'd offered it, the voluntary proof of his name and address, initiated by him.

"No, this doesn't make sense," Belle protested, forever living in the delusion that most people had good intentions. It was something I both loved and worried about when it came to her.

I shook my head, wondering why on top of everything I'd been through last night—the embarrassment, the disappointment, etc.—I had to somehow be comforting someone else. "Belle, sometimes things don't make sense. It doesn't make them any less real. But that guy I was supposed to meet and have an epic love story with—doesn't exist. And if anything, last night should prove that. Now tell me more about the squishy, ugly baby. I need to be prepared for when I visit and have to lay on the fake pleasantries."

Hearing about Hayley's baby was the last thing I wanted to do, but it would take the focus from me and that was what I wanted. Besides, Belle would probably have a million and one questions about Lincoln I couldn't answer, and I wasn't in the mood to feel dumber than I already did.

It had felt so . . . real.

The attraction, the ease of our conversation, how amazing it felt when he'd kissed me—all of it had been so effortless. Which was why I guess I still felt weird about it. Mourning the loss of something I hadn't even had.

Thankfully, Belle took the hint and launched into a full, gory description of the birth and the baby. I could've probably been spared all the details about the episiotomy and subsequent stitching but whatever helped me get through the morning was welcomed.

After Belle had successfully convinced me never to have a child of my own, we moved out of my room and into the kitchen where we had breakfast. It was still early morning but Belle was tired from her eventful night so decided to go to bed and sleep. Meanwhile, I decided to gather my collection of strewn clothes from the living room, which had given Belle the wrong idea.

It wasn't like me to be lazy or messy, which was probably why she'd assumed it had been done in the throes of passion. But, no, I'd just been tired and was giving myself permission to act like a normal twenty-eight-year-old.

My clutch was still on the floor, the clasp having been knocked open when I dropped it and spilling the contents onto the carpet. Loose change surrounded his business card like a sunburst, adding insult to injury as I picked up the card and tossed it in the trash.

There wasn't a chance I was calling him, and I didn't need the temptation of having his number if I somehow lost my mind. I'd never been one of those girls who drunk-dialed ex-boyfriends, but I also knew how amazing that kiss had felt and didn't trust myself with lowered inhibitions.

With the living room back in order, my dirty clothes in the hamper, and my gavel in the prime location on top of my dresser, I decided to go out for a run. Well, not a run really, because I was far from an athlete. More a fast-paced walk/jog that elevated my heartrate. It was as close to exercise as I got with no time for the gym, and meant I could still eat what I wanted and be fit enough to outrun a zombie apocalypse should it happen.

The sun was warm on my muscles as sweat glistened on my skin. It felt good to clear my head and get lost in my own world, my headphones drowning out the noise of the city and traffic.

And while the time outside hadn't really solved anything, it did give me a new sense of perspective. Other than feeling foolish, no real harm had been done and as for bad decisions, I was well under my quota for someone my age.

I couldn't help but smile as I flung open my apartment door, Britney Spears singing in my ears—I'm a fan, and that girl had definitely been screwed over—and I was looking forward to a warm shower and about three thousand calories in the form of loaded fries. I figured Belle would need to carb load after her long eventful night, and french fries smothered in cheese and other wondrous things was the best kind of cure all.

"Never would've taken you for a Britney fan."

That voice.

Lincoln Archer.

Goddamn it.

That was all it took to undo the work of all those marvelous endorphins, my upbeat and positive mood taking a nosedive as I came face-to-face with the very guy I'd vowed to forget.

"Well, I never would've taken you for desperate and pathetic yet here you are in my apartment. The temptation was too great, huh? Guess I should be thankful you waited until today and didn't come begging on my doorstep the minute your driver reported back to you."

I didn't even care I looked like a hot mess, too preoccupied with making sure Lincoln knew how displeased I was. Other women might have thought the stalker routine was cute, but I wasn't one of them. It was bad enough I'd entertained feelings for the guy even after knowing he'd been a creep; going gaga over his boundary issues was *not* happening.

"Ha!" He laughed, not the least bit offended. "But I don't beg on doorsteps. Though if you want to give me a sexy rendition of *Oops . . . I did it again*, I might just sit like a good boy."

"Wow! Sooooo glad I dodged that bullet last night," I huffed out, wondering what I had even seen in him in the first place.

"And you still haven't told me what you are doing here." I tapped my foot impatiently, counting down the seconds until I could toss him out. It was coming, as soon as I got an explanation, he was gone. And I wasn't going to feel bad about it either.

"I called him." Belle emerged from the kitchen carrying two cups of coffee. "I found his card in the trash can."

Oh.

My.

God.

Of all the stuff Belle had pulled over the years, that was easily in the top five.

So on top of seeing a guy I didn't want to see, I was also going to have to plan my sister's funeral.

It was going to be a busier afternoon than I expected.

Chapter 8

Lincoln

I'll admit when I got the call from Belle, I was curious.

I'd assumed I'd eventually hear from Zara, but I'd been prepared to bide my time. And honestly, the part about not begging women was absolutely the truth.

I didn't beg.

Ever.

And if for some reason it turned out that I'd imagined the chemistry between us and we never saw each other again, I'd make my peace with it. Not to say I'd be ecstatic that possibly the hottest, most intriguing woman I'd ever met had disappeared from my life. But I wasn't going to shackle her in my basement and Stockholm her until she agreed to date me.

But like Zara had mentioned, Belle wasn't any easy woman to say no to. And no matter how I tried to maneuver the conversation, she kept steering it back to me, coming to their apartment, and apologizing to her sister.

I'd assumed that I'd not only done that last night, but any further efforts wouldn't be welcomed. But Belle wouldn't be swayed, threatening to call me every hour, on the hour, until I got my fake-Bostonian ass to their Greenwich apartment. Oh, and if I could pick up some vanilla creamer on the way because they were out.

I wasn't even sure what the hell I was doing until I buzzed at their apartment building, the goddamn vanilla creamer housed in my palm.

"You did what?" Zara leveled her sister with a stare, her hands on her lycra'd hips as she sucked in slow measured breaths.

It had been clear she'd been running.

If her long tight running pants and crop top weren't a tip off, the sheen of sweat and the Britney playlist were. And while her face was flushed and her hair was a mess, I couldn't help but notice how incredibly beautiful she was in the daylight.

"I called him. You said he was a jerk, and he needs to say sorry. So I made him come here to apologize," Belle answered matter-of-factly.

"And you guys were out of creamer," I added, accepting the cup of coffee from Belle thankfully without that hideously sweet stuff she hypnotized me into buying.

Zara's brows knitted, apparently our shared version of events not making any sense. Not that I blamed her, I was on the other side of the conversation with Belle and still wasn't sure what I was doing there.

Belle laughed, lifting her cup to her lips and blowing across the surface. "And yeah, we were out of vanilla creamer."

"I would have picked some up if you'd texted me." Zara shook her phone at her sister, the screen displaying no missed calls or messages. "And you," she directed her attention to me, "we said everything we needed to say to each other last night."

I shrugged, not willing to get involved in their sibling tussle. "Well, I guess you gave Belle a different version, because apparently there's still things that need to be said."

I wasn't apologizing again.

I'd already done that.

And since I hadn't been entirely sorry—the deceit part wasn't my finest moment but everything else had been completely above board—I didn't want to offer fake platitudes.

But if there was a further need for an exchange of words, then I wasn't running away from it either. And if taking the chance to see Zara again made me an opportunist, then I was good with that distinction too.

"Belle, can you give us a minute?" She turned to her sister, her expression so unreadable I wasn't sure if I should be turned on or worried.

Belle sighed dramatically. "You know our apartment isn't that big and I'm going to hear anyway. Why can't I just stay and watch?"

"Because I don't want to make you an accessory." Zara sucked in a breath. "Also, anything you hear and not see is unreliable and wouldn't be admissible in court. Trust me, it's better for everyone if you don't need to take the stand."

I laughed, unable to help myself as she delivered all of that with a straight face. I didn't doubt she'd be fierce on a cross-examination. And while I hoped I got to see it someday, I'd prefer if it wasn't on an attempted murder trial. Namely, my own.

"Sorry." I cleared my throat, shaking off the glare Zara was shooting me. "But she is right, Belle."

"Fine!" Belle sipped her coffee, rolling her eyes as she ambled out of the room. "But at least talk loudly so I can hear you. I called this meeting, the fact I've been excluded is really very rude."

"She do that a lot?" I asked, tipping my head in the direction her sister had disappeared to.

Zara nodded, taking another calming breath. "Be overly dramatic or get involved in business that doesn't involve her? The answer would be yes to both."

"I'll remember that next time she calls and gives me her shopping list." I chuckled, not at all upset at where I'd found myself on a Saturday afternoon.

I'd spent most of the night thinking about Zara after she'd left. Replaying those kisses as I lied awake, still feeling the weight of her against me and the smoothness of her skin. The scent of her shampoo had haunted me while I tossed and turned for hours.

Her lids slid closed, pausing a beat before her beautiful eyes opened and rested on me. "Why are you here, Lincoln? Because we both know it's not to say sorry."

"No, it's not." I swallowed, unable to lie. "But pretending last night didn't happen isn't going to work either."

I wanted to touch her.

Wanted to take her in my arms and kiss her exactly like I had last night.

But mostly, I wanted to get to know her and have her know me.

And I was used to taking big risks for a potential big pay-off.

"Why?" she asked, like she was genuinely surprised I hadn't already moved on.

I moved closer, not so much that I was crowding her personal space but enough so she could reach out and touch me if she wanted. "Because you weren't kissing anyone but me last night, Zara, and I won't believe any different."

Her eyes flared wide, and I wasn't sure if it was lust or something else she was feeling. "Are you done?" she asked, her voice betraying nothing.

"That depends." I grinned, wanting nothing more than to kiss her exactly like I had last night. "Have you given any more thought to my proposal?"

"What proposal?" called out Belle from around the corner, letting us know while she might not be in the room, she was listening. "And you *kissed* him? Why wasn't I told?"

Zara rolled her eyes, wiping off the beads of sweat that still dotted her forehead. "Belle, not *that* kind of proposal. And can't you eavesdrop without interjecting like a regular person?"

Belle peered from around the corner. "No. Not when you leave out all the good parts. Sooooo you kissed, huh?" She looked at me with suspicion. "What else did you do?"

"Belle!" Zara huffed before turning to me. "Do not answer that."

I didn't kiss and tell.

Locker room talk bored me. Assholes embellished their exploits because really, they weren't getting shit in the sack, and I had no time or interest in it. But the temptation to tease Zara was proving too great.

"What's in it for me?"

"What?" she choked out.

I tipped my head to the side, suppressing my grin. "You want my silence, what's in it for me?"

She laughed, probably amused at my audacity. And while I had no intention of telling her sister *anything*, it was way too much fun to stop.

"Wow, extortion. Let's just add that to the list of things I don't like about you."

My smile edged wider. "This list sounds intriguing. Sounds different to the list you had last night."

"Are you guys going to rip each other's clothes off right now?" Belle chuckled. "Because if that's where this is heading, I'll leave for real."

"No. We're not ripping each other's clothes off, we are not talking about last night, and we are not going to try and find the real Edwin Carlisle." Zara lifted her hands, putting any debate to rest.

Except.

"Wait! You can find the real Edwin and you're not?" Belle's voice rose an octave. "Again, something that should've been mentioned. Annnnnnnd something I think we should definitely do."

Zara silently swore, her lips moving as the ghost of the words she didn't say teased me. And as much as she would've loved to blame someone else, she couldn't.

"Of course we should," I agreed, doubling down on yesterday's commitment. "I even offered my unwavering dedication to the cause."

I'd still yet to find out why it was so important, but I already didn't like the guy.

"You know what, fine." Zara shook her head, calmer than I'd expected. "You both want to find him so badly, have at it. I'll leave you to it. In the meantime, I'm going to go get a shower."

And with more attitude than should be legal for a pair of hips, she swayed her way out of the living room.

To go shower, presumably.

Great.

Because seeing her sweaty and beautiful wasn't enough, now I had to imagine her naked and wet.

And if she looked half as good as she'd felt last night—

"So?" Belle asked, interrupting the indecent thoughts I was having about her sister. "How are you going to find him?"

I cleared my throat, trying to ignore my cock who was suddenly very interested with the sound of running water. She wasn't kidding about that shower. "I have my sources, and it shouldn't be too hard."

At the very least, talk of the moron—whoever he was—would help the situation in my jeans.

"Good. And you'll keep me updated, right? You'll call me if you find him."

Wait.

Getting friendly with Belle hadn't been the plan.

And while I had zero interest in her other than she was Zara's sister, I didn't need there to be any miscommunications or misunderstandings.

"Yeah, that's not how I work. I'll find him, but if you want to know anything, you're going to have to get it from Zara."

Her brow rose, folding her slender arms against her tiny frame. "Oh, really? Tell me again why you pretended to be someone else and ruined my sister's evening."

"Hey, I didn't pretend. I just didn't correct her assumption. Different things."

She scoffed, the family resemblance to her sister making itself known even though they looked nothing alike. "Pfffft, this isn't a murder trial, douchebag. Save your posturing for a jury."

"You called me, remember?"

We were stopped from further deliberation by the sound of the water shutting off.

It had been a quick shower.

Or she'd never really taken one in the first place.

My train of thought completely derailed, wondering if she was going to walk out in a towel.

"Lincoln." Belle snapped her fingers in front of my face, my head having unconsciously turned to the doorway anticipating Zara's entrance. "Stop being a pervert and listen to me. Find this guy, bring him to Zara, don't be a jerk."

It was bewildering to me how someone so small could make such big demands. And as much as she was trying to monopolize my attention, she was—like her height—coming up short.

"Oh, I'll find him alright. But not because you want me to."

I'd been perfectly fine until the asshole and I had become accidentally intertwined. And I wasn't sure exactly whether or not to thank him, or hope he got audited by the IRS. In any case,

I was going to solve the riddle, and hopefully in the process find out a little more about Zara.

Even knowing seeing her half-naked was a possibility, I was unprepared for the reality. Zara emerged with a huge white bath towel wrapped around her body, her skin flushed pink. She had a smaller one around her head like a turban, striding out with confidence and knowing how hot she looked.

"You're still here?" she deadpanned. "Belle, I thought I told you to put away your playthings."

"I was already leaving." I swallowed, pretending to be unaffected while rocking a hard-on. "But I have no doubt we'll see each other again. And this time, Zara, it won't be Belle who calls me, it will be you."

And leaving her to ponder that little nugget, I turned around and left.

She wanted to play, we could play.

And baby, I played better than anyone I knew.

Chapter 9

Zara

Being angry at Belle never lasted long.

I tried to hold out, laying on the silent treatment and trying to guilt her into feeling bad, but she always wore me down.

She was my only weakness.

The only human alive who could literally do the worst possible thing and I'd probably *still* forgive her. A sister's love is both a blessing and a curse, which was why it only took me a day before forgiving her for calling Lincoln and trying to involve herself in what had been one giant mistake.

Because that was what Lincoln Archer was, a mistake.

"What do you think he's going to do when he finds him?" Belle asked, putting the finishing touches on a gift basket she'd made for Hayley. "Surely, he'll let us know, right?"

"I don't care what he does," I lied, taking the huge organza bow and tying it on for her. "It's a free country, he can do what he wants. Now, you sure you've got enough pink stuff in here?"

True to nature, Belle had gone overboard, and Hayley's new daughter was going to be wearing every shade of pink from blush to fuchsia from now until she turned three.

"Oh, hush! It's never enough pink. Why don't you come to the hospital with me and see Hayley's ugly baby?" She looked at me with hope, batting her eyelashes like she was fifteen and needed me to give her a ride to a friend's house even though it was after curfew.

"I already told you I was coming, Belle." I shook my head. "My schedule is so crazy it's either go see the little goober now or it will be her first birthday before we meet."

Being made a senior associate came with responsibilities, and working overtime was not only assumed but expected. It would eventually all pay off, but for the moment, I was resigned to the fact I'd have zero social life and most of my free time would be cozying up to legal briefs.

And while Hayley was Belle's best friend, I had to admire the way she stepped up and owned it. She was raising her baby by herself, worked right up until she delivered, and was already negotiating with directors for her return to the stage. She refused to accept motherhood meant her life was over. And I respected a woman who could do that so fearlessly, even if they weren't the same choices I'd make for myself. Also showed me that I could possibly have a family of my own someday while still chasing my dreams. Assuming I found someone I loved and I wanted to make babies with. Not Lincoln, of course, someone *other* than him.

"I was just making sure. I didn't want you still being mad and leaving me to wrestle this gift basket into a cab all by myself." She lifted the basket in question, hiding herself entirely behind the cellophane-wrapped gift.

"Belle, don't pretend like you wouldn't have people lining up to help you. I still can't believe you convinced Lincoln to buy your freaking creamer."

"I already told you. We were out and he was coming over anyway." She shrugged like it made perfect sense to her. "I still think you should call him. He was really good-looking."

"I hadn't noticed," I feigned disinterest, pretending like he wasn't the hottest guy I'd seen in a long time. And his kiss . . . wowza. Anyway, none of that mattered, he was in the past and we were never going to see each other again.

Belle collected her oversized handbag while I slipped on my shoes. Unlike last time—when we'd made a mercy dash to the hospital—I wasn't wearing heels and a dress. Instead I was wearing my favorite pair of jeans, a faded bar T-shirt from the place I worked at all the way through undergrad, and a pair of runners. It was the perfect Sunday attire, no structured suits or sky-high stilettos which formed most of my weekly wardrobe.

Together we carried the large basket down the stairs and hailed a cab to the hospital. Belle talked the whole way there, trying to prepare me for this baby who apparently looked like an extra from a horror movie.

"Belle!" Hayley's eyes lit up when we entered the room. "And you brought the entire baby section of Target with you."

"Hi, Hayley," I smiled, my hands occupied by the oversized basket Belle had forgotten she was helping to carry. "I can't believe you had a baby less than two days ago, you look amazing."

That wasn't me trying to make her feel better either, she did look great. Her skin was clear and her eyes sparkling, and if there was ever an advertisement to sell motherhood, Hayley should be starring in it.

"Oh, thank you. Bobbie is honestly a dream baby. I'm not sure what I did to deserve it, but so far, all she does is sleep and eat. Barely any fussing at all." Hayley's face got animated talking about her new little girl.

"Bobbie? You settled on a name?" Belle whisper-yelled, doing her best not to wake the baby who was swaddled in what looked to be a plastic tub.

Hayley nodded, smiling broadly as she added, "Well, I really wanted to name her after my gran. She bought me my first pointe shoes and paid for all my ballet lessons until I was eighteen. She always believed in me even when I didn't believe in myself. But Roberta is such an old-fashioned name, I decided to call her Bobbie instead. You want to see her? She's sleeping but you can pick her up and she doesn't even blink."

"Ummm," Belle stuttered. "Shouldn't we just let her sleep? I don't want her to cry and break her winning streak."

"Okay, maybe later," Hayley agreed, laying back in the bed. "Now let's talk about regular stuff. I don't want to turn into that woman who only talks about her baby."

Belle happily launched into animated conversation, barely taking a breath as she filled Hayley in on everything from the weather, to the cab driver we'd had on the ride over. And while she was chatting, I dared to steal a look at the rumored hideous baby.

"She's really cute." I tried to hide my surprise as I peered underneath the fluffy blanket. Her eyes were scrunched up tight, oblivious to what was going on around her.

Belle must have been high, or traumatized, because Bobbie wasn't even close to being ugly.

"Awww thanks," cooed Hayley. "I think so too but I think every parent says that."

Belle looked at me bewildered, scooting over to see Bobbie. "Wow." She caught herself, recovering quickly. "Well, of course she's cute. Didn't I say that?"

I tried not to laugh, my sister eyeing me hard not to say anything different. "Hey, we should get some coffees or something." Belle tugged me toward the door. "You could probably use the caffeine, right?"

"I would kill for a decent coffee right now," Hayley moaned. "But not from the hospital cafeteria, that place is the worst."

After getting Hayley's coffee order, and Belle assuring her we'd be right back, she pulled me out of the hospital room and into the hall.

"What was that? Can they switch babies on you? Because that was *not* the kid that came out of her vagina." Belle almost hyperventilated. "We have to tell her there's been a mix-up. Maybe you should flag down a doctor and see if they can do a DNA test."

I laughed, putting a hand on my sister's arm to try and calm her. "Could it be that maybe no baby would look cute the minute they were born? I'm almost positive that is Hayley's baby, and I think it would be really hard to try and get a doctor to do a DNA test on a baby and her mother."

Obviously Bobbie just needed a day to "get cute," Lord knows, we've all been there. "Can we go back inside and you not act weird?" I asked Belle, hoping she wasn't going to try and sneak a hair sample from Hayley and the baby and run it down to a lab. "Because I think it's bad enough we just got here and we're out in the hall instead of visiting like we should."

"Well, we have to go get coffee first. I only suggested it as a means to talk to you privately." Her eyes got wide, horrified her friend might learn the truth. "I know I'm a terrible person for saying all of that stuff about the baby, but I was tired. Please don't tell Hayley, I don't want her to hate me."

"Like I would do that? Come on, Belle." I rolled my eyes slightly offended she would think I'd sell her out. "Go back into the room, hold the baby and be the loving, caring friend you are, and *I* will go get the coffees."

"Really? You'd do that?"

"Of course, there's a place right around the corner. Coffee is great and they have desserts as well." I didn't bother telling her *how* I knew, and how it had been the venue for my fake date with Edwin . . . Lincoln. All that mattered was I knew it existed, and it was close enough I could run and get coffees and be back before they got cold.

"You're the best sister ever." She threw her arms around me, her over-the-top gratitude earning us stares from people walking through the halls.

I hugged her back before pulling myself free. "Yeah, yeah, I know. Now go back and be with Hayley. I'll be quick."

She twirled, mouthing me another *thank you* over her shoulder before disappearing back into the room. And since I had a mission, I walked with purpose through the corridors and down to the main exit, finding myself outside on the street.

It didn't take long for me to find Cups, the cute little coffee shop I'd visited with Lincoln. Molly, the waitress, smiled as I walked in, and I wasn't sure if it was because she recognized me or was just generally cheery.

"Hi!" She grinned. "Where's your fiancé?" The mystery why she was smiling, solved. "You must be so happy. He is one of the nicest customers ever and so good-looking. I honestly thought he and Nate were. . ." She leaned in closer. "Well, you know."

Uhhhhhhhh.

And there was another complication I didn't need.

It was supposed to be a quick coffee run. Get in, get out, and go back to Belle, Hayley and the baby. But while I anticipated Molly might recognize me, I hadn't expected a full-blown conversation. Nor needing to confirm my pretend relationship status. It had been amusing, and maybe even a little cute that first night. But those were feelings I no longer had.

Of course, with any luck I wouldn't be near the hospital and therefore the coffee shop again anytime soon. So was it really worth the effort to tell her the truth? No, no it wasn't, resolving to pretend to be Lincoln's future bride if it meant I could get in and out faster.

"Thank you so much, we're so blissfully happy," I lied, plastering on my fake smile. "And Nate will be our best man.

81

He's so great, one of these days he's going to make the right guy an amazing husband."

The lies passed so easily from my lips, my smile and gaze not dropping as I pretended to be pathetically *in love*.

"I'm so glad." Her tone sweetened to match mine as she looked me over. "Well, what can I get you today?"

I rattled off my name with our order for three coffees to go and three oversized chocolate chip cookies. I'd wanted to get another piece of that amazing Key Lime pie I'd tasted the other night but carrying coffee and three slices of pie would have been difficult. Anyway, the cookies looked just as good.

Molly bagged up my cookies before moving to the coffee machine to whip up our order, and I stepped to the side to allow her to serve other customers while I looked enviably at the cake counter. I silently mourned the fact I'd never taste any of them again. Not only because I hoped my hospital visits in the future were few and far between, but obviously now I was a compulsive liar, I could never come back again.

I hadn't realized I'd zoned out until I heard Molly excitedly call out my name. I assumed it was because my order was ready and she *really* loved her job, until I looked up and saw a super fit, tall, and really good-looking guy wearing hospital scrubs.

Oh. Shit.

And judging from the look of utter bewilderment he was giving me, there was no need to guess who the hot doc was.

Nate.

Of course, it's fucking Nate.

Why, God, Why?

The one time I tell a lie, and I'm cursed to eternal damnation.

"What a coincidence." Molly shimmered, her joy so palpable she was almost levitating. "We were just talking about you. And really, there is no greater choice for the best man."

Nate coughed, raising his brow at me before looking back at Molly. I was positive he thought either one or both of us was tripping and wondering if he needed to get out the Narcan.

"Hi, Nate." I waved, because seriously, why stop now. I'd already committed to the shitshow which was this situation, what was another few extra offenses. "Fancy meeting you here."

"Hiiiiiii," he responded cautiously, no doubt trying to work out my angle. "Yeah, small world."

And either Nate didn't want me to suffer any more than I already had, or he honestly thought he could possibly know me. I mean, he was an ER doctor, right? Wasn't that what Lincoln had said? He must be used to working on the fly and meeting a lot of people. Totally conceivable that we knew each other and he just couldn't place me.

Or he was an angel.

I'd be happy with either outcome, as long as I could get my coffee and get gone as soon as possible and not look like the biggest fraud in town.

He gave Molly his order—cappuccino, light on the foam—paid and then came to join me at the cake counter. And while I'd been whispering thanks earlier, my thoughts of gratitude might have been a tiny bit short-lived.

"So best man, huh? Better get my tux dry cleaned." He smiled, making it clear that my quick and easy getaway was no longer an option. "Oh, and you'll have to let me know where you and . . ." He waved his hand, looking at me with expectation, "are registered."

"Lincoln," I coughed out, hoping Molly couldn't hear us.

"Lincoln?" he asked, his brows receding into his hairline before I nodded. "Well, *that* is interesting."

"It's just a small misunderstanding," I started to explain, cursing myself for not setting Molly straight from the beginning.

"Well, considering my best friend hasn't told me he's getting married, I'd say the misunderstanding is pretty big." He folded his arms across his chest.

"It was a stupid joke, he thought I was going to propose and then made a big deal about it. And then when we came here for coffee, he thought it would be funny to tell Molly we were engaged."

It sounded insane when I said it out loud, and honestly, I'm not sure how I found it cute in the first place. Had we been deranged? Because none of the other night's activities—especially concluding with me going to his hotel room—were the actions of sane people.

"Ummm, he thought *you* were going to propose? How long have you been dating?" He chuckled, less shocked than I'd have expected.

"Okay, so we're not. Well, not really. We had one date. And honestly, we're probably never going to see each other again. But I hear you're a really nice guy and if we were getting married, you'd absolutely be the best man. I mean, anyone would have to be better than Lincoln, right?" The words flew out of my mouth in a rush as I lost all composure.

I could argue in front of a jury, deal with a judge who hated women, and present my briefs to the senior partners, all without working up a sweat. Why I'd become a hot mess was beyond me.

"Oh really?" He tilted his head. "What did he do to piss you off?"

"Zara, coffees are ready!" Molly called out, my silent thanks offered to the heavens.

"It honestly doesn't matter. Anyway, I'll never be back here again so I'll let him decide how he wants to stage our breakup. Although I think Molly might be secretly holding a torch for him, so it might work out in his favor. Nice meeting you, have a nice life." I took a huge gasp of air, plastered a smile on my face and walked to where my coffees were waiting.

With any luck I could collect the paper cups and continue walking without breaking my stride, the allure of disappearing into oblivion so tempting it was almost a turn on.

"Wait!" Nate called after me, my hands just about to grasp the paper tray filled with caffeine goodness.

"Shit," I cursed under my breath. "Yeah?" I turned around, continuing the ruse for Molly's benefit.

"Let me walk with you." He winked, collecting his coffee which was now miraculously ready too.

Really Molly? You couldn't just have been a little less efficient.

"Surrreeeeee," I heard myself say, regretting it immediately. "I was heading back to the hospital anyway."

Well done, Zara.

Well.

Fucking.

Done.

Chapter 10

Lincoln

It took two days to locate Edwin Carlisle.

Thirty-eight hours if you wanted to get technical, and I couldn't have been less impressed with my findings.

I'd assumed he'd be some eighty-year-old retiree with no hair and a heart condition. Or a middle-aged guy with a receding hairline and an unflattering paunch.

But Edwin Carlisle was a thirty-year-old investment banker from Manhattan who came from old money. And when I say he was from Manhattan, I mean his family owned four high-rises across the island. He'd been named after his grandfather, got an MBA from Wharton, and while being engaged a couple of times, he was currently single.

The guy wasn't even ugly, working out at least five times a week according to his profile in *Business Weekly's* 30 under 30 and had a disappointingly full head of hair.

Perfect.

So not only was the piece of shit young, but he was also rich, successful, handsome and fucking single.

And while Zara—or Belle—hadn't fessed up as to why finding him had been so important, I could string together the general idea. He was obviously some dude she was supposedly trying to hook up with. I wasn't sure if it was some random missed connection, an online dating match that fell through, or some childhood pen pal that she lost contact with, but she had feelings for this guy.

Clearly, they hadn't ever met, or she would've known I wasn't him. Because in addition to me not being born with a silver spoon up my ass, I also didn't have blond hair or drive a Maserati.

I bet this guy had a really small dick.

Anyway, none of it really mattered other than I had a fucking decision to make.

Well, it was more of conundrum.

Did I take the information I'd gathered, including his residential address, and hand it over to Zara? Or did I dump everything into the industrial shredder and pretend like it never happened? It's not like she even asked for it, hell, pretty sure she said she didn't want to know.

Or that she'd find him herself.

Or some other bullshit which basically spelled out that she didn't want me involved.

So, if I was to toss the dossier I'd compiled in the trash and forgot it ever happened, what would be the harm? I sure as hell wasn't going to gift wrap the bastard for her and hoped things worked out for them. And if that made me bitter and twisted, I was fine with that.

I didn't even have to meet the guy to know he didn't deserve Zara. He'd want a trophy wife, some silicone inflated Barbie doll who could suck his dick on demand and still look good on the society pages. And fuck having a career, her duties would be popping out two or three Carlisle heirs and chairing a few noted charities. She could kiss that Supreme Court Justice idea goodbye.

Oh, he'd be charming at the start. Tell her everything she wanted to hear about how he'd support her fucking ambition and how he found powerful women sexy. But the minute her heart was involved, he'd change his fucking tune pretty damn quick.

Amazing how I'd mapped out the whole scenario, and I didn't know either of them well. Except, as weird as it was to admit, I felt like I did know her. At least, the parts that were important.

And yeah, I knew I was acting like a dick, assuming she'd even fall for that asshole. But I knew how fucking sweet that kiss we'd shared had been, and even the slight chance he might get a taste of that was too much for me to handle.

Anyone else.

If we never saw each other, and she went on to live a long happy life with some other guy, I think I'd be able to deal.

Just not him.

Not the guy she thought I was.

It was irrational and more than a little ridiculous, but I didn't care.

Anyway, I'd made it clear that if she wanted to see me again, she was going to have to call me. And since there were no guarantees that would happen, all of it could be one big moot point. At least that was the lie I told myself knowing there was no way I wasn't ever seeing her again. Nope, I wouldn't force her, but I'd find a goddamn way.

Deciding to stick the folder into a drawer and letting it be a problem for another day, I poured myself a scotch.

I'd left Zara and Belle's Greenwich Village apartment on Saturday and hadn't heard from either of them since. I'd been working from my hotel room, checking up on a floundering company that Locke and Collins were looking to acquire. They had some cash flow problems but were otherwise sound, so I had set up a meeting with their board for tomorrow. If all went well, I'd submit my findings to the partners by the end of the day and I'd have the rest of the week all to myself.

Of course, there was always the possibility I'd be called back early. With my work wrapped up, there was no valid reason to stick around New York. But having family upstate meant I got to play a little fast and loose with my return date. They gave me some leeway so I could go home and see the folks and I flew in and out of the city as much as they needed. It was a fair deal that usually worked well for me, and the current circumstances were no different. Though I doubted I'd be making it to Rochester this time around, sorry Mom and Dad.

The scotch went down easy as I sunk into the plush sofa in my room. My phone buzzed beside me, the ringer having been turned off a few hours ago. I'd intended to ignore it, having given myself the night off from work, but I stupidly picked it up. Deep down I hoped it was Zara even though my gut told me it wasn't. I just couldn't get her out of my head.

"Hey!" I answered, glad to see it was Nate, happy to take a social call rather than one from the firm. "To what do I owe this pleasure?"

We usually saw each other a couple of times whenever I was in town but both of us had crazy-ass schedules. He worked rotating shifts in the ER, and it wasn't unusual for me to be logged into the company portal until the early hours of the morning.

"Was wondering if you'd had dinner yet? I've got a night off from the hospital and figured we could catch up a little more than we did the other night."

"Dinner? Well, that sounds fancy," I laughed, our get-togethers usually at the coffee shop around the corner from the hospital or in the bar of whatever hotel I was staying at.

"Yes, moron. And not at a bar. Somewhere that has tablecloths, and the menus aren't laminated, and I have an excuse to wear a suit. You can pay of course because you sold your soul to Satan and saving lives doesn't pay as well."

I laughed, glad for both the distraction and a chance to leave my room. I'd have probably ordered room service again. "Nathaniel Baxter, are you asking me out on a date? How many times am I going to have to turn you down, buddy? I don't care how much you love cock, you're still not going to be able to handle mine."

"You are such a jerk." Nate chuckled. "And I wouldn't date you if you were the last man on earth."

I mock gasped, pretending to be offended. "Well, now you're just being hurtful."

"Learned from the best." I could hear the grin in his voice. "Now stop wasting time and meet me down in the lobby. I've got reservations at Matteo's."

I straightened my tie, and other than shucking my jacket earlier, I was still wearing most of my suit. Nate probably already knew that, my reputation for being ready to hit a courtroom at a moment's notice, something he'd given me shit about more than once.

"And if I'd said no?"

He chuckled softly. "Please, Archer. When have you ever turned down a nice dinner with good-looking company? You were a sure thing."

"I'll be down in ten."

I ended the call, grabbed my jacket, wallet and phone and took one last mouthful of scotch. My fingers thumbed through my phone, calling my driver as I locked my hotel room. I was glad I didn't have to drive, free to drink a little more as the evening progressed without worrying about a DUI. And thinking about Zara with Edwin—which I still was—made me want to reach for more than just another scotch.

The elevator opened to the ornate lobby of the Four Seasons and it didn't take long to locate Nate. Not sure how he still had the energy to smile and look so goddam optimistic when he spent most of his time dealing with one emergency after another. Guess it further reaffirmed I'd made the right call by leaving medicine.

"Wow, Archer. Five minutes notice and you still stroll in devastatingly handsome. Have you no shame?" Nate rolled his eyes. "I like this scruff thing you've got going on." He pointed to my chin. "Sexy in that *I'm going to destroy your life and sleep with your wife* kind of way."

I smirked, straightening my jacket as we waited for the driver. "Stop hitting on me, Nate. You already said you wouldn't date me if I was the last man on earth. You can't backtrack now."

We made small talk as we waited for the car, the conversation between us always easy. I'd never cared that he was gay, or worried he was going to try and seduce me or some shit. He'd been one of the most dependable and honorable guys I'd ever met, and that was all that mattered to me.

Which meant . . .

"So there's something I want to run past you," I said as we slid into the waiting car.

Nate told the driver where we were heading before turning back to me. "If this is about any kind of rash, it needs to wait until after dinner."

"Not a rash." I unconsciously reached to my neck and worked the muscles that had bunched at the base of my skull. "It's about a woman."

"Really?" Nate's brow rose but didn't look incredibly surprised. "And no one knows women like a gay man, right? Thanks for perpetuating the stereotype."

"Oh har-har," I mock laughed. "And it is about one in particular. I swear, I think there's something wrong with me because she's all up in my head."

Nate waved his hand urging me to go on.

My eyes flicked to the driver who was mostly ignoring us. He was on a huge retainer with Locke and Collins and wouldn't risk his cushy paycheck to spread gossip about me. Still, I wasn't in the habit of showing anyone weakness, so I swallowed before continuing.

"I met her a few nights ago, at the hospital, actually." Heat traveled up my neck just thinking about her. "She's beautiful. Not just a pretty face but the body and brains to match. She's quick with her mouth and funny, and even though I hardly know her, I can't stop thinking about her."

Nate nodded but stayed silent.

"I asked her out, we had coffee. She's a lawyer too if you can believe it, and everything was going really great."

"And?" Nate asked, rightly guessing it didn't have a happy ending.

"I might not have been totally honest about who I was." I grimaced. "I didn't lie," I added quickly, wanting the record to show that I wasn't going out of my way to deceive her. "But she thought I was someone else and I let her believe it."

He listened without comment as I recounted the night, and then all about the next day at their apartment. And even how I'd found the cocksucker—I mean Edwin Carlisle—fully intending on showing I was a man of my word.

But.

But, but, but.

"You think she's going to meet the real Edwin and fall in love with him?" he asked drily.

"No. I mean, I don't know. He is probably a decent guy," I lied. Because I didn't believe he was decent at all. I'd already concocted my version of events, and he was a shady piece of shit with more money than personality.

"Right," Nate deadpanned. "Decent guy is *exactly* what you think about him."

To be fair, I hadn't really sold it. Mainly because it was Nate, and his tolerance for bullshit was low. And I'd obviously told him about Zara because I wanted his input so lying about it wasn't going to help.

I rolled my eyes and let it fly. "Fine, he's a jerk-off. I don't know him, but trust me I know the type. New York, Boston, Chicago—all the major cities are full of these little pricks who bought their way into college or business on Daddy's coin. They wouldn't know what to do without a trust fund and their idea of foreplay is showing a woman their overpriced sports car."

Nate coughed out a laugh. "Wow, tell me how you really feel. Also, don't *you* own a Jaguar?"

"It's a '74 E-Type and a classic, not the same thing," I scoffed, the comparisons between them laughable. "And I bought it as an investment, not to help me get women into bed." Considering the amount of time I actually got to drive the thing, it might as well be on blocks in some fancy garage. But I got to stretch her legs a little whenever I was home and not working weekends.

"Yeah, totally not the same thing. Completely different. Not even remotely close. I'm sure you clarify its investment potential whenever you show it to a woman. Elaborate on its scope for appreciation in the current market's climate." Nate smirked.

"Anyway, this isn't about me," I pointed out, not wanting to get sidetracked. "This is about Zara, and whether or not I tell her about this guy."

Originally, I'd intended to.

All part of the mea culpa and to prove I wasn't a complete jerk.

But things change.

And maybe integrity was overrated.

Nate leveled me with a stare that told me he was about to lay down some realness. "We both know you're going to tell her. Because as much as you pretend to be like those bastards you work for, you have a conscience and a heart. And you're not going to lie your way to an advantage. If you were going to do that, you'd have slept with her, and ghosted when you blew out of town. Not like she would've been able to track you down."

He was right.

Of course, he was right.

It was clear where we'd been heading that night, and I had the perfect excuse never to see her again.

I was leaving.

She'd have never known who I was, or if she found out later I wasn't Edwin, I'd be somewhere else not dealing with the fall out.

"Could you not just lie to me, pretend to be a team player?" I sighed, not all that surprised. "Just once, Nate."

"Maybe if *you'd* asked me to be your best man instead of me hearing it from your fake fiancée, I'd have been nicer." His shit-eating grin spread across his incredibly smug face.

"What?" I asked, wondering if I'd heard right. Since there was nothing wrong with my hearing and Nate wasn't in the habit of misspeaking, it meant . . . "Start talking, Nate. And I mean, right now."

Of course that was the exact moment we'd arrived at the restaurant, the stupid traffic not giving me five more fucking minutes before the driver turned around and announced we'd reached our destination.

I quickly—and probably rudely—thanked him, hustling out of the car and hoping Nate did the same. I wasn't above pulling him out the door and planting him on the sidewalk beside me. And while he was only an inch or so shorter and not that much lighter, I was more than confident I was capable.

"Talk," I barked, watching the blacked-out SUV that had driven us disappearing back into traffic.

"Why don't we go in, sit at the table and have a conversation like civilized people?" Nate smirked, edging toward the door.

"You're a complete dick," I huffed out, annoyed he clearly knew more than he was letting on and was making me wait.

He chuckled, heading toward the door of the restaurant and holding it open. "Nah, a complete dick wouldn't be able to resuscitate you. I, dear friend, can."

I rolled my eyes, walking into Matteo's while he followed closely behind.

"Resuscitate? Why—" I didn't get to finish the sentence, my eyes snagging on her from across the room.

Zara.

Jesus.

Fucking.

Christ.

Chapter 11

Zara

Dinner with Nate and Lincoln was the last thing I thought I'd ever do.

Mainly because up until two days ago I hadn't even met Nate, which was right around the time I was convinced I'd never see Lincoln again.

But Sunday had been full of revelations.

So when Nate called me Monday afternoon to invite me to dinner—telling me Lincoln would be there—I hadn't immediately said no like I'd assumed.

My mouth was open, the word right there in my throat.

Except when it left my lips it had been a "yes" instead.

Damn him.

I swear, he was a male, much taller version of Belle.

He'd been charming, funny and warm on our shared walk back to the hospital, and more surprisingly, hadn't asked about Lincoln.

Which of course made me super curious.

I had pretended to be engaged to his best friend.

Implicated him in my web of deceit.

And he *didn't* have questions?

What was wrong with him?

And more importantly, what the hell was wrong with me that I couldn't accept what was obviously a gift—spared the inquisition and probably judgment—and move the hell on. Which made him a riddle I needed to crack, with the added incentive of gathering further intelligence on Lincoln, which I'd convinced myself I didn't want but for some reason desperately needed.

I was a smart woman, so why I was acting like a teenager was beyond me.

Numbers were exchanged—much to both of our surprise—my parting flippant remark of having dinner together sometime with Lincoln, the last thing I'd said.

Because of course I had to have the last word.

And a referee seemed smart.

Also there was less chance of us ripping each other's clothes off because even though I'd convinced myself I was repulsed by Lincoln, I couldn't stop thinking about him.

But wow, reality was a huuuuuuge wakeup call and wasn't as neat as it had been in my head.

Firstly, he'd somehow gotten *better* looking since I said goodbye to him.

Despite wearing a suit—which did fabulous things for his body —his hair was ruffled like he'd just rolled out of bed. His scruff-covered chin played into the fantasy, looking like he'd been doing some heavy-duty battle in the boardroom—and bedroom—before gracing us with his presence.

And if the widening of his midnight blue eyes were anything to go by, I'd say he hadn't known I was going to be there.

Nate, I might have fallen a little bit in love with you. The advantage and the slight upper hand it gave me, one of the sexiest things ever.

"Gentlemen." I stood, both of them stopping at our cozy round table. "Nate, the menu looks delicious, I can't believe I've never eaten here before." I smiled, watching as Lincoln tried to get his shit together.

It was so rewarding to watch.

A man who could no doubt fly by the seat of his pants in most circumstances, and could smooth talk his way out of anything, was at a loss for words and I had something to do with it.

Lincoln's eyes raked up and down my body, his Adam's apple bobbing slowly as he took a big swallow. "Zara, you look . . ." He paused, taking an even more measured perusal, "beautiful tonight."

I smiled even though I was partly disappointed he was able to string that together. "Thanks." I waved casually, my heart beating madly in my chest. "You look hideous, you let yourself go in the last few days?"

Lies.

So many lies, but I'd never been so grateful to be spilling them because the truth—that he looked amazing and I wanted to wrap myself around his body and kiss him again—wasn't going to be repeated.

To think I'd convinced myself I'd been high or hypnotized or something else on Saturday night and he hadn't been that attractive. Yeah, well that theory was a bust.

He wasn't just attractive, he was mouth-watering. So freaking delectable I couldn't decide which—the more polished version from the hospital or the I-just-had-sex-and-threw-on-this-suit—I liked better.

"Thank you, so glad you noticed." He grinned, completely unperturbed by my insult. Like he knew I hadn't meant it, or if I did, he didn't believe me or care.

So much for that upper hand.

"Zara." Nate moved to my side and gave me a hug. "Linc is right, you look beautiful."

His touch was friendly without being sexual and strangely comforting. I wasn't usually so trusting of people I didn't know, but Nate had something about him that was immediately likeable and sincere. I bet he was an excellent doctor, able to give you bad news like you had a week to live and still make it sound half-decent. Which was probably why I'd lost my mind and agreed to the dinner in the first place.

That hypnotic calm and the allure of seeing Lincoln again.

The reasons *why* I wanted to see him were still up for debate, and I wasn't even going to pretend that I wasn't still attracted to him.

"Thanks, Nate." I smiled, accepting his compliment and the hug. "I almost didn't recognize you out of scrubs."

I'd meant to tell him how handsome he was, how sexy he looked in civilian clothes, and all of that would've been the truth. But seeing him standing next to Lincoln made it hard for me to trust my mouth.

Nate was attractive.

Lincoln was ridiculously hot.

And since I wasn't ready to volunteer that information, I thought it best to go with a safer option.

Nate winked, returning my smile with one of his own before he gestured to my seat. Both men waited until I was sitting before taking their own. It was a little old school but I could appreciate the manners, and knowing they were on their best behavior made it easier to be on mine.

Or so was the plan.

"So, Lincoln, any other women you've deceived in the last few days? I'm happy to start a support group if it's needed."

I'd lasted not even sixty seconds.

Partly because I genuinely couldn't help myself but also because I was curious. If he'd left me and found a more willing candidate. It wouldn't have been too hard, women probably throwing themselves at him every opportunity they got.

I hated them.

And hated how irrationally jealous I was of these fictional women when I'd obviously been the one to turn him down.

Still, logic wasn't an argument I was looking to make with myself, desperate to know the answer one way or another.

"Zara." He breathed out my name and I had no idea what he was going to say next. "Isn't the first thing they teach you in law school not to assume you know anything about anyone? Even with mounting evidence, it's important to make your own findings *before* making judgments."

Oh, that was fucking rich.

Pinning it on me like I was the one to blame.

"You are such a—"

"Really?" Nate interrupted. "We haven't even ordered yet and you two are already going at it. Let's eat first, you can tear each other apart after dessert like regular people."

Lincoln bit his lip, not looking at all offended by Nate's reprimand. "I'll play nice. Zara?"

And as much as it pained me to agree, I wasn't going to be the one who looked unreasonable. "Of course." I laughed, waving my hand casually like I didn't want to wrap my fingers around his neck and choke him.

Or rip his shirt off.

Or kiss him.

The conflict was very real.

"Now what's good here?" I picked up the menu, losing myself in the words I had no interest in reading while I pretended not to give a shit about the man sitting across from me.

Nate coughed, clearing his throat like he didn't buy it. "Everything is delicious. Even more so since Lincoln is paying."

"Wait, no." I held up my hand, wanting to make sure there weren't any misconceptions. I'd agreed to dinner, and in truth, probably looked forward to seeing him. But I didn't want to owe

Lincoln anything, or worse, have him think it was a date. "I'm more than capable of paying for my own dinner, but thanks."

"I'm positive you are *more than capable*, Zara." Lincoln's brow rose in suggestion. "Matteo's is a little pretentious and they don't split the check. But if you feel that strongly about it, you can repay me later."

There was no discussion as to what that repayment might entail, and I had a hunch he didn't mean Venmo.

"Fine," I agreed, because if he thought buying me one lousy dinner got him anything other than a thank you, he was sorely mistaken. "Suit yourself."

While he was doing his best to exude the cool and collected exterior he was so fond of, I could tell he was a little rattled.

"Then let's order." He smirked, picking up his own menu and perusing the offerings.

I wasn't sure if he'd been here before, or he'd already decided what he was having, but his attention wasn't on the specials.

Oh, his eyes glanced down, giving the illusion of him reading, but unless he had special optical processing skills there was no way he'd seen what was listed on those two pages.

Of course, neither had I, and I was staring down at my hardbacked binder like it had the secret to younger looking skin and a smaller ass. Guess we were both distracted, pretending like we weren't checking each other out and refusing to admit it.

There was a heavy silence, no one speaking as we continued the ruse. All the while I mentally tried to formulate rebuttals for yet to be formulated arguments.

A waiter approached, pulling from his pocket a small notepad and pencil. "Is the table ready to order?" He directed his question to Nate and Lincoln, because clearly such an important decision couldn't be handled by a lowly woman.

"Yes, we are." I closed my menu dramatically, refusing to sit quietly and buy into whatever stereotype the guy had in his head. Maybe it was social convention to ask men, or maybe he just figured they looked less decisive? Or maybe he was just a sexist prick and he drew the short straw tonight because I wasn't going to be polite and spare him his feelings. And while I had no intention of being deliberately rude, I wasn't going to allow him to ignore me either.

"Oh, hey." The waiter blinked, looking at the two men for some kind of sign before returning his focus back to me. "Ummm, would you like to start?"

"Yes, thank you." *See, not being rude.* "I'd like to have a Mojito and the pan-roasted halibut."

It was honestly the first thing that I'd seen, and I couldn't recheck the menu after I'd just told the guy I was ready. Surely, they couldn't screw up a basic flat fish.

"And for you gentlemen?" He turned, hesitating.

"New York Strip. Medium rare." Lincoln eased back into his seat before winking at me. "He'll have the same. And a serving each of the baked potato and the lobster mac and cheese."

"And two beers. Imported. Whatever you have from Germany or Italy is fine." Nate grinned.

The waiter's brow rose at our strange table dynamic, but didn't linger, taking our menus and leaving as quickly as he could.

"Probably why people think we're a couple when we're together." Nate shrugged, "It doesn't totally suck though as there are worse people I could be in a fake relationship with."

"Don't lie, Nate, you love it." Lincoln grinned. "Besides, fake relationships seem to be where I excel."

"Hmmm, why do you think that is?" I asked, both curious and liking that we were focusing on his deficiencies and not that I'd been a total idiot.

Because honestly, I *had* been an idiot.

And not that I'd ever admit it to him—because there would be a cold day in hell before I did—but it hadn't been *totally* his fault.

Mostly.

But not entirely.

Lincoln didn't miss a beat. "Because I excel at everything. And a fake relationship is no exception."

Smug.

Ass.

Bastard.

"You know, I'm really glad you *aren't* Edwin Carlisle. Saved myself from making the biggest mistake of my life."

It was more honest than I'd intended but I wasn't taking it back.

Lincoln opened his mouth, and I had no idea what he was going to say because before he did, Nate interjected.

"Ah, yes, the infamous *Edwin Carlisle*." Nate chuckled before turning to Lincoln. "So are you going to tell her or am I?"

Lincoln swallowed hard, cursing under his breath before running his hand through his hair. That would explain why his hair had been a mess.

"Tell me what?" I asked, both excited and terrified by what seemed to be a big reveal.

Lincoln locked eyes with me, taking a breath before slowly exhaling. "I've found him."

"*Him?*"

"Edwin Carlisle. The one who'd been at the hospital that night."

Chapter 12

Zara

Of all the things I'd expected to come out of Lincoln's mouth, the name of the guy he'd pretended to be wasn't one of them.

Hell, I'd prefer if we forgot all about Edwin Carlisle, my stupid lapse in judgment, and refocused on more important things.

Like why I apparently couldn't just leave well enough alone.

Well enough code for Lincoln in the current instance.

"Oh?" I tried not to gag as I tamped down my surprise. "And didn't I tell you that if I wanted to find him, I'd have done so myself."

I mean, I'd had years to dumpster dive the internet and find my mystery man if I'd wanted to. And clearly I hadn't.

Wanted to or searched.

"Yeah, you told me, but I didn't listen." He responded with zero apology. "I've found him. So if you want to continue to hate me you'll have to find some other reason."

I laughed, amused that he believed I felt anything toward him.

Fine, he *was* right, but I wasn't admitting it.

And it wasn't hate, it was more like . . . a strong dislike.

Okay, okay, I didn't dislike him it all. I thought he was hot, and wanted to do stupid things like sit on his beautiful smug face.

But—which incidentally was pretty freaking great too—it had been a really, *really* long time since I'd allowed a man to get the better of me. And *that* was a dangerous game I wasn't sure I wanted to play.

I'd fought all the way through college, and the initial years at the firm, proving I not only had what it took but could do it better, smarter, and with less emotion than everyone else. Because, despite our grandmas carrying placards fighting for our rights to be somewhere, there were still enough misogynistic good-ole-boys who believed we shouldn't. And most of them worked in law firms.

But Lincoln just proved how careless I'd been. Not only was he not who he'd implied to be, but he was a lawyer too. And rival firm or not, there was no room to be distracted or show weakness, not if I wanted a seat at the big table.

"I don't hate you, Lincoln," I admitted. "Hate would imply I have feelings for you. Which I don't. But if it makes you sleep better at night to earn my forgiveness, then I'll suffer through whatever it is you need to do."

So many lies, and I wasn't sure which was the biggest.

Firstly, there'd be no suffering. I wanted to see what his next move was going to be and I was positive I wasn't going to hate it. Mostly because I was crazy attracted to him.

There were *a lot* of smart men in New York.

There were *a lot* of good-looking men in New York.

Hell, there was even a decent amount of smart *and* good-looking men in New York.

But *all* the ones I'd met usually had a chip on their shoulder or couldn't handle a woman like me. They wanted smart and beautiful, but just not too ambitious. And not too smart or too beautiful either because that would just feed their insecurities. And don't let *Vogue* tell you that women are the only ones who have them, men are just as insecure. They just learned really early on that the easiest way to make themselves feel better is to overcompensate and fake the hell out of it.

Which meant when it came to women like me . . . yeah, I wasn't a good fit. Except with Lincoln, who seemed like he could handle me just fucking fine and not break a sweat. And that was sexxxxxy.

His smirk widened, not at all affected by my apparent lack of feelings. "So charitable. I hadn't pegged you for such a philanthropist, but I guess we didn't have much time to talk."

There was a deep rumble in his voice, alluding that he was thinking about that night and what we'd done when we weren't *talking*. I hated how much I liked it, how excited it made me to be sparring with Lincoln as well as flirting.

"I'm full of surprises, Lincoln. Pity you aren't sticking around to see them." It was as much of a reminder for me as it was for him.

Even if I did lose my ever-loving mind and slept with him— because smart girls could want dirty hot sex too—he wasn't in town to stay.

A week? Slightly more? I probably had milk in my refrigerator that had a longer expiration date. And we definitely knew too much about each other for it to be a meaningless fling, not to mention we'd gone way past the boundaries for a one-night stand.

"Oh, I don't know, Zara." He leaned back into his chair. "I might be around longer than you think. The firm has me on a very long leash, and short of pledging my allegiance to Wall Street, I can pretty much do what I want."

I tried not to imagine what he'd look like with a leash, or how ridiculously excited the idea made me. Funny how I'd never been into bondage, but I bet I'd make one hell of a dominatrix.

"But you *are* leaving," I pointed out. "So why don't you just tell me what you're apparently dying to tell me about the *real* Edwin Carlisle and hurry back to Boston."

"Uh-hmm." Nate cleared his throat. "No wonder you guys were fake engaged; you already act like most married people I know." He leaned forward, a grin edging across his lips as he whispered, "They're not having sex either."

Lincoln laughed, and while I tried to resist, I couldn't help laughing too. It was oddly strange how comfortable I felt with both these men and how willing I was to stay. Most guys who wasted my time wouldn't have gotten a second chance, and I sure as hell wouldn't sit through a dinner just to be polite.

And yessssss, I'd had a point to prove, wanting to have the last word or illustrate I wasn't some air-head moron who just fell into bed with men. But not even I'd believe that would be my sole reason to stay.

No, I was intrigued and attracted to Lincoln, and it had been a really long time since I'd felt that. Add in he was smart, just-the-right-amount of cocky, and his best friend was incredibly endearing, and I'd probably agree to more than just one dinner.

"Fine, so tell me about this guy." I waved my hand dramatically, agreeing that I'd been more than a little curious. "Was he at the hospital for his hip replacement? Or a heart attack?"

I was fairly sure that anyone named *Edwin* also held a membership card for the AARP. Judgey, a little, sure, but thinking he'd be a hot guy my age with a great sense of humor had been a little *too* optimistic.

Nate laughed, and it wasn't from his previous "married couple" joke. "Hmmm, not exactly."

So obviously he knew, which meant I definitely had to know. It was *me* who apparently had the connection with Edwin Carlisle, I should've known before either of them.

"I haven't narrowed down the reason for his hospital visit, but I don't think it was health related." Lincoln's words were even and unemotive. "He's an investment banker, lives in Manhattan. Comes from old money." It felt like he was giving a deposition, keeping to the facts and not editorializing.

Which meant there was *more* he wasn't telling me. Because I might have blindly been fooled once by Lincoln, but I was a quick learner. And he wouldn't get a second chance.

"And?" I nodded, urging him to continue.

Our waiter arrived, interrupting the conversation with plates covered with food. The moment I'd seen the New York Strip I immediately regretted my choice with the halibut. Still, I had more important things to worry about other than dinner. Like who Edwin was, and why Lincoln was being so cagey about him.

"I thought you said if you'd wanted to, you'd have found him yourself." Lincoln answered drily after the waiter had left. "What more is there to know?"

As for details, Lincoln had given me the bare minimum.

We both knew it.

And as far as revealing more, neither of us seemed to bend.

"He's obviously successful," I guessed, assuming that had been the reason. "How many millions does he have in his bank account?" I grinned.

"I already said he was 'old money', Zara. That's not a surprise." He rolled his eyes, either annoyed or bored I'd picked the most obvious lead to follow.

So, he was rich, not like that didn't describe a ton of guys in the city. Was he married? An eccentric billionaire who owned an island off the coast of Fiji? A mafia hitman who had a real diverse portfolio? Rich and successful wouldn't be enough to even get a response from Lincoln. And he was very much invested.

"Ooooooo whatever it is you're not telling me, must be pretty interesting." I leaned in closer, hoping it would reveal more about Lincoln than it would about Edwin. "So spill, Lincoln, or I'll get it out of Nate." I grinned at his best friend who was looking enviably at his plate but hadn't started eating.

"Knows me for five minutes and already knows I'm the weakest link." Nate laughed. "Okay, Your Honor, I'll admit I'm the worst at keeping a secret." He finished with a wink.

God, I really hoped when it was over—whatever it was we were doing—I'd still be friends with Nate. I didn't trust easily, or quickly, and somehow, he just made me want to do both.

Granted, I'd started that trend with Lincoln, but I could see how they were such good friends even though they lived in different cities. It was something I wasn't sure I'd be able to achieve.

"So, Edwin?" I asked, not willing to let it go or give Lincoln the chance to change the subject. He'd been a master at distraction when we first met, and he wasn't getting the better of me a second time.

"He lives in Manhattan and won't be retiring anytime soon," Lincoln answered.

Won't be retiring soon?

Oh?

Ohhhhhhhhhhhhh.

He wasn't an old man like I'd assumed. And judging by how cagey Lincoln was being, I assumed he was probably close to my age.

"Well, that *is* interesting." I took a sip from my water glass. "Hmmmm, maybe I should find him. We should meet. You know, just out of curiosity."

I'll admit I wasn't so much as curious about Edwin, as to why Lincoln hadn't handed me the dossier he'd probably compiled.

And no, he hadn't told me one existed but of course it did. It's what I would've done, and I assumed any attorney worth his or her salt would've done exactly the same.

So, I had no doubt Lincoln not only knew he lived in *Manhattan* but had an exact address, any parking infringements he might've accumulated in the last few years, and a list of all his previous employers and girlfriends. And I said *girlfriends* because if Edwin had been married, it would've been one of the first things Lincoln would've mentioned. Or at least I assumed.

Could Lincoln be jealous?

Of a guy I hadn't even met.

Or was Edwin so shady that he felt honor bound to protect me?

Well, I didn't need protecting from anyone and if he was jealous, then I wanted to explore that. And yes, I knew what that sounded like. Maybe I wasn't ready to let go of whatever ridiculous connection we had either. Hello, I was sitting at dinner with two men I barely knew, clearly I was craving adventure or had lost my ever-loving mind.

"So now you want to meet him?" Lincoln's face was devoid of emotion, his voice so schooled in its intonation I wasn't sure if he was surprised or glad. I bet he was amazing in a court room, keeping opposing counsel guessing and playing to the jury like he was about to win a Tony.

I nodded, doing my best to give him as little reaction as he'd given me. I wasn't going to be polishing a gold statuette anytime soon, but I could hold my own. "Yes, I think we should meet. You went to all this trouble. It feels like it would be the right thing to do."

His jaw ticked.

Not a lot, just enough I could tell it wasn't what he wanted to hear.

And as silly as it was, it made me feel empowered to know I'd been responsible for the crack in his usually perfect façade.

"Then it's settled. Mr. Carlisle will be attending a fundraiser next week. Conveniently enough, it will be for Nate's hospital, I'll get tickets. And we can *all* meet him together. Sounds like fun, doesn't it?" Lincoln grinned.

But it was too late for me to buy that he was happy or even excited about it. Whether he'd intended to or not, he'd let his wall down for a split second, and I'd seen the tension in his face. That smile was a complete cover.

"So much fun." I grinned back, and unlike him, mine was sincere.

Nate shook his head, clocking us both with a look. "Can we eat now? When I asked you both to dinner, I'd assumed we'd actually eat. I'm starving."

Lincoln didn't take his eyes off me, my body heating with excitement as he answered his friend. "That makes two of us."

I had no idea what I'd just agreed to, but meeting Edwin was the least of it.

Chapter 13

Lincoln

Nate was surprisingly quiet on the drive home. It wasn't like him not to tell me exactly what was on his mind and I was sure he had a lot to say.

Dinner had been interesting.

I hadn't expected our additional guest, but fuck me, I was excited to see her. Of course, Nate could've given me a heads-up, something I'd deal with later. But Jesus, I hadn't realized how much I'd wanted to see her until she was standing in front of me.

It made no sense how attracted I was to her.

She was beautiful, but I'd been with beautiful women before. But it was what was underneath that stunning exterior that really turned me on. Quick with her mouth, smart and more importantly, confident, she had no problem telling me what she thought. And I wasn't even aware how much I craved a woman who could challenge me.

I wanted it, desperately. Wanting all that sass and whatever else she had lurking underneath. I was positive she had a brilliant mind, and I wanted to explore every inch of it like the rest of her body.

"Nothing?" I asked Nate, the silence in the car making me edgy. "You have nothing to say after you blindsided me?"

Nate scoffed, shaking his head. "Oh, I think the charity gala threesome you signed us all up for trumps my harmless dinner."

"Fine, so it wasn't my best idea." I ran my hand through my hair willing to admit I might've panicked slightly. But Zara had been so goddamn excited to meet that asshole when she'd found out he wasn't some senior citizen with a pacemaker, I had to think quickly.

"Wasn't your best idea?" Nate laughed. "Those tickets are five grand a pop. You couldn't have thought of a cheaper way to make your point?"

I rolled my eyes, not even concerned about the fifteen K I'd apparently signed up to part with. "Really, Dr. Baxter? Think of all the sick kids we're going to help. And it's *your* hospital. I'd have thought you'd be more supportive of my philanthropic efforts."

"It's for the cardiology unit expansion, dumbass. Not kids." Nate laughed.

I shrugged, my mind unchanged. "Is the money going to be helping people? Yes, yes it is. Besides, I could use it as an opportunity to canvass for clients. I see no negatives here."

"Yeah, *clients*." It was Nate's turn to roll his eyes. "Didn't realize your firm was expanding to New York. Or that you were changing your specialty to malpractice suits."

"There will be high-profile donors," I argued back. "Like this cocksucker, Carlisle."

It had been one of the last things I'd read before heading down to meet Nate for dinner. Apparently he needed a bigger tax deduction for the current financial year and was attending the gala with his checkbook in tow. A little harsh perhaps, but if he had been as charitable as he expected us to believe, he wouldn't have mentioned it on his social media page. Not that I could talk, my excuse for giving also came with an ulterior motive, but at least I wasn't bragging about it.

"Say I believe you—which I don't." Nate's head turned in my direction. "What exactly are you going to do? Chaperone her like she's an eighteenth-century virgin? And you still haven't told me what role I'm supposed to play."

"Weren't you going anyway?"

"Do I look like I own a fucking yacht, Linc? And I'm not a cardiologist. Five grand is too rich for my blood." Nate laughed. "But thanks, I always did enjoy surgical events, those elitist bastards get so annoyed when the riff-raff shows up."

"See, look at all the good I'm doing." I waved my hand with a flourish.

"Yeah, such a *giver*. And you still haven't told me what you hope to achieve." Nate held up his palm. "Don't tell me it was for sick people or doing business either."

"Tell me how she ended up at dinner," I asked, not having had the opportunity before. "If information needs to be shared, you should lead with *that*."

My mind might've moved on to other things but it hadn't escaped my attention that prior to me telling Nate in the car on our way to Matteo's, I hadn't mentioned Zara. Or the irrational attraction I had to her. And unless he was moonlighting doing tea leaf readings and predicting the future, there was no way he could've known I was going to fess up either.

Which meant he knew from another source.

And I needed to know *everything*.

"I met her a few days ago when I went for a coffee run," he admitted with a grin. "Molly had some strange idea that the two of you were engaged. Funny, huh? And what was even more hilarious was your fake fiancée didn't set her straight. So of course I had to get involved. Someone has to help save you from yourself."

Well that *was* interesting.

I'd have assumed Zara would've been quick to correct Molly on our relationship status, but she hadn't. And she didn't seem to have a problem setting anyone straight. So maybe there was more to it than she was letting on.

I coughed. "Please, when have *I* ever needed saving?" And more importantly, what was she doing back at the coffee place? Was she hoping to see me?

"Lincoln, I love you, man, but you suck when it comes to women." His hand landed on my shoulder.

"What are you talking about? I've dated plenty of amazing women."

Not to brag, but I could score a date any time I wanted. Dating was the least of my problems.

"And how many of these women have you kept around? Like dated for longer than a couple of months," he clarified.

I shrugged, not understanding how my relationship history had anything to do with him and Zara. "A few."

"Bullshit. You dated that one girl in college for the first year of medical school who dumped you when you switched majors. Broke your heart too as I remember it. Everyone else has been passing through. You're a transit lounge. Don't let anyone get too close."

"Kimora did us both a favor." Not that I thought that at the time.

He was right, she had broken my heart. I thought I was in love with her, but turns out she was more in love with dating a future doctor than who I really was. "And who I date and how long it lasts hasn't seemed to bother you before."

"Because you seemed happy. But the last few times you've come to New York." He shook his head. "I don't know. You just seem so . . . empty."

My mouth opened to argue but I shut it again. I wasn't sure he was entirely wrong, even if I didn't want to admit it.

Work had been my focus.

Making money, being successful, and doing what I wanted to do.

It was no accident that the woman who'd walked out on me had been my one and only serious relationship. I remembered how much it stung, and how easy she'd switched me out for some other guy. I wasn't doing that again.

Fuck.

That.

If women wanted some dude with deep pockets, knew how to make them come fifty different ways, and looked decent in a suit, then I had that locked down. As for love, relationships, or whatever else Hallmark was peddling, I wasn't interested. I'd rather know exactly where I stood. It didn't make me jaded, it made me fucking honest. And no, I wasn't worried about ending up alone. I had every intention of eventually putting a ring on it. Marriage was just another contract and I sure as hell didn't go into a negotiation thinking with anything other than my head. But until then, I was going to enjoy playing.

"I'm happy with the way things are." At least, I thought I was. It was the first time in a long while I'd questioned it. "Zara would just make my time here more entertaining."

"Oh? All you wanted was to be entertained? Well, I guess that's a good thing. Should make things easier when she meets the new guy and forgets all about you." Nate chuckled, his sarcasm not missed.

"Guess we'll find out one way or another, right?" I shrugged, the idea of Zara with some other guy making me irrationally annoyed.

Nate side-eyed me, not buying any of my bullshit. "Yeah, *that's* the point you're trying to prove."

"And what is my point?" I asked, wondering when Nate changed his specialty from Emergency medicine to psychology.

"Oh, I don't know." He rolled his eyes. "You finally meet a woman who holds your interest beyond what she can do in bed, and you're not testing to see if she trades you for another guy? Sure, that's not fucked up."

Was that what I was doing?

No.

No, I wasn't a bag of hurt feelings '*boo-hooing*' in the corner because I got dumped—once—a lifetime ago.

"Maybe it is a test," I conceded, but not in the way he was thinking. "To prove that she wants me just as much as I want her. And it had nothing to do with her thinking I was someone else."

That was exactly what it was.

She could say whatever she wanted, pretend to be indifferent, but underneath it all, she wanted me to kiss her. She wanted more than that too, all of which I'd happily give her as soon as she admitted it. And no rich boy from the Upper East Side was going to change that.

"Seems like a lot of effort." Nate stroked his chin as we pulled up to his apartment building. "But okay, whatever. I'll get my tux dry cleaned." His hand went to the door handle. "I'm sure we'll iron out the details in the next few days."

I lifted my hand in a wave as he exited the car. "Let me know if you want to bring a date, I'm feeling generous. Might give you something else to focus on instead of me."

Nate shook his head. "And miss out on watching you make a fool of yourself with this woman? Please, I'm not going to want to miss a second."

He was wrong, but I didn't prolong the goodbye, watching Nate disappear into his building before the car headed back to my hotel.

After it was established we'd all be meeting Edwin Carlisle, which meant I'd be escorting her to the gala, dinner had been great. She'd let her walls down a little—or at least that's how it seemed—and the conversation had been easy and relaxed. And other than Nate being with us, it felt like we were back at the coffee shop like that first night. She genuinely seemed interested in what I had to say, and I couldn't get enough of her.

She was infectious, and so goddamn captivating I wanted to keep talking to her all night. It wasn't just that she was smart or driven, something I found incredibly attractive. But she was funny and witty too. And as for beautiful, she defied the definition. She was the entire package, something I wasn't even sure existed, so saying goodbye at the end of the night had really sucked. I'd even offered her a ride, hoping to spend more time with her.

But Zara politely declined, thanking me for dinner and giving Nate another hug—his second for the evening. And while she didn't offer me the same, meaning our contact was reduced to a warm but platonic handshake, she did hand me her number. Under the guise of me contacting her regarding the gala or whatever, she'd given me her business card with her handwritten cell number on the back. I didn't care what excuse she needed to tell herself, or whether it had been genuinely to facilitate our next "date." All that mattered was I had her number, and it had been honestly obtained.

Her card was pulled out from my pocket as the car approached the hotel, my fingers tapping the edges as we came to a stop.

"Will that be all for this evening, sir?" Terry—the driver— opened my door.

I slid out of the car, anxious to get back to my room. "Yes, thanks, Terry. I have a late meeting at eleven tomorrow so you can take most of the morning off. I'll call you if my plans change."

He gave me a curt nod, shutting the door behind me before returning to the driver's side. I didn't always get the same driver whenever I was in town, but I liked Terry. He knew how to keep his mouth shut but wasn't a robot either, important with the amount of sensitive conversations I had in the car. Case in point, he hadn't asked me about Zara when he'd driven her home and it was obvious he'd heard Nate and I talking about her.

The firm might be picking up the tab, but he was earning an extra big tip from me.

Nodding to the doorman as I entered, I went straight to the elevator and headed up to my floor. I wanted out of the suit, and wondered if she was doing the same, peeling that dress off her gorgeous body. The thought of it got me hard, my cock bobbing against the fly of my pants as I headed to my room.

I wondered if she knew how sexy she was, and how much I wanted to run my hands all over those curves.

My chest rose, pushing out a hard breath as I closed the door and switched on the light, a soft glow flooding the living area of my suite. I didn't waste any time, taking off my clothes as I moved through the space, tossing them onto the couch. Normally, I'd head to the shower, jerk off and then go to sleep, but I didn't want to rush it.

I didn't want the distraction of the spray beating down on my skin, or the sound of the water taking me from my fantasy, reaching down and palming myself when I was fully naked.

My knotted fist slid up and down my shaft slowly, the friction of skin on skin adding a slight bite of pain as I sunk down onto the couch.

Mmmmmmmmmm, I wanted her.

Wanted it to be her hand—no, her *mouth*, around my cock, watching her as she swallowed me down into her throat.

I imagined what she'd look like, how she'd stare at me with those intense beautiful eyes of hers and how insane she'd make me.

She would tease me, keeping her movements slow and steady, making me suck in desperate breaths as I fought the urge to beg.

I'd want to. Hell, I'd want to do it so damn much, but I'd resist, so damn curious to see how long she'd draw it out.

My chest heaved as my breathing quickened, my hand moving up and down my shaft faster and tighter as I indulged the fantasy.

I was desperate for her, wanting her mouth and body more than I wanted my own orgasm, but I was chasing it down all the same.

"Fuck," I groaned, closing my eyes and recalling her in vivid detail.

There wasn't a thing about her I would change, turned on by her in so many ways I was positive she could tell me to go fuck myself and I'd still find it the sexiest thing ever.

"Yeah, baby," I breathed out, the conjured-up images of her dark attitude-filled eyes making me harder than I could stand. "God, I want you."

There were no delusions it was my hand and not hers, but as my balls drew up and my fist pumped, it was thoughts of her that had me begging to come.

Heat jacked up my spine, my legs kicking out as my ass lifted off the sofa, my hand tight around my cock.

It was her name I shouted out, the image of her on her knees in front of me had me coming so fucking hard I almost couldn't breathe. Hot jets pulsed from my dick as I spilled my load onto my stomach. My other hand cupped my balls, squeezing a little as I continued to throb, the orgasm nowhere near as satisfying as I'd hoped.

Sure, it had knocked the edge off, loosened my muscles and eased the tension, but it only reinforced how much I didn't want a substitute.

It was her, and only her, and I could jerk off five more times and I was certain I'd always end up with the same result.

Well.

Fuck.

Chapter 14

Zara

It wasn't a date.

I wasn't exactly sure what it *was,* but it was *not* a date, at least that was what I'd told myself as I avoided calling or texting him.

Dinner with Nate and Lincoln had been unexpected.

I'd gone in assuming it would be weird and awkward, but I had a point to prove. Not that I was clear on what that point was anymore, but I'd definitely had an objective.

Having a good time hadn't been it.

And yet, try as I might to avoid his goddamn charm and keep my head in the game, I'd found myself actually enjoying his company.

He was funny and smart, and the ease with which he could slip between different topics of conversation was impressive. Seriously, he could seamlessly move from some obscure precedent he'd found to support a case he'd worked on three months ago to his stance on cats being assholes. He wasn't a fan apparently and wasn't shy about voicing it. And all the way through it—even though he'd regained his usual cockiness—he was attentive, interested in my thoughts while being sure to include Nate as well.

It was oddly arousing, the contradiction of this man who was confident, well-spoken and incredibly sexy with an underlying awareness and consideration. It was a lethal mix, and one which reinforced why I'd been so attracted to him in the first place.

But I also wasn't stupid. And while I was no longer angry about his earlier deception when we'd met, I still felt conflicted about wanting more with him.

There was no scope for a long-term relationship. It was hard enough when you lived in the same city, dealing with conflicting schedules, and demanding caseloads and everything else that went with life. Add in miles and forced separation and you had a recipe for disaster. And a man like Lincoln didn't seem like the kind of guy who'd be happy with something long distance. Not when he could have a different woman in his bed every night.

And little-known fact about me, I had a tendency to get jealous. Crazy, because mostly it seemed I was so ambivalent about love and relationships. But that was because I'd never really invested too deeply, knowing how much of myself I'd have to give. I was a perfectionist, and if I did lose my mind and fell in love, I worried it would consume me. So, not sure I wanted to live in the unhealthy reality where I'd be constantly wondering if he was with someone else.

Therefore, the only option would be a casual fling.

The set-up was perfect.

He was gorgeous and he'd eventually leave which meant no messy breakup. Yet, even knowing that, I couldn't understand why it still felt like a mistake.

Indecision made me uncomfortable, the churning in my gut reason enough for letting it go to voicemail when he called me to organize our weekend gala "date." I listened to his low sexy voice as he asked me to call him back, allowing myself only to text him a response.

> Sorry, swamped. Some of us have work to do and haven't got time to play. What time do you want me to meet you on Saturday? The Prince George Ballroom, right?

I'd done enough research on the gala to know where it was and that tickets started at five thousand dollars. Not sure he knew the price tag when making his grand declaration for all of us to go meet a man whose significance he had no idea about. And either he had more money than sense, willing to part with a few grand to prove a point. Or he was just as stubborn as I was, unwilling to admit defeat. I didn't have to wait too long for his reply.

> Zara, there's always time to play. But if you need help with time management, all you have to do is ask. And I'll pick you up at 6.

I rolled my eyes, only partially annoyed at his jab.

> There's nothing wrong with my time management, and you are the last person I need help from. Also, more than capable of getting my own ride.

> Wow, the *last* person? Surely there's other people on that list. Serial killers? Arsonists? Tax attorneys—I mean could they be any more boring? But if you need to lie to make yourself feel better, okay we'll go with it. And picking you up was for Terry's benefit, not mine.

I laughed, shaking my head at his response. I was fairly secure in myself but he took confidence to a new level.

Umm, who is Terry? I thought it was just you, me and Nate?

Terry is my driver. And while I've told him you're not interested, he's gotten rather smitten. You don't want to break the poor guy's heart, do you?

My brows scrunched in confusion. I wasn't even sure if I'd even introduced myself to his driver, and we'd definitely not had a conversation.

Your driver? I barely said two words to him when he drove me home. Not sure how smitten he could have gotten in a silent, brief and single interaction.

***Two* interactions. He drove us to my hotel before he drove you home. And he likes his women strong and silent, who may potentially rip off his balls. Personally, I think he's crazy, but the heart wants what the heart wants. So 6. Your place. I'll even tell him to ignore you so not to make you uncomfortable with his obviously one-sided affections. ;-)**

You know you have issues, right? Fine, tell Terry I'll be ready at 6.

Excellent, it will be the highlight of his night.

My fingers hesitated over the glass, not wanting the conversation to end but having no real purpose to continue.

We'd needed to make plans and we'd done that, all that was left was to say goodbye. But I didn't want to, both glad and annoyed I hadn't called him. I was still mentally debating what to say next when his next text arrived.

You know, you can tell me, Zara.

Huh? Short of him hearing my thoughts, he couldn't know my feelings were conflicted. Or that secretly I was desperately wanting to see him again. I held my breath as I sent my response.

Tell you what?

Why Edwin Carlisle was so important.

I breathed out a sigh of relief, glad it was just his curiosity over Edwin and not something else. Maybe I should just come clean? Tell him the whole ridiculous story. He'd no doubt think I was a moron for chasing after a man whose name I'd been given at a carnival sideshow when I was a teenager. Maybe he'd lose interest, seeing how ridiculous the situation had been. Think *I* was ridiculous, and not bother to show up on Saturday. It would let me off the hook, and whether or not I kissed him again wouldn't even be an issue. Because honestly, I really, *really* wanted to. And I wasn't sure I'd be able to stop at just kissing.

Before I could stop myself, I pressed call and held the phone up against my ear. I was still shaking my head when I heard it connect.

"Zara." His voice was low and gravelly, and my name had never sounded sexier. I had to take a breath and refocus, reminding myself why I'd called in the first place.

"Belle and I saw this fortune teller woman at Coney Island when we were kids. She said *Edwin Carlisle* was the name of the guy I'm supposed to fall in love with and marry." I sucked in air, barely taking a break before continuing. "Of course, *I* knew she was full of shit, but Belle was convinced. So when we heard the name over the speaker at the hospital, we got curious. And before you say anything, I know how ridiculous it sounds. But it was easier to go along with it, prove to Belle there was no secret out-of-this-world force at work than argue. So there you have it."

I waited, the silence on the other end making me more edgy than I liked. But if it was all going to unravel, I'd rather it happen before we were riding to a gala, having committed to spending an evening together.

"Well, that is an interesting story. Thanks for sharing it with me."

The sarcasm was missing from his voice, but I wasn't sure if he was being sincere. He could totally be humoring me, holding back his laughter and being polite, and I'd have no idea. And somehow that made it worse.

"Yeah, okay, so I'll see you at six on Saturday." I did my best to sound indifferent, more than a little disappointed by his response. I hadn't wanted for him to think I was crazy, but I'd expected *something*. Even if it was a little friendly teasing.

"Six. I'll look forward to it."

And before I knew what was happening, the call had ended.

I should've been relieved, saved from the ridicule which was probably appropriate, given the circumstances. Hell, I was involved and *I* thought it was ridiculous, I could only imagine what someone from the outside must think.

Shaking it off, I lowered the phone and went back to my work. I'd been home for over an hour and was still going over briefs. Not that I could concentrate anymore, reading the same sentence three times before I finally gave up.

What was he thinking? And why did I even care? I didn't even have to go on this date—which wasn't a date—on Saturday if I didn't want to. I hadn't been the one to tell him to spend the money on tickets, and even if I had, it was my prerogative to change my mind.

But as much as I tried to talk myself into calling him back and canceling, I couldn't. Wanting to see him again, and possibly demanding to know why he hadn't said anything when I'd finally confessed the truth.

Screw him.

Screw him and his opinion—or lack thereof—and the stupid attraction I clearly still had. It was a silly, unhealthy addiction I needed to shake.

I'd find someone else.

Anyone else.

And have random, hot sex with a guy who I didn't have complicated entanglements with. Maybe it would be the *real* Edwin Carlisle. Or maybe I was completely done with all things to do with that man and should go find myself a guy I barely knew and lose myself in a screaming orgasm.

Yes.

That was exactly what I'd do.

Because clearly boredom or sexual frustration was to blame for why I was so hung up on a guy I barely knew.

My hand tightened around my phone, fighting the urge to call him back even though I knew it was a totally bad idea.

Nope.

Not going to happen.

Instead, I lifted myself off my bed and walked out to the living room where Belle was camped out with a script she was working on for an audition.

"Hey, you want to go out?" I asked, not completely sold on the idea but not wanting to sit at home either.

"On a Thursday?" Belle's eyes widened in surprise before fishing out her phone and looking at the time display. "At ten o'clock at night?"

"I've gone out during the week before, Belle, don't act like I'm tucked up in bed with a cup of warm milk every night," I scoffed, folding my arms across my chest.

"Sure, for a firm function or a date, or some other obligation that you can't weasel out of. But voluntarily going out on a *school night*," Belle shook her head, "yeah, not something you've done in a while."

"Well then that's a problem because the last thing I want to be is predictable and boring." *And wasn't that the truth.* "So let's get dressed and go out somewhere. We live in one of the best cities in the world, and I've got my entire life to sit at home going through depositions."

Belle stood up, flattening her palm against my forehead. "You're not sick, are you? This isn't some fever-induced psychosis, is it? Because it's usually *me* trying to drag you out, and *you* giving me a line about how we should be responsible."

She had a point, and usually I hated being out late when I had to wake up early for work. The partners expected my A game, and that meant getting there before nine and staying well after five. And being tired or hungover from a night of partying wasn't conducive to any of that.

"Okay, so maybe I've decided that I want to do something different."

"This wouldn't have anything to do with certain hot lawyer from Boston, would it?" Her brow rose in suspicion. "I'm fine with it if we're trying to make him jealous, I just would prefer to know."

My hands anchored themselves on my hips, my sister too observant for her own good "No, this is nothing to do with him. And how am I going to make him jealous? He doesn't even know I'm going out."

Would he even care?

Other than potentially being annoyed I was with someone else other than him, it wasn't like he had feelings for me other than physical attraction. And who knew if he was—more than likely—entertaining a string of other women while I was sitting at home working my ass off. It wasn't like our upcoming "date" qualified for anything that required his monogamy.

Belle didn't seem convinced, eyeing me with the same look she did when she knew I wasn't being honest. The head tip to the side was added in case she wasn't being dramatic enough.

"Oh, really? So the guy you said you had no interest in, who you've been out to dinner with earlier this week and have plans with for some fancy ball this Saturday, has *nothing* to do with this sudden need to go out?" She lifted her finger, stopping me from interjecting before continuing. "And before you answer I'll remind you that the walls aren't that thick and I heard you were just on the phone with him."

"I thought you were going over lines for an audition?" I asked drily.

"Oh, I am but I can multitask." She smirked. "And you know I can't help myself but be invested in this. If it wasn't for me, you wouldn't have even met him. So the way I see it, I'm involved in this too."

Belle really needed her own relationship, then she could stop being so interested in mine. Not that I was in a relationship. Or even looking for one. Or . . . something even close to a relationship.

"So maybe I have some complicated feelings about Lincoln," I admitted, deciding there was no point trying to hide the truth. She was the only person who could read me like a book. Not even our parents had that skill, and it was something I'd guarded closely.

"Complicated how?" Her script was tossed to the side as she turned all her attention to me.

"I like him."

The words had left my mouth before I could sensor them, making me sound so vulnerable and slightly immature. They weren't qualified within the confines of time and knowledge, hell, I barely knew him at all. But whether or not I felt they were valid, it didn't make them any less true.

I liked him.

I did.

And I wanted to know him in all the ways that mattered.

Belle sighed, patting the sofa beside her and inviting me to take a seat. "Well then, we're not going out. Instead we're going to sit here and you're going to do what you've always done. Find a way to make it work."

She was right. I needed to find a way to make it work.

I just wasn't sure if that meant getting involved, or forgetting him entirely.

Chapter 15

Lincoln

I'd never been the kind of guy to count down to a date.

There was never a knot of anticipation in my gut, and not since college had I had any confusion as to how I thought it was going to end.

But Zara was different, and the unpredictability wasn't only exciting but made her even more attractive. So when Saturday finally arrived, it came as no surprise I was watching the clock.

I'd arrived at her apartment just before six and waited downstairs like she'd instructed. Why she wouldn't buzz me up so I could wait inside was beyond me, so instead I stood on the pavement outside the exterior door like a stalker. She didn't seem like she was in a hurry either, taking her time before she finally made an appearance.

My hand was ready on the buzzer, about to press it again, when she pulled the door open.

Jesus.

Christ.

She was beautiful.

Breathtakingly gorgeous in a full-length red gown that gathered at both shoulders and dipped low at her cleavage. It looked expensive and classy, and sexier than should be allowed.

"Sorry to keep you waiting." She smirked, not looking at all sorry as she stepped outside.

My eyes floated up and down her body, stalling as they landed on her tits. I wasn't sure whose benefit the dress was for—mine or Edwin—but I was currently reaping the rewards. And despite the possibility it had been for him, I was refusing to entertain the negativity, preferring the version I had in my head where she'd worn it just for me.

"No problem, happy to wait," I lied, wanting nothing more than to kiss her. Instead, I pressed my hand against her back unable to stop myself from touching and using the excuse to guide her to the car.

"Where's Terry?" she asked, stopping in front of the black Aston Martin Vantage I'd driven.

"Had to fire him." I pressed the fob, unlocking the door and holding it open so she could slide inside. "Figured it was easier than you breaking his heart when you turned him down."

She laughed, shaking her head as she swung her legs into the car. The split at the side of her dress slid open, flashing a good amount of thigh before she adjusted the fabric. I didn't even pretend not to notice, doing my best not to lick my lips as I waited until she was properly situated before closing the door and moving to the driver's side.

"Flashy rental?" she asked, looking around the pristine interior. I wasn't sure if expensive cars impressed her, and secretly hoped they didn't.

"Car club." I fastened my seatbelt. "One of our partners is an enthusiast and has a corporate membership. Means I get access to the keys of the toys whenever I need them. Figured tonight was as good of an excuse as any."

"Especially since you fired your poor driver." The smile edged wider on her lips.

I nodded, moving my hands to the ignition. "Exactly. Not like we could turn up to this gala in a cab or an Uber."

"What about Nate?" She glanced at the lack of back seats before returning her eyes to me. "I'm sure the trunk of this car is five star, but I think that would be pushing the friendship a little, even for you."

I laughed, loving how easy and quick she tossed those comebacks. She was a worthy adversary, someone who I'd absolutely love to go a few rounds with in a courtroom.

Or the bedroom.

Hell, I'd take both if that was on offer.

"Nate will meet us there. I'm sure he'll be glad to hear of your concern."

The engine roared to life, the V8 protesting we were still stationary as I eased away from the curb and headed to the Flatiron District.

She adjusted in her seat, her leg exposed as the fabric of her dress slipped off her thigh again. She didn't bother to fix it, leaving her hands folded in her lap as her heeled feet stretched out in front of her.

"How's your week been?" I asked, attempting to make conversation and distract myself from her gorgeous fucking legs.

She let out a contented sigh that ran down to my balls. "Pretty good. I'm assisting on a corporate merger. It's different from being in a courtroom, and not my preferred branch of law, but diversity is what the partners want. They'll also allow me to do more pro bono work if we close on some of these bigger clients. So I guess it's good for everyone."

I wasn't surprised to hear she was invested in pro bono work. While most attorneys did it to fill a quota, or earn favor with the firm, I imagined she was driven by her sense of social justice. I liked that about her, and it was a quality I hadn't seen in a while. That kind of attitude was in short supply at Locke and Collins.

"Well, corporate law is my specialty. Let me know if there's anything I can help you with."

Lame.

And possibly a little insulting. But the offer had been genuine and not because I thought she wasn't capable.

"Thanks, I've got it covered." She smiled, thankfully not taking offense as she lowered her voice seductively. "But I'll keep you in mind if I have any hostile takeovers."

My cock throbbed, and I was fairly sure we weren't talking about the law anymore. I cleared my throat, keeping my eyes on the road as we sat in traffic.

"What about you? You wrap up your case? You must be heading back soon?" Her tone was light, conversational, lacking any emotion at the idea of me leaving.

And why the hell did that disappoint me?

I didn't like emotional, clingy women, in fact, I actively avoided them. So why the lack of concern about my impending departure was bothering me, I had no idea.

"Almost done," I answered honestly, knowing the only reason I hadn't wrapped it up on Friday was because I was dragging my feet. "I'll be around a little while longer."

My head turned, hoping to catch her reaction, but she didn't give me one, her face impassive as her eyes flicked to mine. "I'm sure Nate's pleased."

"He is."

The air in the car thickened, the tension palpable between us. And while she wasn't giving me a lot to work with, it was obvious whatever I was feeling, she was too.

My fingers tightened around the steering wheel annoyed they had a job to do and couldn't reach across and pull her lips onto mine. I was almost positive she wouldn't have stopped me, and I wanted to feel how desperate that mouth was for mine.

Fuck me and my bright ideas.

The car behind me blasted its horn, prompting me to refocus on the road. The light had changed from red to green and we'd been sitting still for longer than the two seconds New Yorkers were willing to wait. Guess it was a blessing in a way, giving me something else to concentrate on and hopefully get rid of my hard-on before we got to the gala.

We rode the rest of the way in a weird silence. Zara turned on the car stereo, a symphony blaring out of the speakers on a preset classical channel. She didn't bother looking for anything else, and I had enough trouble keeping the car on the road without worrying about the goddamn sound system.

I was relieved when we pulled up in front of The Prince George Ballroom, the entrance to the beautifully ornate 20th Century hotel lined with important people handing over their keys to valets.

"We're here," I announced unnecessarily, slowing to a stop before cutting the engine.

I wanted to touch her, to feel my hands against her skin while looking into her eyes, but I also knew there was a chance her attention could soon be diverted elsewhere. To *him*. It was a gamble I was willing to take, desperate to spend more time with her as I walked around to the passenger side, holding open the door and watching as Zara carefully slid out. Even the valet was mesmerized, his grin widening when he got a view of her legs.

"There you go." I dangled the keys between my fingers with one hand as I slipped the other around Zara's waist. "Thanks." My tight grin hopefully hinting that he should stop looking at my date and pay more attention to my ride.

"My pleasure." The guy nodded, taking the keys and handing me a ticket. Amazing how he could be talking to me and yet looking at her. "Have an enjoyable evening."

Honestly, as irritated as it made me, I couldn't blame him.

Zara was beautiful. No, it was more than just beautiful, she was breathtaking. And even with Manhattan's elite on display, there wasn't any woman close to how gorgeous she was.

Ignoring that technically I had no reason to keep holding her, I left my hand on her hip as we walked through the doors. And if she had a problem with its location, she didn't mention it, sidling in close to me as I handed over our tickets and strode inside.

Round tables were set up, covered with red linens and white folded napkins. It wasn't unlike any other social event/ fundraiser I'd been to before except I'd never really cared who'd been my plus-one.

"It's so beautiful," Zara whispered as we moved through the room, her eyes restless as she took it all in

"No, you're beautiful," I whispered back, loving how she leaned into me. I wasn't even sure she'd noticed she was doing it, her body responding to my touch, telling me she liked it. I was almost disappointed when I caught sight of Nate at one of the tables. "We're over here."

Nate stood, giving us a smile as we got closer, straightening his bow tie. "About time you got here." He gave Zara a brief hug before turning to shake my hand. "There's a set of golf clubs that are listed in the silent action. Be a pal, Linc, and place a bid."

"You don't even play golf, asshole." I rolled my eyes, wondering if I bought him those clubs if he'd leave me alone with Zara.

It had been my stupid idea to invite Nate, assuming it would make it seem less like a date for Zara. But since seeing her walk out of her apartment, all I could think of was being with her and only her.

"Oh, I know I don't play, but it will really piss off the cardiac surgeons if I win them and they don't. I'm not above being petty." Nate laughed as he collected three flutes of champagne from a passing waiter's tray and handed them out. "Carlisle is at the head table, in case you were wondering."

Just the mention of his name sent ice through my veins.

I hadn't forgotten why we were there and who we were meant to see. And even though the piece of shit was somehow responsible for me meeting the most amazing woman ever, I wasn't feeling very grateful.

In fact, I didn't have *any* good feelings when it came to Edwin Carlisle and considering I'd yet to even see him, that wasn't a good sign.

Zara's head turned instinctively, her eyes tracking the guests at the main table and landing on the prick I knew to be Carlisle.

He looked just like his editorial in *Forbes*—smug grin on his face with no trace of humility in his eyes. His glossy blond hair catching the light like a shampoo commercial as he laughed with what I was sure was zero sincerity.

"That's him?" Zara's eyes widened, directing the question to me while clearly keeping her eyes on him.

I'd assumed she would've Googled him.

Done some kind of search, if for no other reason than not to go into the situation blind. So I wasn't sure what to make of it that she hadn't, and if that was a positive or a negative.

On one hand, it showed a level of disinterest. Her commitment to getting to know the guy who supposedly she was going to marry, not very high. And while I didn't believe some random woman in a tent had the ability to see the future, the jury was still out exactly where Zara sat on the issue.

There was a counter argument, however. And perhaps she hadn't searched for him, wanting the meeting—and the possible connection—to be organic. Like ours had been when she'd assumed I was him.

"That's him," I confirmed, trying to keep the bite of agitation out of my tone. "We should go over and say hello before dinner starts."

On the list of things I wanted to do, going over and shaking that asshole's hand ranked dead last. We hadn't even sat at our table yet, standing around it, sipping champagne like all the other guests who were either mingling or posturing. But I was already annoyed and fighting the urge to punch the guy in the face—for no other reason than who he was—and I couldn't see that situation improving as the night progressed.

Nope, it was best to get it over with. And let whatever was going to happen, happen. Oh, and in case it wasn't clear just how stupid the idea was, it was further reinforced as she glanced back over at him and the piece of shit caught her stare and smiled.

Great.

Fucking perfect.

Chapter 16

Zara

God, he was hot.

Eyes that could liquefy your insides and a smolder that should be illegal in all fifty states. And currently he looked so goddamn delicious I was questioning my own judgment.

No, not Edwin Carlisle—who, other than a passing interest, I really didn't care about—but Lincoln Archer.

I'd tried to reason with myself, reaffirm all the reasons why doing *anything* with him would be a bad idea. But I was struggling with the motivation.

And it wasn't just because he was good-looking, although that certainly wasn't helping my cause. But there was something else—an aura, a vibration, a magnetism—that spoke to me in a way no other attraction had.

No, it was more than just his hot body and handsome face, and I was compelled to find out what the hell it was. Which was why in any other circumstance I'd have downloaded every public record available on Edwin Carlisle, and instead I'd spent my time researching Lincoln James Archer. Middle name totally found without very much effort.

"Looks like he's coming over." Nate coughed into his hand.

I hadn't even noticed I'd been staring, my eyes blinking and shifting back to Lincoln. He hadn't been looking at Edwin, his gaze intently fixed on me.

"Well." I did my best to keep my voice level and unemotive. "That's why we're here, right? And it's probably easier if he comes to us."

Easier wasn't always better, and I wasn't exactly known for taking the easier route. But admitting that I really didn't care to meet the man who was the catalyst for the whole grand adventure seemed unintelligent.

Lincoln's brow lifted, asking a question he hadn't vocalized, and I couldn't be sure he didn't know. That he hadn't seen through my casual throwaway attitude and was about to call me on my bullshit. That was *not* what I wanted. Especially not in front of Nate with New York's elite as a willing audience.

"Sure, *easier*." He lingered over the word like he knew it was a lie, turning to Edwin who was making steady strides toward us.

He was handsome in that manicured Upper East Side kind of way. Tailored suit, hair slicked back, and a smile that said, *I can buy anything I want*, without opening his mouth. I was positive it was arrogance that had afforded him the confidence, his eyes twinkling like he hadn't been told "no" in a while.

"Have we met?" he asked, ignoring Nate and Lincoln as his eyes traveled up and down my dress. He wasn't even trying to hide he was checking me out, probably assuming I'd thank him later for his honesty. "I couldn't help noticing you looking at me, but yours isn't a face I'd so easily forget."

In my peripheral vision I saw Lincoln roll his eyes, silently mouthing something I couldn't make out. I'd assumed he'd step forward, thrust out his hand and try to take charge of the situation like most men did, but he didn't. Instead he stood back, cocked his head to the side and waited to see what I did next, and I couldn't help but feel like it was some kind of test.

I nodded, acknowledging him as I chuckled casually. "No, we haven't met. And I was actually looking at Dr. Brown who you were talking to. I hear his work with robotics could change cardiac surgeries drastically in the next few years. Fascinating, isn't it?"

When I said I hadn't downloaded everything on public record on Edwin Carlisle, I hadn't been lying. But I wasn't going to a gala without at least knowing who the chair of the foundation and visiting keynote speaker were, a quick study all I needed to ensure I could at least be conversational. It was something I was used to from law functions, not willing to be caught unaware and potentially snub a judge whose courtroom I might one day visit. And Dr. Brown—visiting from Oxford—was easy information to grab onto.

Lincoln grinned, seeming to be impressed. "Riveting stuff," he agreed.

Edwin's eyes widened like he couldn't believe I hadn't been gawking at him. Which to be fair, I had been, but I wasn't about to admit that. Especially when he'd assume it meant something it didn't.

"Yes, a very worthwhile enterprise." Edwin recovered quickly, holding out his palm. "I'm Edwin Carlisle, a pleasure to meet you."

It was so surreal to hear that name—one that had obviously been in the back of my mind for years—from the man it belonged to.

He was real.

A living, breathing man who existed outside of a fantasy, and I needed a moment just to take that in, even though I still didn't believe he was my destiny.

"Zara Mathews." I gave him a polite shake, recovering quickly. "And this is Nathan Baxter and Lincoln Archer." I gestured to the two guys who were paying more attention to our interaction than I would've liked.

Each of them took a turn in shaking Edwin's hand, Lincoln surprisingly silent during the exchange.

Edwin didn't waste any more time, turning his attention back to me. "Well, since I've had the pleasure of meeting your friends, Ms. Mathews, maybe I could introduce you to mine. I'm positive Lance would love to meet such a beautiful fan of his work."

Uhhhhhhh, great.

I was being hit on by the guy I was supposed to have a life-long lasting relationship with, in front of the guy who I was actually interested in but who had no long-term prospects. No wonder I been so resistant to relationships. Clearly when it came to making smart choices, I sucked at it. That's why casual, non-emotional flings were preferable, and sadly neither of them would be suitable for that.

"Sure," I heard myself say, thinking I had to at least pretend to be interested, considering I was masquerading as a fan. "But I also graduated summa cum laude from Harvard and I'm sure Dr. Brown would appreciate *that* more than my beautiful face. And call me, Zara."

Ok, so I wasn't going to totally lose my mind and allow this man to assume because I was attractive that I wasn't intelligent. Sure, I knew zero about robotics, cardiology, and basic science in general, but he didn't know that. If it was one thing being an attorney taught me, it was knowing how to present a case to demonstrate your point of view. And my point of view was I wasn't an airhead.

Edwin laughed, my little backhanded comment not offending him. "Oh, he's definitely going to like you." He held out his elbow in a gesture that I wasn't sure was still used outside of Regency novels. "Shall we?"

Lincoln straightened, his eyes connecting with mine as his lips thinned. He wasn't saying anything, neither encouraging me to go nor asserting his place as my date. Granted, the whole reason we were there was to meet Edwin, which we were currently doing. But I assumed he wouldn't be so willing to let me just walk away with another guy either, which just gave me more conflicting emotions to deal with.

Obviously, I didn't want or need a man's permission to do anything, nor was I the kind of girl who wanted to be fought over. That kind of drama was what Belle lived for, and what I'd been trying to avoid most of my life. But with Lincoln, I guess I secretly wanted him to be a little annoyed. Maybe even slightly jealous. Or at the very least add some wisecrack of his own before I linked my arm with some other guy who'd called me beautiful.

"I won't be long." I turned to Lincoln, assuming it would prompt a response.

His brow rose, a smile I wasn't sure was genuine spread across his lips as he gestured to the room. "Take as long as you need."

And as accommodating as that sounded, it still pissed me off. For all the reasons I'd previously mentioned. Which is why I had no choice *but* to leave and go spend time with Edwin Carlisle, whether I wanted to or not.

Denying Edwin's elbow my linked hand or arm, I stepped forward in the direction of the visiting keynote speaker. He took the hint and followed, leaving Nate and Lincoln back at our table as we both strode with purpose to the main table.

"Are you in the medical field?" he asked, his smile widening. "Because I'd assume if you were a donor, I'd have seen you at one of these events before. And I'd hate to have missed any previous opportunities to make a new friend."

It was smooth, I'll give him that. And while it was obviously a pickup line, I had to admire his confidence. I imagined he'd been to a hundred or more similar events and he seemed pretty damn sure he hadn't seen me. He was either extremely perceptive or incredibly cocky and at the moment, I didn't really care which.

"No, I'm a lawyer." I saw no reason to lie. "But it's a worthwhile cause." Also not a lie.

"It is," he agreed as we got closer to the table. "But I'd be lying if I didn't say that I'm especially grateful you picked this one to support. You are very beautiful."

We pulled up short just before we reached the table's edge, my body turning to face his. "Aren't you even slightly concerned I'm dating one of the men I was with?" Surely he had to be even a little bit curious.

"Are you?" His smiled didn't drop.

I hesitated, wondering if it would be easier just to say that I was. "No, they're just friends."

And while it was technically the truth, it wasn't really how I felt. Weird considering I didn't know either of them very well. And yet, in such a small amount of time a strange connection had been made.

"Good." His hand made a move like it was going to shift to my waist, stopping and retreating before it made contact. "That's very good."

With his effort to touch me thwarted, he repositioned himself at my side and cleared his throat. Dr. Brown, or Lance, as Edwin called him, was approximately fifty with feathered white hair that refused to be obedient. His dark-rimmed glasses were thick and practical as was his black and unremarkable tuxedo. His conversation with some dark-suited older guy had ended and was now looking at us with curiosity. "Was wondering where you ran off to so fast, now I can see why you left."

Edwin laughed, straightening his tie. "Lance, I'd like you to meet the charming Zara. She's a big fan of your work."

Dr. Brown's eyes widened like he wasn't sure he'd heard correctly, flicking Edwin a gaze before returning back to me. "Big fan, hey? Robotic surgical systems don't often attract fans."

"Well, that's a shame." I chose to continue perpetuating the lie. I mean, I'd come this far, why back out now? "Not even nerdy fan boys? At least one of them has to have asked for your help to defeat one of the Robot Death Battle machines. Save a life, take a life—they don't have to be mutually exclusive."

Dr. Brown laughed, his head shaking. "Edwin wasn't kidding, you are delightful. I'm Lance, and as much as it pains my soul to admit it, I don't even have nerdy fan boys. A pleasure, Zara." He held out his hand but instead of shaking it when I offered mine, he kissed my knuckles.

It was cute in that non-threatening way, and I wasn't the only one who could be accused of being delightful. He obviously had a good sense of humor and I was glad he wasn't a weirdo I was going to have to pretend to like.

"Excuse me, Dr. Brown, there's someone you need to meet before we sit down for dinner." An impeccably dressed brunette interrupted us. "So sorry, Edwin, I'm going to have to steal him for a moment." She smiled at him, her eyes darting to me but didn't offer any acknowledgement.

"Of course, Delia. Lance, I'll be sure to keep Zara entertained until you can rejoin us."

Wait, what?

DELIA?

My eyes narrowed as I discounted how much of a coincidence it could be that Madame Delia had predicted my great love affair with Edwin Carlisle, and here we all were, together like a band reunion.

And with the additional information, the mental calculation of the years between our meetings, it was obvious that it wasn't as random as it sounded.

Delia—who'd looked like she spent way too much time in a chair getting lip fillers—looked remarkably similar to the *Madame Delia* Belle and I had met on Coney Island. Sure, she was older—weren't we all—but even without the cheap knock-off turban and low mood lighting, it was clear they were one in the same.

The flash of recognition was mine, and mine alone as Delia—AKA Madame Delia—led Dr. Brown away to a group of men who looked rich and important. Instead I was left alone with Edwin, trying to work out the connection.

"Is that Dr. Brown's assistant?" I asked, noticing she hadn't been on the list of organizers when I did my brief but informative web investigation.

"Delia?" Edwin chuckled. "God, no. She's my sister-in-law."

Oh, really? Well, shit just got more interesting. "Oh?" I threw out casually, not trying to sound too interested.

"Yeah, my older brother Harold—I know, our names are terrible—and I are both representing the family here tonight. And Delia is so used to playing hostess, she finds it hard to switch off. She couldn't be any more perfect for Hal, loves working a crowd and they've known each other since college. Anyway, she probably wants to show Lance off to someone important." His smile grew wider. "And I appreciate the chance to get to know you a little better while we're alone."

Well that was just fucking great.

Not only was I right about Madame Delia being a fraud and full of shit all those years ago, but she picked the name of the one guy who I'd probably never meet. Her elitist future brother-in-law who was probably sleeping with vapid rich girls. And even though I'd known—now confirmed—that her prediction about my love life was a fabrication of the highest order, I was still unreasonably angry.

Fuck Madame Delia.

"Zara?" Edwin moved closer, his hand brushing my arm. And from the look on his face, I couldn't be sure that was the first time he'd said my name. "You okay?"

"Sorry." I shook my head, giving him a rehearsed smile. "She just looked like someone I knew a while ago. I was mentally trying to place her."

Oh, I'd placed her alright. I knew exactly where, when, and how, with such detailed accuracy I could even remember the shade of candy pink lipstick she'd been wearing. But I still hadn't decided how I was going to play it, and if confronting her was going to be as satisfying as it felt in my head. I also didn't want to look like a complete crazy person, which there was definitely a danger of. That wasn't taking into account Lincoln who was still waiting for me at our table.

Could my personal life get any more complicated?

"You know Delia?" Edwin raised his brow. "Why don't you sit with me as my guest, and I'll do a proper introduction while we're having dinner."

"No, I couldn't do that." I laughed, the idea of being his plus-one so hilarious I was positive I hadn't heard him right. "I'm here with friends. Ditching them would be very rude."

"But neither is your *boyfriend*, correct?" The emphasis on the word not missed. "Because surely they wouldn't have a problem with you meeting new people, making *new* friends."

I glanced over at the two men I'd walked in with, not having spent nearly enough time with them as I would have liked. Lincoln's eyes were on me, the expression on his face unreadable as I looked for a sign.

"Sure, maybe I'll stay for a little while," I agreed, deciding that I could at the very least give Madame Delia a piece of my mind. "I'll just go let them know."

Edwin grinned, probably so accustomed to getting his own way he wasn't even surprised. And since he didn't seem concerned about whether it would upset the seating configurations, I tried to go with it too. But deep down it ate at me, and not just because I wasn't with Lincoln and Nate.

People with money often did what they liked without regarding the consequences, so while I was sure there was an event planner who was going to need a Xanax, Edwin wouldn't care. Which is why no matter how charming he turned out to be, he'd never be the soulmate I'd been promised.

No, I needed someone who cared about people less fortunate than themselves. Who worked to make sure pensions were honored when companies were dismantled. Who negotiated the busy schedule of an ER doctor whenever he was in town even though his own schedule was probably a nightmare. And who was kind and conversational to wait staff in small coffee shops.

Shit.

Edwin Carlisle didn't stand a chance, because the only man I really wanted was the man I'd walked in with.

The guy I'd been infatuated with since the moment I'd laid eyes on him.

And there was no mistake as to what his name was.

I wanted Lincoln Archer.

Chapter 17

Lincoln

"What do you think they're talking about?" The words were directed at Nate even though I hadn't taken my eyes off Zara. She'd glanced my way a few times, and I had a hunch I knew where it was going.

He—the cocksucker—was going to invite her to be his guest, because that was what men like him did. Even if he'd arrived with someone else, he'd find an excuse to have her whisked away by an assistant and Zara seated in her place. I'd seen it a million times, married men trading their wives for mistresses, players juggling different girlfriends like no one's feelings got hurt. And it annoyed the hell out of me and not just because I wanted Zara for myself.

She deserved more than that, more than the cheap pseudo emotions a man like Carlisle could give her. And even though I was aware I knew nothing about him other than what I'd read, there wasn't a litigator on earth who could convince me he was good enough for her. Hell, I was positive *I* wasn't good enough for her, but I wasn't stupid enough to get hung up on the technicality.

She was gorgeous, and smart, and funny, and so many other things the list became too endless to count. And even though I knew it wasn't practical, I wanted her more than to win my next case. Which was saying a lot since work had pretty much been my life.

Had I told her how beautiful she'd looked? How that dress curled around her body like it had been designed only for her? Why hadn't I just kissed her when I'd gotten her alone in that car, told her the real reason I hadn't wanted a driver was because I didn't want to share her the whole night. I'd wanted to reach over and take her lips, to stop playing the stupid game we'd somehow found ourselves in. But there was a tiny part of me that didn't trust myself. That knew once I'd kissed her again—really kissed her, with no misunderstandings between us—I'd have a hard time walking away. And I wasn't sure how she'd feel about that.

Fuuuuuuuuck, it had been so long since I'd really cared about a woman, I wasn't even sure how it was supposed to feel. Was I supposed to be so consumed by her? Obsessed? Want to go and rip off the fucking asshole's arms she was talking to because he looked like he wanted to touch her?

"Why are you even asking me if you don't care enough to listen?" Nate chuckled as he tossed back some more champagne. "Or was the question for yourself?"

"Sorry." I shook my thoughts loose, not liking what was going on in my head. "What did you say?"

"I said, he was probably boring her to death with talk of his flashy sports car and yacht. Isn't that what you accused men like him of doing? Or are you now doubting your own defense?"

I hated when Nate was observant, his retort earning a side-eye and an under-my-breath "Fuck you."

He laughed, handing off his empty champagne flute to a nearby waiter and taking mine from my hand. "Listen, aren't we here for her to meet this guy? I mean, this was your idea, right? Surely you have a strategy? Because counselor, it's unlike you to go into anything unprepared."

And he was right.

While it always seemed like I played fast and loose, I didn't usually go into a situation without having calculated the outcome. It was what made me a good lawyer, the ability to think on my feet while still controlling the narrative. But I was flying blind with this one, doubting I was doing anything right as everything I knew seemed to be called into question. What the hell was I even doing waiting around for another guy to make a move on the woman I was interested in? Had I left my balls in Boston?

"She's too smart to fall for his bullshit." I wasn't sure if I was trying to convince him or myself. "Ten minutes with him and she's going to tell us she's ready to leave."

"Not before the main course," Nate scoffed. "Did you see the menu and who the chef was? Gabriele Matisse is a gastronomic genius, and there's a six-month wait at his restaurant."

"You don't need us to hold your hand, Nate." I rolled my eyes. "If you get lonely you can get Terry to come sit with you and listen to your menu critique, I'm paying him double tonight." While I hadn't needed him to drive me, I made sure Nate didn't have to worry about dealing with a cab. And since it was a Saturday night he'd have probably preferred to spend it with his friends and/or family, I wanted to make sitting around waiting for a call worth his while.

"He'd probably be better company," Nate sighed. "Less moody."

I flipped him off—discreetly of course because I wasn't totally uncouth—when I noticed Zara was on her way back. "Finally." The grin spread across my face. "I knew she'd see through his bullshit."

Nate chugged what was left of my champagne and gave me a thumbs up.

"So?" I asked as Zara stopped just inches from me, the urge to touch her too overwhelming as I rested my hand on her hip. "Was he everything you imagined? Belle is going to be so pissed I got to hear all about it before her."

Her hand rested on my chest as she smiled back at me. "You know her so well. I'm surprised she hasn't texted you for updates. You know she saved your number to her phone, apparently you're her new favorite personal shopper."

"Bring the woman creamer one time and she automatically typecasts you." I pretended to look hurt as my hand clasped the one she had on my chest. "And I thought only defense lawyers were so ruthless."

Honestly, I didn't care what her sister asked me to bring them. If it gave me an excuse to see Zara, I'd happily play delivery boy.

Zara looked at where our hands were, promptly moving hers as she glanced over her shoulder at Carlisle. "Actually, Edwin invited me to sit at his table."

"Did he?" Cue my lack of fucking surprise. "Didn't he bring a date?"

Something flashed behind those beautiful eyes like she hadn't considered the possibility. And while she shook her head, she didn't seem sure. "No, I believe he came alone."

"You believe or you know?" I asked, knowing she wasn't that naïve. "Did you ask him if he was alone? Or did you assume he was because there wasn't a woman hanging off him at that particular time?"

My words had a bite, sounding harsher than I'd meant to.

"I wasn't aware this was a cross examination." She kicked up her chin, unwilling to be intimidated. "Or that it was any of your business."

"It's not." I peeled my hand off her hip, annoyed I was literally driving her into that piece of shit's arms. "I just," *hoped you'd choose me,* "don't want you to get hurt. I brought you here and I feel responsible."

It was so not what I wanted to say, not even close to what I was feeling. But Nate was giving me side-eye and Carlisle was watching us like I might scuff the paint on his new ride and Zara. . . well, I had no idea what was going on in her beautiful head.

Did she want to go to him?

Had I been wrong?

Did she spend five minutes with that douchebag and decide that he really *was* what she'd been looking for. That she didn't want to waste a perfectly good evening with someone like me?

"You're not responsible, Lincoln. Free will, remember?" she argued, like that would somehow make me less accountable when that asshole slept with her and then promptly forgot her. Or worse, if he broke her heart.

"Anyway." She glanced over her shoulder again before her eyes returned to me. "I just wanted to let you know so you didn't think I was ditching you. I promise I'll be back by dessert."

My throat felt dry, speechless for the first time in possibly forever. But showing vulnerability wasn't something that was easy for me, and I was incredibly out of practice.

"No." I grabbed her hand as she turned to leave, her eyes widening as I pulled her forward, my growl surprising us both. "Don't leave."

"Um, Linc, easy with that hand, buddy," Nate warned, his head tipping to my tight grasp around her wrist. Nate had to know I'd never do anything to hurt Zara—or any other woman for that matter—but he wasn't going to let me manhandle her on his watch either.

My fingers loosened, gently grazing her skin as they maintained contact. "Stay with me, Zara. Please. Don't go to him."

I hated the way the words sounded and the weakness they represented. But I also wasn't willing to let her just walk away either. Not without putting up a fight.

"You want me to stay?" Her voice softened like she hadn't been sure it's what I'd been desperate for since the moment I'd laid eyes on her in that ER. "But I thought we were here—"

"Fuck why we're here, Zara," I cursed, moving closer and brushing the hair off her shoulder. "I'm not interested in anything other than you right now."

And without asking her whether she wanted me to or not, I kissed her. My hand finding her jaw and pulling her close as I took her mouth in full view of the guy she was apparently leaving me to sit with. I tasted her lips, feeling them move under mine as she answered with a kiss of her own, her hand hitting my chest as she fisted my shirt.

I didn't care how it looked, or that we had an audience, or what anyone might say. My lips had been dying to be on hers all night and I wasn't willing to waste another second without the pleasure.

Her body softened against mine, her tits pressing against my chest as I wrapped an arm around her and gently pulled her closer. I loved the way she fit, how natural it felt to have her against me like that, and how much I wanted more of it.

She whimpered, her mouth opening wider as my tongue slid in. I needed more contact, to feel more of her against me. "Zara." Her name breathed out between kisses. "Want you."

Nate cleared his throat, reminding us we weren't alone like I'd forgotten where we were.

I hadn't.

I just no longer cared.

Zara pulled away first, my mouth chasing hers, unwilling to release it so soon. Not since it had taken me so long to make it happen, and not when there was the slight possibility it might not happen again.

"Lincoln." She sucked in a breath, taking a small step back. "Did you just kiss me so I wouldn't go sit with Edwin?"

"No," I answered, because there wasn't a chance I was going to let that asshole take the credit. "I kissed you because I couldn't stand another second not kissing you. Because I've wanted to kiss you again since the first time. And even though I've done it just now, it hasn't lessened the urge."

There was something about her that made me more honest than I wanted to be, that fought against my instinct to only show her the side most everyone knew. But Nate was right, if I'd wanted to keep lying to her, I'd have done it that first night.

Her fingers traced her lips, the ghost of the kiss we'd just shared still fresh. "We need to talk."

"Fine," I agreed, willing to do whatever she wanted to do as long as it involved her being with me. "Why don't we step out into the hall where we can have some privacy. Or do you want to leave, and we can chat in the car?"

I knew what my preference was, and the hall wasn't it. But despite attacking her mouth without warning, I wasn't a total Neanderthal. So I was giving her the choice, hoping she was having similar feelings.

"Hall."

Ugh, okay fine. "After you." I waved to the exit, ignoring Nate and Edwin who were both watching us intently. And funnily enough I didn't care what either of them was thinking.

Zara kicked up her chin, as she turned toward the door. I didn't waste any time following her, matching her strides with my own as we both left the ballroom together.

Her eyes darted left and right, looking for a pocket of privacy. The hall hadn't been the oasis of seclusion we'd hoped, people milling around as donors were ushered inside and volunteers smiled brightly in an effort to offer assistance.

"Over here." Our shoes echoed off the intricate tiled floor. "There's a bridal suite."

It might not have been my first function at the Prince George Ballroom, but it was the first time I'd hoped the adjacent rooms were unlocked. I assumed they'd kept them ready in case their paid guests needed some privacy or a moment to collect themselves before a speech. And if I happened to be wrong, I was leading her to the loading dock.

Success, the door gave way as I yanked on the handle, the brightly lit room welcoming us as I closed and locked the door behind us.

"Won't you get in trouble for that?" She folded her arms across her chest as she watched me move back to her. "Or is this part of your usual routine since you know the layout so well?"

I both loved and hated that she asked the question, assuming I'd had done it with another woman. Loving the fact she said exactly what was on her mind, but hating she'd think that about me.

"Casey, Nate's sister, got married here. I was responsible for delivering her new shoes when the ones she'd been wearing had cracked a heel. You know how hard it is to charm a sales associate at Bergdorf to keep the store open for you while you negotiate traffic? If she'd given me half the appreciation she'd given those Manolo Blahnik's I'd have been happy."

"You went out and got Nate's sister new shoes on her wedding day?" Her eyes widened either impressed or just plain surprised.

"Of course, I did. Nate was busy with his maid of honor duties, and if Casey had just bought the real deal instead of cheap knockoffs, she wouldn't have cracked the heel. Figured it was an easy fix and no one noticed me sneaking off. And other than the displeased middle-aged saleswoman who wasn't willing to forgo the commission on the high-priced shoes, it was relatively painless."

She swallowed like she wasn't sure what to say. And I liked that something so trivial seemed to impress her. "I've not been here with anyone else, Zara. And if being in this room with you gets me in trouble, I'll take the repercussions."

Her body moved closer to mine as her hands unfurled from her chest, taking it as an invitation, and wrapping my arms around her and brushing my lips against her mouth. "I know you said you wanted to talk, Zara, but I meant it when I said I wanted to kiss you."

Heat traveled up my spine as we made contact, my fingers tracing up her back and finding themselves knotted in her hair. I didn't care what happened after, but in that moment, I wanted to take more, to be with her like I'd been dying to do and denying myself for days.

When she didn't stop me, I deepened the kiss, my teeth pulling against her bottom lip. It was more than I'd had yet still not enough, her body undulating against mine as contented whimpers spilled out between breaths.

There was a gray couch that had probably seen its share of action pushed against the back wall, and I steered us toward it. I wasn't going to do anything she wasn't okay with, but kissing her and making her feel good was definitely on my agenda.

I sank heavily into the couch as the back of my legs felt the fabric, pulling her down on top of me as I kept our mouths connected. I loved the feel of her, the desperation in her own kisses as she hitched up the bottom of her dress allowing her thighs to straddle me.

She was wild, unrestrained and not second-guessing herself. There was no hesitation in the way her hands threaded in my hair or the rock of her hips as she ground against me.

I liked that side of her and knew it lurked underneath. I'd seen a glimpse of it the first night when she'd made out with a relative stranger and asked me to take her to my hotel room.

But watching her take what she wanted this time around was infinitely more satisfying.

"I said we'd talk." She pulled back my head and kissed me again like she was struggling with her own rules and regulations. "I'm not fucking you in some back room."

My hands locked around her hips, encouraging her to keep riding me. "It's the bridal suite, sweetheart, and I guarantee you it's seen its fair share of fucking."

Her teeth grazed my jaw while her fingers followed in their wake. "I don't care, I'm not fucking you here even though I really want to. There's something about you that drives me crazy, Lincoln, but I'm not totally throwing away all my common sense."

"Then let me take you to my bed, Zara." My hand palmed her tit and I felt the tip get hard against my touch. "We both want this, why we're fighting so hard against it is what really doesn't make sense."

That conversation was going to have to wait because I couldn't even think straight anymore. Not when she was pressed against me, using the ridge in my pants to get herself off. Not when I could feel how primed she was for my touch, and when I knew one flick of my tongue against her hot little clit would have her screaming for more.

"Your terms, baby." I arched against her, letting her feel how hard I was for her. How the length of my cock was straining against my suit pants, desperate to get out. "Let me take you to my hotel, Zara and I promise, you won't regret it. Then once I've made you come, we can talk as long as you want. I won't even fuck you yet, if that's not what you want. Just let me lick you, let my mouth kiss that heat between your legs, Zara, and make you unravel while you pull my hair."

Fuck, I was getting off just talking about it, the idea of going down on her more than I could stand. I wanted my mouth on her so badly, to map every inch of her skin with my lips and tongue, I'd be recalling it by memory hours after stopping.

She moaned, her hips rocking more desperately against my crotch as my words sunk in. "Tell me what you want, Zara. Because I want to give it to you. I'll give you anything, right now. You just have to ask."

It wasn't a line, or even an exaggeration, my body and mind so worked up, I'd agree to almost anything at that moment. She could've asked me to leave my firm in Boston and start a not-for-profit in Anchorage, Alaska, and I'd be booking a goddamn flight. Anything to have her not stop kissing me, and for those desperate whimpers to reach their crescendo.

I bet she screamed when she came—loud, wild and completely out of control. I didn't doubt for a second that she was amazing between the sheets, and that sex with anyone else before or after would never measure up.

"Tell me." I nipped at her neck, wanting to mark her beautiful, flawless skin like some sick pervert. "I want you. I'll beg if I have to."

"We can't just leave." She moaned against my mouth not convincing me we couldn't or shouldn't.

"Why? You need to go tell Carlisle you're not going to be sitting beside him? Or are you worried about Nate? Give me the problem and I'll give you the solution." Because I could almost promise that whatever she thought was stopping us from leaving wouldn't stand a chance.

"You're so sure of yourself." She laughed, kissing me despite her words. "But yeah, I'm more worried about Nate than anyone else. Being a jerk isn't natural for me."

"You should try it, it's actually a lot of fun. And Nate will live. I'll even give him my checkbook so he can spend obscene amounts of my money on the silent auction. Trust me, he'll forgive me." Her concerns for Nate being angry completely unnecessary. "What else? Edwin? We can both go tell him if you like, I want to make sure there's no misunderstanding as to what I am to you."

"Oh yeah? And what are you?" she asked stopping my mouth with her hand as she pulled away.

"We can deliberate the verdict back in my room. As for right now, I'm the man who is going to make you come more times than you can count." It wasn't all I wanted from her, but it was what I was willing to settle for at that moment. Because telling her I wanted to wake up with her every day and feel her go to sleep against me every night was too intense, even if it was the truth.

Her body rolled, taking her pleasure even though she'd stopped kissing me. "One night, Lincoln. That's all it can be." The negotiation had started, and I hadn't even gotten her naked yet.

Yeah, one night wasn't going to be enough, but I wasn't about to argue. Not when I knew I could be more convincing *after* she'd been in my bed. "I said I'd give you whatever you want, Zara, and if all you want is one night, that's what I'll give you."

It was the first time I'd willingly lied to her, saying words I knew weren't true. Because even if she was positive she could walk away in the morning, I wasn't sure I could.

"Good." She leaned down to kiss me, that beautiful mouth finally back where I'd wanted it. "Then take me back to your hotel, Lincoln. This time, I'm not going to ask to go home."

My hands anchored on her hips, watching her eyes darken as I ground against her. "Zara, when I get you back to my hotel, you're not going to *want* to go home."

That was a promise, and one I intended to keep.

Chapter 18

Lincoln

Nate couldn't have been more thrilled when we'd told him we were leaving. He was either bored with my half-assed effort to be interested in the cause—I still wasn't sure what the gala was supporting nor did I care—or was tired of my lack of appreciation for the food and wine that five grand a ticket got you. So when we told him we were leaving and I gave him the parting gift of a blank check and told him to buy himself something nice, he stopped short at pushing us out the door.

Edwin wasn't so understanding.

In our absence, dinner service had started. He was seated at the head table with all the other people I didn't really care for with a vacant chair at his side. It was still unclear if he'd had it vacated for Zara's benefit—likely—or if he'd turned up to the event without a plus-one—doubtful. Not that I cared whichever scenario was responsible, other than reinforcing that he wouldn't be spending the evening getting to know the woman I wanted. I'm sure he'd have someone else keep him company before they came to collect the dishes from the first course, something else I didn't care about either.

Zara insisted she go up to him and make her apologies alone, worried I was going to gloat. What she didn't realize was I didn't need to gloat. The fact she was leaving with me was enough of a reward, that he knew about it directly from her, well that was just a bonus.

"How did he take it?" I asked, waiting patiently in the outside hall like she asked. Apparently, my request to watch was in poor taste, and I'd been shoved outside the minute I'd said goodbye to Nate. "Let me guess." I tapped my finger against my lips like I was thinking. "He was disappointed he didn't get to spend the evening with you, but he's given you his card. You know, so you can have a friendly lunch sometime in the future and he wishes you the best."

"How did you know?" Her brow furrowed.

"Because I've worked with a hundred Edwin Carlisles and their M.O. never changes." I didn't bother asking if she was going to hold onto the number or not because it reeked of desperation. And at the moment he was the last thing on my mind, and if I played my cards right, it would be the last thing on hers too.

"And what's your M.O?" she asked, her arms wrapping around my body. "Or is that privileged information?"

My lips found hers as my hands anchored on her hips. "I don't need a playbook, sweetheart, and if I did, it would've been tossed out the window by now."

She was an enigma.

Different from almost every woman I'd ever met.

And whether I wanted to or not, I was flying by the seat of my pants.

There was some throat clearing behind us, a gray-haired woman giving us judgment while we made out in the foyer. I didn't much care what she thought, but it did illustrate the point that we were still not in the car, heading to my room, and that was something that needed remedying.

"Okay, beautiful, let's get out of here before we scandalize the guests." I kissed her one last time before knotting my fingers with hers.

We headed to the exit, handing my ticket to the valet, and were soon back in the car I'd borrowed for the evening. We drove in relative silence, the anticipation crackling between us as I navigated through traffic and got us back to my hotel in record time. I didn't even bother to park, pulling up front and handing the keys to the concierge, asking him to contact the car club and get the car returned. I didn't want the distraction of needing to do it in the morning, and I didn't want heat from Boston because I'd abused my membership privileges.

With the car taken care of, we went straight up to my room. My hands were itching to touch her, but I kept it respectable in the elevator. I wasn't interested in giving some asshole jerk-off material courtesy of the security footage, so as hard as it was not to press her against the wall and fuck her right there, I resisted, knowing the reward would be the greater prize.

I'd barely gotten my room unlocked when my restraint broke. I didn't want to wait anymore, the urge to touch her eating me up since the last time she'd been in there with me. Difference was, there was no mistake about who she was with and what she wanted, and I was taking all of it.

Her body arched into me as I locked the door behind us and tossed my room key aside. My hands found her waist, pressing her against me so she could feel exactly what she did to me. I wasn't just hard, I was throbbing, so desperate to be inside of her my balls ached.

But I wouldn't rush it, oh no. I was going to savor it, draw out the pleasure for hours until we both were crazy. And first I was going to make her come.

"Bed," I ordered, walking her backward through the room until her legs hit the mattress. I didn't bother with any more instructions, my hands finding her zipper and working her out of that fucking beautiful dress.

All it took was a gentle tug and it dropped to the floor, pooling around her sexy heeled feet. I'd get to her shoes in a minute, having fantasized about them sitting on my shoulders while I sunk deep into her, but currently my attention was on her hot body and the scraps of lace that were barely covering it.

Her bra was tiny, half-crescent cups of see-through fabric that pushed up her tits in the most spectacular way. And her panties were almost nonexistent, barely hiding the gift I knew was waiting underneath.

"Mmmmmmmm," I moaned in appreciation, my lips against her skin as I moved down her neck. "Was this for me?"

"No, it was for me." Her body bowed as she relaxed onto the bed. "Smart women can want to feel sexy, it doesn't make us anything less than we are."

"Oh, I completely agree." I did my best not to tear the scraps apart as I pushed down the cup and exposed one of her breasts. "And you are definitely sexy."

My tongue curled around one of her nipples while my hand freed the other. Her eyelashes danced as I gently sucked, a moan spilling from her lips.

"Lincoln."

Fingernails grazed against my scalp as I moved my mouth to her other nipple, her hips impatiently grinding trying to find friction. I liked her like that, needy and unrestrained, not thinking about what she should be doing, but what she needed.

My mouth was replaced by my hands as I moved my lips farther down her torso, kissing and licking my way down to that tiny see-through triangle that was held together by some impressive strings on either side. Sinking to my knees, I took advantage of my angle, positioning her so her legs hung off the bed and giving me unrestricted access.

"Wait." She yanked at my hair stopping my progression down. "Shouldn't we . . . I don't know, get you naked first?" she asked, panting between each word.

I shook my head not willing to stop what I was doing to waste time undressing myself. My cock ached, desperate to be free, but I wanted to taste her more than I wanted my own relief. "There will be plenty of time to get naked after I've made you come, Zara. I've been thinking about it for days, and I really need to make it happen."

My hand disappeared underneath her panties and felt how slick she was for me. Her hips tilted up, arching into my touches as my fingers swirled against her clit.

"Lincoln." It was both a plea and a demand, her hand coming down on mine and pushing it into her. I wasn't sure exactly how expensive her lingerie was, but I was seconds from tearing it off and reducing it to trash.

"Oh God." She panted, her breaths coming out in short, sharp bursts. "More. More exactly like that."

"It's cute you think I need instructions." My teeth nipped at her hip while I slid down her panties with my teeth. My hands had more important things to do and currently they were getting really familiar with one of her tits and the slickness between her legs.

She kicked them off the rest of the way, her dangerously high heels almost doing some extra damage. But I wasn't distracted, flattening my tongue against her heat the moment it was exposed.

"Fuck," she cursed out, lifting her hips to my mouth as I lapped against her. I loved the taste of her, feeling her coating my tongue as I pushed it deeper inside as I thumbed her clit.

It wasn't even close to how amazing I thought it would be, the desperate whimpers as she ground against my face making me so hard, I was glad I was already on my knees.

I thrusted involuntarily, needing to take a minute to reach down and unzip my pants. But that didn't mean I stopped, only needing one hand to free my cock while I worked her with the other and my mouth.

"Yes, Lincoln. Yes." Her breaths got faster and shallower, her body unable to keep still as I returned my full attention to her. My fantasy about her shoes on my shoulders was soon realized as I lifted her legs to straddle both sides of my face. "Oh, I think I'm going to—"

I didn't wait for her to tell me, her body spelling out how close she was as I continued to kiss, suck and fuck her with my hands and my tongue. I wanted to feel her explode, to be looking up at her when she finally lost all control, and then for her to look at me and know I was responsible for that pleasure.

Greedy for all of it, I increased my pace, unrelenting with the contact until she finally gave us what we'd both wanted. Yeses spilled from her lips as tiny pulses echoed against my mouth, my assault slowed but not stopped as the waves of her orgasm washed through her.

Fuck that was good, her sated body sinking into the plush memory foam mattress as whimpers accompanied the subtle shakes of her arms and legs. Her bra was still fastened underneath her tits, shoes still on her feet, but she looked utterly perfect lying there in front of me, and I was dying for another taste.

"Mmmmm." I licked my fingers as I rose to my feet and then gave myself a slow and deliberate tug. Her eyes flashed to my cock, my shaft exposed from the front of my pants.

"Is that just for show or do you know how to use it?" Her brow rose as I slowly unbuttoned the front of my shirt.

I laughed, my shucked jacket dropping to the floor, my shirt following it quickly after. I'd meant to make her wait, for her to watch me as I slowly peeled off the layers of my suit, but I was impatient.

167

Her elbows lifted her off the bed, her vantage giving her a better view. I liked her eyes on me as I undressed, the hungry dark expressive pools framed by inky black lashes not moving from my body as I revealed more and more skin.

It wasn't long before I was naked, standing at the foot of the bed before once again sinking to my knees.

"Wait," she protested. "I want to touch you." Her hand reached out as she shuffled into a sit.

The chuckle escaped my throat as my fingers moved to her ankles. "You can touch me in a minute, sweetheart. Just let me finish what I started."

She watched with interest as I unbuckled the fastening on either side of her ankles and then slid the heels off her feet. Her toes were painted in a deep red, each perfect digit wiggling as I released them. Next was the bra, my fingers tracing up her legs and then hips, following the curves of her body to the swell of her breasts. It was easy to get distracted, to give them the attention they deserved. But I had an objective, and even aroused I could complete a task.

It didn't take more than a flick, the fabric falling away from her back and dropping into her lap. I tossed it to the pile of clothes on the floor before turning my eyes back to her so I could appreciate her completely bare.

Her skin was smooth, the tiniest strip of hair kissing the top of her slit.

A groan spilled from my mouth, sounding more animal than human as my knees planted themselves either side of her.

She was beautiful, and sexy, and so goddamn delicious there was no chance one night was going to be enough with her. Not that I was going to bring that up, willing for the argument to be made after I'd been deep inside her, and made her come at least two more times.

I was about to reach down to my pants for a condom when her head dropped forward, her lips making contact with my cock.

"Fuuuuuuuuuuuuckk." All thoughts paused as tingles moved down my shaft.

What started off as a sweet kiss, got a whole lot dirtier as she sucked me in. Her cheeks hollowed, her lips stretching around my crown as she took as much of my length in as she could, her hands tightening around my girth.

"Jesus, that feels good," I hissed out, my fingers threading in her hair as her head bobbed. The wet pop of her lips made it almost impossible to stay still, my hips gently fucking her mouth as she continued to jerk me off.

Coming in her mouth was something else I'd fantasized about, right along with watching her ride me. But I was torn as to what I wanted first, seeing her bright eyes looking up at me as she took me deeper into her throat almost doing me in.

"Zara."

Her name was all I could manage, not having the ability to form sentences while she was sucking my dick like that, my chest rising and falling as I tried to stave off the high.

"Not coming," I grit out, trying to convince myself more than anyone else as I pulled my cock from her beautiful puffy lips. "Not yet."

"I bet I could make you." Her eyes so full of defiance there wasn't a doubt in my mind.

And fuck me, it was a bet I desperately wanted to take. To see how long I could draw it out, and which of us had the stronger will. But I wasn't feeling particularly masochistic, and I still had a few more orgasms I needed to deliver on.

"You think so, do you?" I taunted back, taking a reprieve from her gorgeous mouth to get that condom. "That get you off, Zara?"

And as much as I wanted to know the answer, I was done talking, tearing the latex from the foil and sheathing myself. I gripped myself hard around the base and tugged, the idea of not being inside of her no longer acceptable.

"Yes." A wispy moan followed out the word as her body softened against the bed. "Yes."

"Yes, to what?" My mouth went to her throat as I flattened myself against her, using the ridge of my erection to rub her clit. "You've got to be more specific, sweetheart."

Her eyes fluttered closed as I moved up and down her slick center, the head of my cock just barely pushing in. "Yes, it gets me off," she ground out, tilting her pelvis to get me in deeper. "The idea of making you lose control turns me on so much."

She wasn't the only one, and I was so turned on that I sunk into her with one firm deep stroke. I'd wanted to go slower, to tease her a little longer. But plans had a way of changing, especially when she was involved.

"Like this?" My elbows accepted my weight, doing my best not to crush her. "You want to see me lose control, Zara?" I pulled out fast, plunging back in, each thrust getting deeper. "Tell me how crazy you want to make me?"

Faster.

Deeper.

Harder.

Her legs wrapped around my hips, tilting her pelvis so I could get in deeper. Her lips were still glossy from having sucked my dick while her perfect perky tits bounced with every thrust.

Jesus.

Christ.

She wanted me out of control and that was exactly what she was going to get, any restraint I'd had falling to the wayside as I pumped into her.

"Tell me." The caged words barely making it past my clenched teeth. "Tell me, Zara, because I'm about to lose my goddamn mind, baby."

"Yes, yes. I want it all. Just like that," she panted, matching each rock of my hips with one of her own. "I want you crazy, Lincoln. So fucking crazy."

The request wasn't needed, she had me exactly where she wanted me and there wasn't a thing I could do about it.

My head reached down and kissed her, our mouths just as hungry as the rest of our bodies as I felt her fall apart underneath me. I swallowed her scream, taking all she had to give me until I couldn't hold out any longer. My body shook as I shot my load, her pussy squeezing my shaft as I came hard, watching her eyes widen as she continued to pulse.

"Zara." Her name whispered between kisses, dragging my hips in and out of her until the last of her tremors had subsided. I wanted to own all of her pleasure and for her to own mine, my lips kissing her until a contented smile spread against them.

Her fingernails grazed against my spine, tracing the contours of my back. "Hmmm, that was good."

"Good?" I scoffed in disbelief. "That was at the very least great. But if you want to turn this into some kind of a challenge, Zara, I'm not the kind of man to back down."

"Fine, fine, it was great." She laughed, pressing her cheek against my chest. "Such an egomaniac. If I tell you it's the best sex I've ever had, will it make you feel better?"

"Would that be the truth?" I asked, wanting to believe it but not conceited enough to assume.

She rolled her eyes, her head relaxing against the pillow as I gently eased out of her. I'd done my best to not smother her under my weight, rolling onto my side and lying beside her. "I'm not interested in platitudes, sweetheart. Because Zara, I'd prefer you tell me what's really on your mind rather than what you think I want to hear."

I'd never cared with other women. Happy to hear them tell me what a good lay I'd been, and not interested in whether it was the truth. Not that I'd ever left anyone unsatisfied, but I'd never given much thought on how I'd stacked up. But with her, I wanted to be the best. To have made her come so hard that she wasn't going to forget it.

The breath slowly pushed past her beautiful lips as she turned onto her side to face me. "You were really, *really* good." Her slow smile lit up those dangerous dark eyes. "But . . . you know, if you feel like you have a point to prove, I'm happy to let you do that."

"Oh, really?" I asked, nipping her playfully on the shoulder. "How generous of you."

Her shoulder lifted in a shrug. "Generosity is just one of my virtues, Lincoln."

"Yeah?" My fingers traced her shoulder, following her smooth skin down the length of her arm. "Let's see what your others are."

Chapter 19

Zara

It was late when I woke up, the bed still warm but empty.

I hadn't planned on spending the night, determined I was just going to have sex with him, get him out of my system and then go home. Then I could move the hell on and hopefully remember why he was such a bad idea to start with. Because avoiding him and trying to forget him hadn't worked out. And maybe he could be a one-night stand even though we'd sailed waaaaaaay beyond casual and he knew too much.

But.

All those decisions had been made *before* I'd slept with him. Before I knew how amazing sex with him was and how incredible he'd make me feel. And I'd had decent sex before, it wasn't like I'd been slumming with average penis my whole life and I'd finally met a man who knew what to do with it. But he was different. Attentive. Deliberate. Slow and also fast. Gentle, yet firm and rough too. He gave it all to me, and when I'd casually mentioned he was the best sex I'd ever had, it was not a joke.

He.

Was.

The.

Best.

Of course, after I'd said it I'd immediately regretted it. Worrying I was inflating his already ridiculously large ego and setting myself up for the biggest cliché of all time. You know the one, the delicate flower who hasn't ever been fucked properly. *"Wow, your cock is so big, how is it ever going to fit,"* and *"Oh, no man has ever made me come sooooooo hard before, I'm totally ruined now."* Eye roll.

Well, one of those was sort of true. He *had* made me come hard, repeatedly, so I knew it wasn't just a fluke. Meant the bar for future sex had definitely been raised.

And after my multiple orgasms and the lack of him asking me to leave—I'd assumed since he'd gotten what he'd wanted, he'd show me the door—I decided to stay.

Mostly, because I was curious. Would it be awkward, with subtle hints that I was overstaying my welcome? Or would he summon his driver while I was in the bathroom and tell me my ride home was ready? Or would he want me to stay? I hated how much I wanted it to be the last option, how easy it was just to curl up with him and go to sleep. Because we couldn't work, right? He was just a silly obsession that started because of a mistake.

Which is why it didn't make sense how happy I was when he wrapped his arms around me and kissed me goodnight. He held me the whole time, his gentle kisses suspending me somewhere between a dream and reality.

So, I was more than a little disappointed when I woke up and those arms—and kisses—were gone, and I was alone between the sheets.

My fingers wrapped around the covers to pull them over my exposed skin, I felt so naked in that room, and I didn't mean just physically. I was halfway between deciding to just get dressed and leave or hang around and see when he was going to come back when the door unlocked, footsteps making their way back toward the bed.

"Good morning, sleepy head." His smile beamed, one hand holding a cardboard drink carrier housing coffee I assumed, and a large paper bag in the other. "I tried to wake you to see if you wanted to go get breakfast, but you told me to *shut the fuck up and go get you a bacon cream cheese bagel.*"

I laughed, my hand flying to my mouth. "Wait, I *actually* said that?" The vague memory of being hungry and really wanting a bagel coming back into focus. We'd ordered some room service throughout the night, but that had been hours ago. And sex made me hungry.

He waved the bag, his grin widening as he sat on the edge of the bed. He was wearing jeans and a T-shirt, looking so just as comfortable being casual as he did in a suit. "I got you two. And a fruit salad, and three chocolate chip cookies. You're kinda mean when you're hungry, I wasn't going to risk coming back in here without adequate supplies."

I shook my head, strangely not embarrassed by my rude and obnoxious demand. He made it easy for me to be myself, to not feel self-conscious about the things I said, did, felt. "Well, you made me leave the gala without staying for dinner."

"Oh, I forgot the part where I took you hostage and forced you to leave." He chuckled, the fake shock thick in his voice. "Also seem to remember the tray of food that was delivered just after midnight, pretty sure I didn't eat it all myself."

"It's not the same as bacon cream cheese bagels," I argued.

"Clearly." He pushed the bag closer. "Which is why I took a cab to the West Village and got you some from Shlasky's. People will argue there are better ones in the city, but they'd be wrong."

"You took a cab?" My hands grabbing for the bag, the smell of salty bacon and freshly baked bagels wafting through the opening. "What happened to Terry?"

He scoffed, taking a coffee for himself before resting the other on the nightstand beside me. "Jesus, Zara, it's Sunday morning, how heartless do you think I am? He drove Nate home last night. I'm not going to wake him up when I can just as easily catch a cab."

It was funny how much his obvious consideration—both for Terry and me—warmed my soul. He could've easily called his driver—since it was literally his job—and asked him to go to the deli. Or just gotten something down the street. There were bagel trucks and delis on almost every street corner. But he'd gone to one he thought was the best.

For me.

I tried not to get caught up in the significance of it, but couldn't help but be touched by his sweetness. Edwin wouldn't have been so thoughtful, probably asking me to order from a room service menu like most guys. But Lincoln was different, and so surprising in all the right ways.

"Thank you." I hugged the paper bag to my chest. "This is . . ." I tried to find the right words without getting overly emotional. The man got me breakfast; it *wasn't* a big deal. "Really nice."

"You're welcome." He took a sip from his coffee while holding out his other hand. "I got myself breakfast too. Mine is the bacon, egg and cheese."

I pulled out the wrapped bundles, peeking through the paper and seeing which was his. He hadn't been kidding when he'd said he'd gotten me two. My bagels lowered onto the bed as I emptied the rest of the bag.

As promised, there was a fruit salad, cookies, and a blueberry muffin he hadn't mentioned. All of it laid out in front of us like a makeshift picnic as we sat cross-legged on the bed. I was still very naked, the sheet dropping as I moved, something I noticed when I caught his eyes staring.

"Anyone would think you haven't seen a pair of breasts before." I yawned, stretching to give him a better view and secretly liking the attention. "I thought we were eating."

He licked his lips, leaning forward to kiss me. "We are, but I can multitask. And your breasts are exquisite, all the others I've seen can't even compare."

He was lying obviously but I didn't care, happy to live in whatever delusional fantasy world he wanted to be in, especially since he'd brought me food.

I kissed him back before giving him a playful shove. "So a blueberry muffin, huh? How did you know they're my favorite?"

He sighed heavily, looking up at the ceiling and cursing softly under his breath. "I knew I should've taken it out of the bag and smuggled it in."

"I'll share my cookies," I offered. "And the fruit salad."

"Just take it all, Zara." He huffed dramatically, pointing at the muffin sitting between us. "But don't even think about putting on a shirt. If I'm going to give up my blueberry muffin, I'm going to get to stare at your spectacular tits while you eat it."

I laughed, arching as I picked it up and took a nibble. "Fair trade."

We ate right there on the bed, my usual concern about crumbs in the sheets missing in action as we relaxed into an easy conversation. I fed him bits of my newly acquired blueberry muffin, and let him taste my superior bacon bagel. He maintained that the bacon, egg, cheese combo was by far the better option, refusing to concede.

He asked about Belle, about Hayley and the baby, and even about my work. And I asked him about his family, if he missed being away and how many meetings he had lined up for the week.

Deep down I knew they were conversations we shouldn't have been having. The interest in each other's lives not conducive to the casual hook-up the night before was supposed to be. It was hard, reminding myself I was eventually going to have to leave, and that as wonderful as it all felt, nothing had really changed.

Why did he have to be so goddamn perfect?

Couldn't he have been an asshole, or less sweet, or even just less amazing in bed. I'd have taken any of those options, finding it more difficult the more time I spent with him to motivate myself to leave.

And I obviously had to leave, I'd been the one who'd insisted it was only going to be one night. He'd probably been on his best behavior, giving me one night of the best version of himself, knowing he'd never have to repeat it.

Now, if only I could make myself believe that.

"You want to go get a shower?" He cleared the trash, smoothing over the sheets and the comforter with his palm. "They come through and clean the room around eleven, and I usually go and take a walk around the city so I'm not in the way. Figured since you're here, you might like to join me."

A walk around the city on a Sunday afternoon sounded fantastic, especially given the company. But that was skating dangerously close to a line I was nervous to cross, especially since I had no idea when he was leaving.

"I should get back home. Belle will require an update, it's easier if I just get it over with." The excuse sounded lame even to me, the disappointment unable to be kept out of my tone.

He nodded, knowing it wasn't a total lie, the stream of unread messages flashing on my phone proof of that. "I could come with you, be your exhibit A."

"What?" I laughed, assuming he'd been joking. "You want to come home with me?"

He shrugged, like it was no big deal. "You worried I'm going to present a different version of events? Besides, surely Belle is going to need cereal or apple juice or tampons, so she'll probably just call me later."

"You'd buy my sister tampons?" I asked, skeptical he'd so willingly fulfill that request.

"Sure, it takes more than just a box of feminine hygiene products to spook me." It was said with so much confidence, I had no choice than to believe him.

He must be really, *really* good in a court room.

Strange how just that thought alone was turning me on.

But he seemed too perfect, and I still wasn't sure if it wasn't partly an act. Sure, I could tell he was into me, but was it because he knew it was temporary? Even broken clocks were right twice a day. And I wouldn't allow myself to be that moron who assumed consideration and kindness meant more than it did. He could still be polite and a player, the two didn't have to be mutually exclusive.

"I think it's better if I go by myself, but thanks. Your commitment is admirable." I did my best to deliver it with as much confidence as he did.

The truth was, I didn't want to go home by myself.

I wanted to walk around the park with him, and talk, and learn more about what made him tick.

I wanted to hear about his work, and his life, and just be in his company.

But I also wanted to sleep with him again, and my mind was cloudy on whether or not that was a good idea.

No.

It was a bad idea.

A really bad idea.

He would leave, and I was already more attached than I should be if he was just a fling, which is why I shouldn't have slept with him in the first place. Not that it would do me much good now since we'd already had sex and it was so freaking amazing, I couldn't think straight but—

"Zara?" Lincoln interrupted my internal thoughts, his quizzical look disarming me.

"Yes?" I answered, not sure if my name had been the first thing he'd said and I'd been too deep in my deliberations to notice.

He moved closer, his hand brushing the hair from my face. "You want to tell me what you're thinking about? Because I think you *do* want me to come back with you. You want to spend the day walking around with me, arguing over which pretzel vendor is best or why my suggestion to go to Central Park is so predictable. But for some reason, you won't say it."

Oh.

My.

God.

I did my best to keep my face neutral, to limit the intake of air to a normal breath, but internally I was reeling. Never had a man read me so quickly and accurately, most of them taking everything I said at face value. I was partly responsible, having schooled myself so diligently to not show my true emotion—more for work purposes than anything else—that they had no reason to assume different. But no one had really questioned it. No one bothered to dig a little deeper, to see what was really underneath.

It excited and terrified me in equal measure, my need to go home by myself no longer hypothetical.

"I wasn't really thinking about anything." I shrugged, giving an award-winning performance as I smiled casually. "Other than the usual stuff, getting home, explaining to Belle, getting ready for work tomorrow." I rattled off acceptable options like they'd been my exact thoughts. "Sorry if I seemed distracted."

He laughed, bringing his mouth closer and kissing me. "*Liar*. But you don't have to tell me if you don't want to, I'll settle for getting my answers from your body instead."

His arms wrapped around me and before I could fully understand what was happening, my traitorous body was pressed against his.

Damn him.

Damn him right to hell.

He laughed against my mouth, my body ready for whatever he had in mind. I was still naked, something that should've made me self-conscious except it just made me relieved. Glad there weren't many layers between us, and that I could feel his warm hands against my skin as he moved them up and down. "Tell me again you don't want to take a shower with me, Zara."

"I want to," I admitted, knowing my body was just going to betray me anyway. "But I need to get back and you already said they'll be coming to clean the room soon."

"I've got a *do not disturb* sign I've been itching to use," he argued, his lips moving to my neck. "Just need a second to slip it on the outside of the door."

Gah, it was so tempting. Tempting to lose myself in his kiss, his touches and everything else his body promised. One more time surely wouldn't hurt, right? The pros and cons were mentally weighed as I palmed his cock and found him hard. The slow glide up and down the ridge in his pants made him hiss as I teased him through the fabric.

"Zara," he warned, his breaths not as controlled as they'd been a minute or two before. "You want me to come in my jeans? Because that's what's going to happen if you keep doing that. I've been hard as a rock watching you eat breakfast naked, so I'm going to need very little encouragement to blow my load."

It gave me a thrill he was also unhinged, that his calm and collected exterior wasn't a true representation.

"Oh?" I giggled, my hand slipping under the waistband and gripping his cock.

No underwear.

Mmmmm, well that was a surprise.

"Zara." His fingers wrapped around my wrist stopping me. "If you want to play a game of control, I'm good with that. But only after I make sure we're not disturbed."

His eyes dared me to tell him I was leaving, for my mouth to say words we both knew would be lies, but I couldn't. And more importantly, I didn't want to.

I wanted to be in that room with him.

To go into that shower.

To get lost like I had through the night and into the early hours of the morning.

"I'll meet you in the shower." My hands gave him one last tug, his restraint around my wrist having loosened as he waited for my response.

He groaned, planting his hands on my hips and stopping me from turning around and heading to the bathroom like I'd planned. "I'm glad you changed your mind. Now let me make sure we won't be interrupted."

Chapter 20

Zara

I eventually made it home sometime in the late afternoon.

Unsure if Belle was still home—I'd texted her and told her I was fine but wasn't coming home for a few hours—I unlocked the door and crept into my apartment. Not sure why I was sneaking into my own home like I was robbing the place, but I winced at each creak and sound like it was the worst thing ever.

Okay, so maybe I wasn't as clueless as I pretended to be as to why I was sneaking. But as much as I loved my sister—and knew the confrontation was inevitable—I wanted to bask in the feel-good glow a little longer.

"Have fun?" She smirked, perched on the edge of my bed like she'd been patiently waiting. "Because it's almost four o'clock and I've been unable to concentrate on anything since two. Oh, and Mom wants you to call her too. Even she agreed it's very unlike you to be out so late and not at least call. But we both approve of you having more fun."

"You called Mom?" I sighed, wondering why being tattled on by my younger sister still made me nervous. "Belle!"

My hope that my sister had been busy with audition prep, or visiting Hayley, or even just doing *Belle things* had been shot to pieces. Not only was she *not* occupied with any of the aforementioned but she had actively given up waiting in her own room and called my mother. She'd also taken up residency in mine to squash even the slightest possibility I'd sneak in without her seeing.

"Pfft, I didn't call her because of you. And I didn't even mention Lincoln." She rolled her eyes, smirking. "She was working a difficult case and I wanted to make sure she was okay."

"Is she?" I asked, giving up my attempt at tiptoeing, tossing the heels I'd slipped off my feet onto the floor. "I know she was helping a young mother move out, and they had to do it while her husband worked the nightshift."

"Yeah. I could never do her job, but I'm glad these people have someone like Mom helping them." Belle hugged my pillow.

Our mom was probably one of the most altruistic people I knew. Not only had she been a social worker for our entire lives, but she went above and beyond to help people. Even if it meant working late, or hiring movers at a premium rate because it was out of regular business hours and paying for it entirely out of her own pocket.

"Good, I'm glad it all went well." I grinned, resolving to give her a call when my head was in a better place.

"Great, now we've got that settled, you can get back to telling me all about Lincoln. Your redirect might work for you in a courtroom, Zara, but I know all your sneaky tactics."

"You know, I don't have to tell you anything." I chuckled, folding my arms across my chest.

She gasped, a mix of real horror with added drama. "Why would you be so horrible to me? I thought you loved me."

"I can still love you and not divulge every detail of my life. Especially my personal life, Belle." I tried in vain to argue, knowing there wasn't much point. Not only would Belle find a way to weasel it out of me, but she was likely to call Lincoln herself. I hadn't forgotten she still had his number. But more importantly, a part of me wanted to share it too.

The buzz was so new and exciting, I wasn't sure I'd ever really felt it before. Not when it came to a man anyway. I'd experienced a similar thrill when it came to my work—when I'd gotten my promotion, when I closed on a really big or pivotal case. But when it came to my relationships, it had all been tempered. I'd been happy of course, excited even. But not to the levels where things just *felt* different. Like the air vibrated around me, and everything just seemed more colorful.

Belle sighed dramatically, throwing herself onto my bed. "Just tell me. You've been gone almost an entire twenty-four hours. I can't even remember the last time you slept over at a guy's place, let alone spent a night *and* a day with him."

I joined her on my bed, flopping down beside her with slightly less drama. "He is really great, Belle." The smile crept on my face even though I tried to fight it. "He's funny and charming, but so incredibly sweet too. And a night wasn't even close to long enough."

Without any more coaxing from Belle, I spilled the details of our short but eventful date. Everything from our ride to the gala in his fancy rented car, to meeting the real Edwin, to both of us realizing we'd been fighting a very real and hot attraction. My skin prickled, reliving my own excitement as I spoke of how he kissed me and then pulled me into the bridal suite at the ballroom. And how I couldn't say no to going back to his hotel and spending the night. I even told her how I'd grouched at him half-asleep and demanded he get me coffee and bagels. And rather than laugh at me and call someone else to meet my demands, he went out and got them himself. Coming back with a bounty that was more than I'd asked for, making me feel so special and wanted.

"Oh my god!" Belle's hand flew to her mouth. "You're in love with him."

I laughed, shaking my head at how ridiculous that was. "Belle, we were together one night and I barely know him, I'm not in *love* with him. Besides, he's leaving. He might not have told me when, but the fact he lives in Boston hasn't changed in the last few days. He will eventually leave."

The words felt bitter in my mouth, and even though they'd been the same ones I'd been telling myself, I hated hearing them out loud. That didn't make them any less true though, even if I was positive I was not in love with him.

"So?" she scoffed, turning toward me like I was the one who was being stupid. "And it wasn't just one night. There was the coffee when you first met, and the dinner with Nate, and when he came to our apartment and brought us creamer."

"Brought *you* creamer," I corrected.

"Me, us, he was here, wasn't he?" She giggled. "And you had the perfect opportunity to blow him off. You could've sat with Edwin, given Delia a piece of your mind—I hope she got old with saggy boobs, I want more details on her later—but you didn't. And come on, but a rich, good-looking, *local* guy wouldn't be a hard sell for most women."

She had a point.

But Lincoln wasn't the kind of guy you could replace, even though I knew I eventually would have to.

"You love him, Zara. Or are falling in love with him. Which you would totally see if you stopped trying to audit every single thought you had."

I hated when Belle was right.

More than that, I hated when I was wrong. And while it didn't happen often, I was fairly sure it was one of those times.

Love? Yeah, I wasn't sure that was it, but there were feelings that were deep, complicated and entangled. The kind of thoughts that knotted your insides and warmed your skin like the sun in July.

Shit.

Shit.

Shit.

"Shit," I cursed, annoyed at myself. "He's leaving, Belle."

I had successfully gone twenty-eight years without falling in love and when I'd finally found someone who was perfect, he was going to leave. Worst thing was, I didn't even know when. It could even be tomorrow, and then what? "Long distance relationships don't work out. Not when you have two career-driven and highly independent people. I'm literally setting myself up for heartbreak."

In a perfect world, he'd tell me his trip had been indefinitely extended. We'd have all kinds of time to work out what we were doing and how we felt about each other, and if my feelings were only one-sided. But I was holding a ticking time bomb, with no idea when it was going to explode, and I didn't want to make a fool of myself when it was more than plausible he didn't feel the same way.

Of course, I knew I wasn't just a good-time, that he'd obviously had some sort of feelings for me too. But having the "what does this all mean?" and "where is this relationship heading?" talk when you weren't even officially dating was ridiculous. Who did that? I'll tell you who, no one. Because if you were stupid enough to initiate those kinds of conversations when you'd only spent one night together, the other party would be crossing state lines before you'd even finished the question.

"So, what are you going to do?" Belle asked, wrongly believing I had the answer.

My hands scrubbed the front of my face, that blissed-out feeling disappearing faster than I'd wanted. And to think, less than an hour ago my biggest problems were deliciously tight well-worn muscles and a lock that could've used some WD-40.

"Obviously, I can't see him again." I sighed, knowing I'd fallen too far, too fast for anything good to come of it.

She turned, her brow raised in question. "So you're going to avoid him, take the coward's way out? Wow, never thought I'd see the day."

"I'm *not* taking the coward's way out," I argued, even if I wasn't exactly convinced. "But seeing him and prolonging the inevitable is stupid. Besides, it's better this way. Then he can finish his work without the added distraction."

Belle laughed, flipping over onto her stomach and poking me in the ribs. "You're so noble. Making all these decisions for the greater good, especially for him."

"Maybe I am." I shrugged, knowing he wouldn't be the only one who'd benefit from the time and space. I'd barely even looked at work all weekend and I couldn't remember the last time I'd had a Saturday and Sunday to myself. Not since graduating, and not something I should be planning on continuing if I wanted to make partner.

"Just don't blow him off, okay? He seems like a nice guy, and who knows what can happen. At the very least, call him and tell him on the phone you aren't seeing him again."

She had a point, and while it was easier to just disappear into thin air, it wasn't exactly practical either. He not only had my phone number, but knew where I lived, as well as a sordid array of other personal information I'd word vomited whenever I seemed to be around him. If my plan had been to go quietly into the night, I'd screwed that right up.

I nodded, agreeing that a call was probably the best way to do it. Lord knows I couldn't trust myself to see him. Too worried he'd touch me or hell, even just look at me and I wouldn't be able to stop myself from kissing him. He'd become a habit alarmingly fast and one I didn't want to break even though it was hazardous to my health. The Surgeon General would definitely not recommend, the graphic warning of the impending heartbreak should've been printed on his beautiful and breathtakingly gorgeous face.

"I'll call him," I promised, the tightness in my chest making me uncomfortable. "But if you ever call me a coward again, I'm going to burn your box of old Broadway Playbills."

"Zara!" Belle gasped. "You wouldn't dare!"

"No, I wouldn't. But you should be nicer to your older sister." I pulled her into a tight hug. "Now get out of my room. I have some sleep to catch up on and am going to attempt to get some work done." I wasn't holding out hope for either of those things, but it was fun to pretend.

Pretend like I had it all together and I wasn't dreading that call. Or that I wasn't disappointed and sad that I'd probably never see Lincoln again.

I'd done it.

Called Lincoln, telling him how much of a good time I'd had. How much I'd enjoyed our amazing dates, but all good things came to an end—blah, blah, blah—and I wished him the best for the future.

It hadn't even been that hard, my voice not wavering from the confident, light and conversational tone I'd been hoping for, the emotions I felt kept locked down as I delivered my—slightly rehearsed—speech.

Of course, it had probably been easier since the entire—and brilliant—delivery had been left on his voicemail, but that hadn't been my intention.

I'd called, fully prepared to speak to him, but it seemed fate had other ideas. Instead I got his sexy—probably hadn't been his intention—voice recording telling me he was unable to take my call but to leave a message and he'd get back to me as soon as he could.

Which was what I did.

I'd done exactly as the man had instructed, leaving him a message with the disclaimer that it didn't really require a call back as we were both really busy, but I hoped he enjoyed the rest of his stay. And if that hadn't been enough, I signed off by telling him to say "hi" to Nate.

Uhhhhhhhhhhhhhhhh.

I was such a coward.

But it was done, and short of hacking into his network, retrieving the message and deleting it, there wasn't much I could do. Besides, I wasn't sure my future attempts would be any better and it was clear the man was too busy to accept calls.

I wasn't sure if my assurance that a return call wasn't necessary was going to be heeded so I prepared myself all the same. But when Monday morning came, and I hadn't received a call or text in response, either through the night or in the morning, I assumed he'd either taken me at my word or was relieved.

Not sure why I was disappointed. I'd literally told the man *not* to call me, and was annoyed he'd done as I'd asked. Not to mention that if I'd been so insistent on hearing what he had to say, I'd have called back at a later time instead of leaving a stupid message.

"Zara, where are last week's depositions?" Joel Bally knocked at my door.

It was still weird having an office, only having just moved in from a cubical, but I loved the small, well-lit space that was completely mine. It made obsessing over a guy I'd dumped—had we ever been really dating?—over voicemail so much more convenient given the privacy. Especially since I was supposed to be doing work, and technically was behind since I'd spent the weekend with my head in the clouds.

"Right here, Joel." I lifted the folder that had been sitting in my outbox. I'd meant to drop it in his office earlier in the morning but had been distracted. You know, when I'd been busy congratulating myself on being so unemotional while secretly being emotional. It was a full-time gig, apparently.

Joel wandered over to my desk, flipping open the folder and glancing at the contents before closing it and focusing on me. "Great. You need to go over anything before your two-thirty? The Wilson merger is pretty stock standard so you can handle this meeting on your own. I'll be there to nut out the final details of course, but I'm excited to see what you can do."

His confidence in me was encouraging even if I was feeling deflated. "I appreciate the opportunity." I stood, handing him some notes I'd been organized enough to take last Friday before I'd completely lost my mind. "Here are the points I want to clarify with the client. Other than that, it seems fairly straight forward. Both parties have agreed they want it done as quickly and as painlessly as possible, I don't foresee any problems."

At least I sounded like I didn't have my head up my ass and was deserving of the faith he'd put in me. Which was good considering I didn't want to screw up the one part of my life that had been pretty much my everything up to that point.

He took my notes, his eyes scanning over them as he brought his hand to his chin. "Good, good. Well, looks like you've got it all covered. I'll be in my office if you need anything else." He held out my notes and gave me a warm smile. "Knock them dead, Mathews."

I gave him an enthusiastic fist pump as he waved me goodbye, the notes tossed back onto my desk as he closed the door behind him.

Well, that was fun.

My ass sunk heavily into my chair as I gazed longingly at my phone.

I wouldn't call, I told myself, rationalizing it was easier for everyone involved if we just left it the way it was.

Lincoln was probably wondering why I'd even bothered to leave the message in the first place. I'd told him at the gala it was going to be a one-time deal, so it wasn't like he'd been expecting a relationship.

Why was I over-thinking it?

Everyone was playing by my own goddamn rules and I was pissed off.

I was momentarily disrupted from my mental tug-of-war when my phone rang. It was the internal line, one of the secretaries from the front desk.

"Hi, Aria."

"Hi, Zara, your eleven-thirty is here."

My eyes flashed to my schedule, an appointment I hadn't recalled making taking up my eleven-thirty spot. "Um, I hadn't realized I had an appointment."

"It was at Joel's request." Well, guess that answered that. "I'll send him down now."

There wasn't any time to ask who the meeting was with or what it was for, Aria ending the call. She didn't even say goodbye, the receiver still pressed against my ear as I listened to dead air.

Joel setting an appointment for me wasn't strange. He'd often palm off clients who didn't need a partner, especially if it was for tedious or monotonous work. Perks of being high in the pecking order I guess, and I was happy for the hand-me-downs.

I stood, straightening my jacket as I waited for my unknown client. My office wasn't far from reception so it wouldn't be long, and I didn't want them to walk in and think I'd been rattled.

The knock came just as expected, striding to my door and affixing a smile on my face as my hand twisted the knob.

"Hi, I'm Zara Math—"

The rest of my greeting lost in my throat as I pulled open the rest of the door and came face-to-face with the sexiest dark-haired, blue-eyed man in a suit—so perfectly cut for his body it showed exactly how hot he was—to ever walk into my office.

Lincoln Archer.

Oh my God.

It felt like I couldn't breathe, my skin tingling hot as my blood ran cold, thankful I still had a decent skeleton capable of keeping me upright.

So much for that return phone call.

Chapter 21

Lincoln

I'd heard the message she'd left me.

Then I listened to it again, looking for the punchline because surely it had been some kind of joke.

Zara had a wicked sense of humor, so I'd laughed at first. The words spoken on to my voicemail so level and unemotive it felt like she was presenting to the bar.

It was only on the third time around that I'd worked out she was serious. Or at least, was *trying* to be serious, the rehearsed speech, one she thought she needed to say rather than what she wanted.

And I wasn't having it.

Yes, I completely remembered what she'd said. It was going to be a one-time deal. But even if that was what she initially believed, surely she'd changed her mind.

We'd spent the most amazing night ever together, and yeah, the sex had been pretty fucking awesome. I'd made her come so many times I'd lost count, just the thought of that look on her face when she was about to explode, enough to get me hard. And it hadn't been a one-sided deal either. I'd moaned her name, the feeling of her body convulsing against mine enough to drive me crazy.

But it wasn't just the mind-blowing orgasms, we had a connection. Crazy intense but no less real, and more than I'd ever had with any other woman. And there was no way it was entirely one-sided.

No.

Fucking.

Way.

So, if she'd genuinely decided she wanted to keep to her original agreement, then she'd need to tell me face-to-face. She didn't get to leave me a voicemail.

Which was where Nate came in.

"Zara Mathews, Lincoln Archer." I held out my hand like I was meeting her for the first time. "I'm your eleven thirty."

Her eyes were wild, lacking the usual locked down composure I'd seen in them before. I liked her like that, the façade of perfection slipping when I was around, the cracks of the real her peeking through underneath.

"Mr. Archer." She accepted my outstretched hand and gave it a firm shake. *Nice, very, very nice.* "Please, won't you come in."

She was all business, those beautiful wild eyes holstered as she slipped into the refined attorney everyone was probably more familiar with.

Not going to lie, her ability to do both was crazy hot.

It didn't take a genius to work out Zara didn't mix the office with her personal life, and I wasn't a big enough asshole to force her to do that in front of people she worked with. Which was why I happily nodded, accepting her invitation inside, pretending I didn't know how good she felt underneath me.

It was only after the door was closed and we were safely away from prying eyes and ears that she dropped the act.

"What the hell are you doing here?" Her voice a mix of shock and surprise. "Lincoln, please tell me you didn't fabricate an appointment to see me."

"Well, it's good to see you too, Zara," I chuckled, wondering if she was as desperate to kiss me as I her. "But no, this isn't a fabricated appointment."

"Really? You're here for *legal advice*?" she asked, her tone mixed with curiosity and disbelief.

"More a consultation." My eyes floated down her body, her corporate wear not unlike what she had on the night we'd met. I liked it. The fit of her tailored skirt and jacket hinted at the bombshell body it hid underneath.

"Well, then you better come sit down." She gestured to the seat opposite her desk. "My billable hours probably aren't as high as yours but can leave just as nasty a sting."

Fuck.

I wanted to kiss her.

To feel that beautiful, smart mouth on mine while my hands were all over her body. But I wouldn't, not at least until I was sure that was what she wanted.

"How would you know what my billable rate is?" I asked, getting closer, the smell of her perfume intoxicating and torturing me in equal measure.

"I know your *type*." Her head tipped, daring me to tell her different. "So, Mr. Archer." The way she said my name sent a shiver up my spine. "What can I do for you?"

Such a loaded question, and one I had a million answers for—none of them professional. But even though her office didn't have any windows—something I was thankful for—I was going to keep it respectful.

Well, for as long as I could.

Trying to ignore how amazing she looked, I strode toward the chair and sat down like she asked. She did the same, the desk a literal and metaphorical buffer between us as she slid into her seat.

My fingers dipped into my inner jacket pocket, pulling out the folded piece of paper. I smoothed it out, holding it out toward her and waited for her to accept it.

"What's this?" Her eyes scanned the document, taking it from me so she could inspect it closer. "You're here for a consultation on a prenup?" Her eyes flashing to mine as her voice rose.

"I am." I nodded, unable to hide my grin. "It seems Nate cannot be left unattended when given access to my bank account and a silent auction. Your firm—like a few others in the city—offered services as part of their donation for the gala. One of them was the formulation and execution of a standard prenuptial agreement. Nate thought it was both hilarious and ironic."

When he'd initially told me, I was ready to kill the man.

I'd expected him to get himself a weekend stay in Napa, or a painting by some brilliant, underrated—yet ridiculously expensive—artist. I knew there were a few larger ticket items so I was really praying he didn't completely lose his mind and saddle me with the bill for a helicopter. But a consultation with Bally and Cobb hadn't even entered into the realm of possibility.

Not only had the "donation" been more sizeable than any prenuptial agreement would've cost, but completely inappropriate. That was until I saw the genius, the appointment—bought, paid for, and totally legitimate—giving me an excuse to stroll into her office and see her.

No partner would ever want to deal with some bullshit charity auction item, so it was either her or one of the other associates. And Joel Bally was predictable, palming it off to the one associate who thrived and enjoyed pro bono work.

Zara Mathews.

Thanks, Nate.

"Wow." She shook her head, reading over the piece of paper, proudly declaring I—the recipient—was entitled to three consultations to draw up and finalize my prenup. "He's diabolical."

"Doctors." I threw up my hands dramatically. "And everyone thinks lawyers are the assholes."

She laughed, the first real smile crossing her lips since I'd walked in. "Yeah, guess that oath *to do no harm* wasn't taken literally. Still, it's pretty funny, though. How much did he pay for this?"

"You mean me, right. How much did *I* pay for it? Because if he'd been using his own cash, he wouldn't have thought it was as funny. And you don't want to know." I shook my head, unwilling to part with that information.

"Oh, but I do." She grinned, arching back in her seat in a move to get more comfortable but was really just sexy as hell. "Or would you rather us start talking about the division of your assets in the event of the dissolution of your future marriage."

"I'd rather talk about the voicemail, and why it was left in the first place."

Her eyes darkened, my request probably not unexpected even if more direct than I'd intended.

"You want to tell me what that was about?" I leaned forward, unwilling to let it go.

She sighed, her lips twitching. "I thought we agreed—"

"Yes, I remember." I cut her off, not needing the refresher. "But you still feel that way? Because I'd like to renegotiate."

"I don't think that's a great idea." She folded her arms across her chest, almost like she was holding herself back from doing something we both wanted. "But I meant what I said on the message. I like you, I had a really good time and—"

"Yes, you wish me the best for the future." I chuckled, wondering if she'd been breaking up with me or giving me a severance package. "Cut the bullshit, Zara, that wasn't you. Now, tell me what's really on your mind."

"Lincoln." She shook her head, her thoughts being reorganized in front of me. "I meant it when I said I like you. And I did have a really good time."

"Good, because those feelings were mutual, Zara. I'm not sure if I didn't make that clear, but spending time with you has been a highlight."

"I'm glad. Honestly, I am." She took a breath, pausing a beat. "I can't do this here, but I really want us to remain friends."

"Friends." I rolled around the word in my mouth and didn't like it. Not when I'd had more with her. But she was right, an ambush wasn't going to get me what I wanted. "Okay, then, let's be friends."

"Really?" She didn't try and hide her surprise, sitting up straighter. "You're cool with that?"

"Of course," I lied, letting the smile ease back on my face. "So, *friend*. Let's have dinner tonight. We'll order in. My hotel, your apartment, I'll let you choose."

She looked at the door, almost as if expecting an interruption or hoping for one. But she wouldn't get so lucky, still plenty of time left on my allocated appointment.

"I thought we agreed to be friends."

"We did. You can have dinner with friends. I have dinner with Nate all the time and don't sleep with him," I offered drily. "But I get it. You don't trust yourself around me, so we could have a chaperone, make it easier for you to keep your hands to yourself. Nate is back on rotation so he's out. What's Belle up to tonight? Should I call and ask?"

"Don't call my sister!" she warned, her hand reaching across the desk and landing on my arm. "I don't need any more heat from her."

"Oh? Belle giving you a hard time?" I asked, not even trying to hide my delight. Her little sister was fast becoming one of my favorite people.

Her eyes flared as she pushed out a breath. "I'll have dinner with you. I'll text you details of where and when later if you agree not to involve anyone else and we can wrap this consultation up early."

Wow, who would have known it would be so easy.

"Sounds reasonable. But you will *call* me and let me know the details, I'm not a fan of your messages." Last thing I wanted was for her to change her mind and let me know via text. What was next? A note left with the reception of my hotel? Nope, if she wanted me to leave her office she had to agree to dinner and a phone call.

She rolled her eyes. "It was one lousy voice message; I've texted you before."

"You did, but your privileges have been revoked since you couldn't behave appropriately," I offered with zero apology. "You've done this to yourself, Zara."

"Fine. I will *call* you. I will call and we will have dinner. Satisfied?"

Not even close.

"For now," I agreed, the outcome better than I'd expected. Not that I'd planned to leave before she reconsidered but a firm commitment to another date was even better. I pushed up the cuff of my jacket, seeing the time was edging toward twelve.

A lunchtime meeting with my client to wrap up my New York dealings was my last order of business, and I was cutting it dangerously close to being late. Not that I had a choice, the only appointment time I could get for Bally and Cobb was either the eleven-thirty I took, or nine a.m. next Monday. And I wasn't waiting until Monday.

As hard as it was to leave without touching her, I rose to my feet. The urge was still there, stronger when she did the same and walked around to my side of the desk.

"So, I'll call you," she offered, her hand fidgeting by her side.

I nodded, distracting myself from the beautiful curl of her smile. "You will."

"Well, let me show you out." She gestured to the door as she stepped ahead and placed her hand on the handle.

She didn't open it though, pausing, her body bracketing the doorway. "What did you do to Nate?"

It was a valid question, and one I'd be happy to answer.

But I didn't want the last few moments with her to be about Nate.

I leaned in, my lips so close to hers I wasn't sure I would stop. But I did, pulling up just short as I hovered over her mouth.

There was a sharp intake of air as those beautiful lips separated just enough that I'd be able to slide my tongue in if I wanted to. And regardless of her declaration of our new status—friends—I doubted she'd stop me.

"I'll tell you at dinner." I pulled away, leaving us both wanting.

It was a dick move, but I needed to be sure. Positive it wasn't her feelings that had changed, and those second thoughts were her just being cautious.

And I was right.

She still wanted me, just as much as I wanted her. All I had to do was decide how I was going to use that information.

My hand reached down to hers, covering it as I opened the door.

"Thanks for your time, Ms. Mathews. I'll look forward to hearing from you."

She straightened, sliding her hand from under mine to create more distance. "My pleasure, Mr. Archer. Have a nice day."

It was all so sanitary, polite, and administrative. Textbook-perfect professionalism HR would get a hard-on over, but I knew better.

I'd bet anything, underneath that cute, conservative skirt that curved her ass so deliciously, she was wet. And she'd be thinking about that kiss that didn't happen all afternoon.

"Same to you." It was my last goodbye, straightening my tie as I stepped out into the hall and headed out toward the exit.

I didn't look back, knowing it would only heighten the anticipation for when I saw her later. And that just made my balls ache even more.

"You're a sadistic son of a bitch, Archer," I chuckled to myself as I found my way back to reception. "And that woman is going to be your undoing."

"Archer!" Robert Phillips slapped me on the back, not at all annoyed I was over thirty minutes late. "We started without you. I'll get the waiter to bring you some champagne."

I'd been dragging my feet with the settlement, taking longer than I needed finalizing contracts, but I'd prolonged it as much as I could. All the details had been ironed out two days after I landed in New York, with only minor negotiations needing to happen. Ordinarily I'd have done it as quickly and painlessly as possible, not in the mood to spend more time with a client or case than was necessary. I got bored easily, always anxious to move onto my next case, looking for the thrill that came with a new set of problems. It was that high that kept me working long hours, neglecting my family, and for the most part, detached. But since meeting Zara, I'd slowed down, reassessing every angle before giving it the rubber stamp in an effort to stop me from getting on a plane and going back home.

Ironic that it didn't feel so welcoming anymore, the idea of flying back to my empty apartment in Boston making my stomach roll. But regardless of my personal feelings on my current address, I couldn't stop the inevitable. Everything was signed, sealed and delivered as of yesterday afternoon, and whether I wanted to admit it or not, my business in New York was done.

I smiled back, not really feeling the jovial mood that was around the table. Five equally white-haired, Caucasian, designer-suit-wearing "Roberts" were joining the original one in raising their glasses. "Good, you're drinking heavily. It will make my bill easier to take."

Robert—the original one, not one of his clones—laughed, sloshing the expensive champagne out of the glass. "You're a real character, Archer, exactly the kind of guy we'd kill to have on our team. Those Boston bastards better watch their backs or we'll steal you right from under them." His obnoxious laugh was met with a chorus of agreement and approval. "You can take the boy out of New York but never New York out of the boy." He winked, wrongly believing that because I'd originally been from *The Empire State*, I was one of them.

I wasn't.

Because even though I was a shark in negotiations and could close more successfully than anyone at the firm, I still gave a shit. I cared about the workers of the companies we dismantled, reassembled, amalgamated, or absorbed. And while I'd become a very rich man doing the very thing I loved, I'd been able to protect some of the people who would've definitely been shafted.

So, *fuck you, Robert*, we were nothing alike.

"You're forgetting I've seen your accounts, Robert." I accepted the glass of champagne I'd been handed by the waiter. "You couldn't afford me."

Cue more ruckus laughing and celebratory backslapping, my need to eye roll at an all-time high.

The remainder of the lunch was as predictable as the start. I listened with fake enthusiasm while each of the men recounted how he was going to celebrate his new windfall. Stories of their glory days at college spoken about like they'd graduated in the last decade, embellished with sordid tales of their sexual conquests. It was always the same mix—money, women, power, wealth—a heady cocktail I'd partaken of more times than I was proud of. But I didn't like it, no longer comfortable with the level of egomaniacal misogynistic bullshit I had to sit through.

What the fuck was I even doing with these clowns?

Had I been delusional, reassuring myself I wasn't like them but really wasn't much better? Nate was right, I had been unhappy. Or at least I'd been stuck on autopilot, doing the shit I'd always done because it made sense.

But it no longer did.

And heading back to Boston was no longer the only thing making me want to lose my lunch.

"When's your flight?" Robert #4 asked, his pudgy fingers shoving an unlit cigar into his mouth. He wouldn't smoke it, the maître d' nervously looking in his direction, but he was going to tell himself he could if he really wanted to. "Heading back soon I'd imagine."

"I've got some other business to attend to before I do." My lips thinned into a line. There wasn't a chance I was mentioning Zara to any of these cocksuckers, even if I'd been obligated to tell them my business. I didn't want her tainted by them, by this, feeling like those two parts of myself were disconnected.

There was a reason I didn't talk about work when I was around her, Nate, or my family. I'd always rationalized I'd kept the different sides compartmentalized so I didn't turn into a heartless bastard, but maybe it was deeper than that. And sitting at a table full of privileged, rich, soulless assholes gave me a front-row seat to my future.

A trophy wife who'd divorce me because I didn't pay her enough attention. Only to marry two or three more times because I got sick of coming back to an empty house I probably hated. Maybe we'd have a couple kids—different wives of course, just to make it interesting—and my relationship with them wouldn't fare much better. They'd toggle between treating me like an ATM to despising me, no doubt blaming me for screwing up their lives. It would be nothing like the childhood I had, the bond between my parents and siblings something I'd forget about by the time I was fifty. Hell, I'd already put the wheels in motion, not bothering to even tell any of my family I was in the state.

Well, that was fucking great.

And to think just a couple of hours earlier I'd been ecstatic, standing in Zara's office, looking forward to our "friendly" dinner.

"Gentlemen." I stood abruptly. "You'll have to excuse me, I have something urgent that needs my attention."

"Of course," laughed Robert #2. "We're going to hide out here a little longer before we have to go back to our wives." Loud groans punctuated his statement.

"Enjoy that." I tipped my head goodbye. "I have something important to do."

And for the first time in a long while, I actually meant it.

Chapter 22

Zara

"You're dating him again?" Belle swung her legs on the edge of my bed, her chin resting on her fists as she watched me get ready. "I don't want to say I told you so, but I kinda predicted this. He's your soulmate. You belong together."

"Belle," I huffed impatiently, hating that I was weirdly nervous about seeing him. We'd had dinner before. Seen each other. Slept together. Why the hell was I nervous? "You did not. In fact, if I'd listened to you, I'd be chasing after Edwin Carlisle and not Lincoln. And we're not dating. We're friends."

"Friends?" She screwed up her face in disgust.

"Yes, friends," I reaffirmed, the idea marinating a little more since our meeting in my office. "He's got a great mind, and he'd be an asset if I ever wanted to bounce ideas off him during a tough case." I listed all the reasons I'd gone over on my way home. "He wouldn't see my asking for help as a sign of weakness and I can be myself around him. I'd trust him to tell me the truth."

"Yeah, his brilliant *mind* is why you're wearing that low-cut dress that shows off your boobs." She rolled her eyes, pointing to my cleavage.

"I can appreciate intelligence and still wear a low-cut dress, Belle. And no, it's not just his mind, he's funny and interesting, and sexy, okay. There I said it. He's sexy."

There was no point denying why I was wearing the dress, because I wasn't fooling anyone. I'd said I wanted to be friends with the man, made a big production about it and yet still thought about how he'd almost kissed me in my office.

And how much I'd wanted it.

Get it together, Zara. You can't have your cake and eat it too, and sending mixed signals isn't smart. And yet, when given the option of staying in the clothes I'd worn earlier or changing into something else, I'd gone solidly with *something else.*

He'd been slightly distracted when I'd called.

Not rude or short, but his voice was lacking the usual teasing tone I loved so much.

We'd agreed to dinner at a restaurant close to his hotel, even though I knew it could spell bad news later. He'd assured me it wasn't for shady non-friendly purposes but that he had a stack of work that needed to be taken care of and was using his room as a make-shift office for the afternoon.

When I'd offered to raincheck dinner for another night, he shut the discussion of a reschedule down. He said he wanted dinner with me, and I'd already agreed, and he didn't trust me not to send a carrier pigeon with another goddamn message where I wished him well. I swear, he was never going to let me live that down. And one night wasn't going to make a difference even if I had been secretly looking forward to seeing him too.

"For the record, I think you're stupid." Belle examined her nails, the bubblegum pink polish chipping at the edges. "Just tell him you like him more than just friends and sort out how this thing is going to happen. You belong together. It's Boston, he doesn't live in another country. And he has family here, he could totally move."

Ahhhhh to have Belle's optimism, where you just believed everything would work out, raining glitter and sparkles. And as much as I hated to quash her bright outlook, sometimes—or always when you were me—you had to live in the real world.

"Belle, he's not *just* an attorney, he's got a highly successful job that he's worked his ass off for. I can't just ask him to move on the *chance* we work out. He'd be risking everything he's been building."

I was fairly sure he'd have no trouble finding a job in New York. A man like Lincoln would be an asset to any firm, Bally and Cobb included. But he'd already established his reputation, and even if he got an offer close to his obviously impressive salary, he'd have to prove himself here. Boston was not New York, and he'd have to re-earn his label of greatness.

"Besides," I continued, knowing it wasn't my only reason not to push the issue. "What if he asks me to move? Then what?"

While my concerns for his career were valid, I held some very real ones for myself. It was entirely plausible that he'd suggest I be the one who uproots and moved. And then what did I say, that I was fine with him tossing away the years he'd built in Boston but I wouldn't consider it for myself? No, I needed to be in New York, I needed to be at Bally and Cobb, and I hadn't suddenly decided I didn't want to sit at the BIG bench sometime in the future. And what the hell happened if we broke up? I'd be in a city I didn't like, away from friends, family and even colleagues. Everything I knew was in New York.

Belle swallowed the possibility obviously not having crossed her mind. "You couldn't leave me, Zara. How would I do anything if you were gone?"

I shook my head, gently pushing her shoulder. "You would do just fine. We'd both hate being away from each other, but we'd survive." A weak smile edged on my lips. "But what I couldn't take is the resentment. From him if he hated it here or had to start over, or the resentment I know I'd have if I walked away from everything here and we ended up history in six months. We could end up hating each other, Belle. Being the worst mistake ever for both of us."

There was just too much at stake, too much we'd have to sacrifice, and it was something I'd never ask. Conversely, selfishly, the idea he'd ask that of me terrified the hell out of me. Which meant, like it or not, we just couldn't work out.

Belle sighed loudly, throwing her hands around my neck and pulling me down with her onto the bed. "I hate this. He makes you happy, why does it have to be so complicated?"

I shrugged, not having the answers. "What does Dad always say? *Nothing worth having is ever easy.* And he was right."

"Great, now you're quoting Dad." Belle chuckled. "Well, I guess go be friends with him then. But I would totally sleep with him again. You have all the time in the world to be friends that don't screw when he's back in Boston."

Couldn't say I disagreed, worried I was already on board with Belle's plan.

To be honest, I wasn't sure how we *weren't* going to end up in bed together again. The attraction between us was off the charts, and neither of us had any restraint. But I was going to do my best to make sure I didn't end up with a crushed heart, and the more I slept with him, the greater the possibility got.

"Why don't you worry about your own sex life instead of focusing on mine." I elbowed her, not wanting to think about Lincoln and whether we'd end up in bed. "His driver is going to be here soon. Please don't make it weird."

She rolled her eyes. "Zara, he's met me. What if his driver asks about me and I didn't ask intrusive questions or make it weird? He'd be suspicious. I have a level I need to maintain now."

I'd barely shuffled into a sit when I heard the buzz at the door. Terry was clinically punctual, right at seven o'clock as Lincoln had promised, my heart doing a weird flip in my chest.

"Okay, don't make it *too* weird. While I have no problem with you terrorizing Lincoln, Terry is a nice guy," I amended, scooting off the bed and slipping into my shoes. "Now tell me I look good." I smoothed the front of my dress.

"You look a-mazing," she sing-songed. "Now go torture the poor man."

Funnily enough, that hadn't been my plan, or not consciously anyway. I left Belle in the bedroom, making my way to the intercom, pressing the external lock for the door and collecting my things ready to leave. I assumed Terry would be downstairs in the front foyer, quickly grabbing my handbag and keys so not to keep him waiting.

"Wow." Lincoln was standing at our front door as I opened it, his eyes traveling up and down my body. He was still wearing the same beautiful suit from earlier but had changed his shirt. His hair was a perfect sexy mess, as was the smattering of stubble on his jaw. I loved the edgier side of him, the *after-hours Lincoln*. "That's some dress." His smile widened, his hand reaching down to my waist and pulling me into his arms. "Don't get too excited, this is a friendly hug and completely allowed."

"Oh, by whose order?" I asked, not bothering to fight him, enjoying the press of his body against mine. "And who says I'd get excited?"

He laughed, the gentle vibrations of his chest making it hard to pull away. "Come on, Zara, we both know *excited* is your middle name."

"Don't be rude." I poked him in the chest, unwrapping myself despite not wanting to. "And I thought Terry was picking me up, wasn't I supposed to be meeting you at your hotel?" At least that had been the original plan because of his meetings.

Lincoln shook his head, a disappointed sigh spilling from his lips. "He's downstairs with the car, and I told you he was in love with you, Zara. I'm here just to make sure there's no impropriety."

"Oh, how selfless of you." My hand fluttered at my chest. "But I'm sure I could've managed."

And I would've, but I was secretly glad he'd come as well. It was irrational how much I liked seeing him, my pulse faster than it should be considering I was standing still. But I knew better than to argue with logic, and I selfishly wanted to soak up every last minute with him even though I knew it would only make it harder.

"Hi, Lincoln!" Belle yelled from behind us. "I hope your intentions are honorable, Zara's already told me you aren't her boyfriend anymore."

"I was your boyfriend?" Lincoln grinned, mock surprise flashing through those beautiful dark blue eyes. "Why am I just finding out about this now?"

"Jesus, Belle." I cringed, trying hard to stop the blush creeping up my cheeks. "I never called him my boyfriend, and what happened to you not acting weird?"

"That wasn't acting weird." Belle grinned. "Weird would be inviting myself to your not-date-date because I haven't eaten yet and I don't like my options in the fridge. I mean, since you guys are only *friends* and all."

Lincoln's eyes connected with me, his brow raised because he had no idea if she was joking or not. "She's not serious. If she was genuinely going to attempt to invite herself to dinner she'd already be in the car," I assured him, silently vowing to give my sister a stern talking to when I got back. "And I seem to remember," I turned to Belle, "you saying you were going to go hang with Hayley and help with the baby."

"Of course I am, I just love that little squishy ball of goo. I was just teasing you. Now get out of here already." She waved us off, almost pushing us out the door. "And behave."

And with her parting warning and gentle shove, Lincoln and I found ourselves out in the hall.

"You ready?" His hand found its way around my waist, my brow rising in question before we moved any further. "What? Your hall lighting is insufficient, and I don't want to trip and sue your building manager for public liability. It's a safety issue."

I laughed because he truly did have an answer for anything and everything. "How you aren't a trial lawyer is beyond me, Lincoln. Now, let's get into the car before you trip over your big feet in this horribly dangerous lighting."

My body leaned into his touch as we made our way down to the exterior door. Terry was waiting by the car, ready to help us inside even though it wasn't necessary.

"Hi, Terry." I smiled enthusiastically, shuffling along the seat while he held open the door. "Hope you had a lovely day."

"Stop flirting with my driver, Zara," Lincoln whispered as he scooted in behind me, giving my arm a playful squeeze as he shut the door behind us. "He's already feeling fragile when it comes to you, toying with his emotions is just plain cruel."

Thankfully Terry was too busy getting behind the wheel to hear, me elbowing Lincoln intentionally as I pulled on my seat belt. "I already regret this newfound friendship, no wonder your best friend lives in another state."

He clasped his chest dramatically. "Wow, Zara, right for the jugular. But I'll have you know our friendship is more for his benefit than mine. He'd be lost without me."

Even though I knew he was kidding, I could see some truth in it. Lincoln and Nate had a special friendship that didn't come around every day, similar to what I had with Belle, but unlike us, they weren't tied by DNA.

I had friends, good ones even, but nothing like what I shared with Belle. It was hard to navigate. The hours, the work, the dedication I needed to achieve my goal wasn't something that was easily understood, so I missed a lot of movie nights/birthdays/dinners. They didn't complain, but as time went on, the invitations dwindled. So Belle was my best friend, and that's how I saw Lincoln and Nate.

"I'll take care of him after you're gone." I squeezed his hand, knowing that I couldn't forget about that charismatic ER doctor even if I tried.

"Jesus, Zara. I'm not dying, and you can't have Nate. He's mine," he warned as the car started to move into traffic.

We really did our best not to touch each other while we rode in the car, my fingers gravitating toward him all the same. By the time we'd gotten to the hotel we were holding hands, and more important than the contact, was how natural it felt.

I'd never been a hand-holder, never been the woman to constantly seek out affection. But I wanted it from him, which is why I'd assumed a clean break would be easier. Except it wasn't, my body and soul craving him.

"I thought we were going to a restaurant?" I asked, looking at the front of the Four Seasons. "Lincoln." I shook my head, knowing the minute we were in his room I'd cave. "Please don't make this harder than it is."

My plea wasn't an attempt at humor, but an honest request. There was a higher than average chance I'd end up in his bed by the end of the night, but I didn't want it to start that way. Nor did I want to relegate myself to a cheap hook-up. It was more than sex. *We* were more than sex. At least, that's what I thought.

He brought my knuckles to his lips, the contact warming my skin all over. "We're just making a pit stop, I promise." Sincerity shone in his eyes and I knew it wasn't a line. "I have one more thing that needs to be taken care of, and then I'll take you out. If it makes you uncomfortable, Terry can take you to the restaurant and then come back for me. Or you can wait in the lobby, or in the car."

It was such a sweet offer, and one I probably should've accepted. One, it removed temptation and two, it gave him the opportunity to make his call in private.

But I didn't want to go without him. Or wait in the lobby or the car.

"Will you be breaking privilege if I join you?" I asked, not completely having lost my mind.

"Awwww, you want to save me from getting disbarred, thanks *friend*." He mock punched my shoulder. "But it's an email, so unless you plan on reading over my shoulder, we'll be safe."

I nodded, following him out of the car as he exited. He retook my hand, knotting our fingers together as we strolled through the lobby, taking one of the elevators as we headed to his room.

The confined space amplified what was already a thick sexual tension between us, our bodies closer than they needed to be since we were the only ones in the elevator. It was a welcome reprieve when we got to his floor, a silent prayer of thanks offered as the metal doors slid open and we got into the hall.

"I would've waited," I confessed; his hand was still clasped with mine as the other unlocked his door. "If you wanted to finish or you were going to be late, you could've called."

He laughed, shaking his head. "No, you would've tried to convince me that we'd do it another time. Or some other excuse. Honestly, Zara, if I could avoid this, I would. But I wasn't giving up dinner with you tonight, even if I have to get creative."

And he was probably right, I'd have tried to cancel, but only because I understood. And had been there too many times myself. Needing to make after-hour calls, or wrap something up even after I'd left the office, so I knew it wasn't personal. "I wish to maintain my Fifth Amendment right at this time."

"Words of a guilty woman." He chuckled as he led me into the room and switched on the lights. "Now keep out of trouble while I take care of this."

We were close, alone, and yet he didn't try and kiss me, unwrapping his hand from mine and walking over to the desk.

I watched with interest as he loosened his tie and shucked his jacket, hanging it over the back of the chair before sitting down.

The room was quiet as I made my way over to the sofa, taking a seat while he opened his laptop and started tapping on the keys.

What amazed me more than anything was how easy it felt. To be in that room, that space, even while he was doing something else. And I knew I'd have to finally ask the question I'd been putting off asking.

When was he leaving?

My chest rose, pushing out a heavy breath as I tried to concentrate on something else but couldn't get my mind off the words.

And while it would be easier not to know, to live in a suspended state of reality where he might hang around forever, it was unlike me to choose ignorance.

"Lincoln?" I took another breath, hoping if we had the conversation while he was in the middle of something it might seem more casual.

"Hmmm?" He nodded, not looking up from his screen as he continued to type.

I swallowed, turning so I could see his beautiful profile.

Goddamn it, I was so in love with him.

"When are you leaving?"

Chapter 23

Lincoln

Fuck.

Fuck.

I'd been hoping to avoid the question, willing to let it be the elephant in the room we didn't talk about. Sure, I assumed she'd eventually ask, but the longer we could prolong it, the better.

My fingers stopped typing, noticing she was watching me. Shit.

She wanted to know, and this wasn't going to be a conversation I'd easily be able to maneuver out of.

"Are you anxious to get rid of me?" I tried to laugh. "Or just making conversation?"

"I need to know." She rose from her seat, moving toward me with such sexy strides it was hard focusing on anything other than the sway of her hips.

Oh, I knew we were trying to be friends, keeping the contact platonic. I'd been blatantly flaunting the rules by touching her, but I wouldn't make myself stop. I hadn't kissed her though, suffering through that hell more than I'd have liked.

"When?" she asked again, making it clear that she wasn't letting it go.

She was going to leave.

The moment she knew I already had a plane ticket she was going to walk out the door.

And as much as I wanted to find a work around, a creative way where I avoided or didn't attempt the truth, I couldn't make my mouth do it.

"My case is over and I'm flying back tomorrow."

Her eyes flared in surprise. "Tomorrow? Were you going to tell me?"

Was I?

"I wasn't going to just leave. But I didn't want to ruin tonight."

Because honestly, after she knew, things would change.

They already had, I could see it in her face. And she only knew half of it.

Her head tipped to my laptop as she stopped in front of me. "Is it sent?"

"Errr," I stalled, knowing whatever resolve I had was fast running out. "Almost." Even if I wasn't done, I'd be wrapping it up. Not like I could think about work when she was standing in front of me like that.

"Then finish and tell Terry we'll be staying here. We'll order in."

"Zara." I pushed away from the desk, ignoring the unsent email and abandoning the laptop. "You sure that's what you want to do? Because I feel like I'm supposed to argue or something, and I'm not going to."

"Good, so we agree on something. Make the call." Her hand dropped to her hip as she watched me send Terry the text. "And send the email."

"Fuck the email." I took the two steps and closed the gap, grabbing her face and just fucking kissing her.

I didn't ask if that was what she wanted or worry about violating our stupid "friend" agreement. It was pure instinct, the need for a connection bigger than anything I was going to say or do.

She moaned in my mouth putting to rest any doubts as she clung to my shirt. She wanted it too, her hungry lips seeking mine as I slid in my tongue. "Lincoln."

"Yeah, baby?" I panted, pulling her body against mine.

"In case there's any confusion, this isn't me just being *friendly.*"

I laughed, reaching down and squeezing her ass. I was already hard, my cock pushing against the front of my pants like it was begging to get out. "Well, I hope not, but I wasn't about to complain."

Having wasted enough time with words, I pulled her against me. I wanted there to be no confusion that we'd moved well beyond the friend zone and I wasn't intending on going back there.

She arched into me, hooking one of her legs onto my hip, forcing the bottom of her dress to bunch up and expose her tiny black panties. She definitely had a thing for barely-there underwear, and I was a huge supporter of the trend.

"Yes, Lincoln." The words were tossed out on a breath, her hips grinding against me as she tried to get herself off. "Oh my God, I'm so close."

I wasn't surprised, my own need gnawing at me like a hungry beast. The office had been foreplay, and we were both primed.

"Not like that." My hands moved to her waist, keeping her still. "I want to be the one who makes you come."

"Then you better do something about it." She clawed at my shirt, her fingers busy with the buttons.

"Yeah?" I hauled her off the floor, lifting her against me. "Should I wish you all the best for the future, Zara?" I nipped at the exposed skin of her neck. "Maybe I'll leave you a voice message."

Her legs wrapped around me as I carried her to the bed, the tips of her fingernails biting into my skin as she desperately tore off my shirt. "You're such a jerk."

She was right, I was a jerk and I loved that I didn't have to be anything other than myself when I was around her.

I dropped her to the mattress, her body bouncing as my hands moved to her feet. One pump was removed, then the other, my fingers traveling up her beautiful smooth legs as I went to work getting the rest of her clothes off.

"Your pants," she panted against my chest as I moved on top of her, my main objective getting her out of that sexy as hell dress. "Let me—"

"When I'm done," I insisted, not concerned that I was still mostly clothed as I found the zipper and yanked it down. "Fuck, you're not wearing a bra."

My brain went into freefall as I peeled away the dress and revealed her perfect beautiful tits. The pink tips were hard, ready and waiting for my mouth as she shimmied out of the bunched-up fabric and my lips curled around one of her nipples.

"Oh, Lincoln." Her eyelashes fluttered as her head rolled back, my fingers and mouth worshiping her tits one at a time.

"That's it, baby." One of my hands dropped between her legs, sliding under the slip of lace. "I love it when you say my name."

She was wet, her swollen clit begging for attention as my thumb circled it lightly. Her legs fell open, giving me better access as my mouth kissed its way down her body, both of us needing more.

"Just get them off." She yanked impatiently at her panties, pulling them down her legs and tossing them to the floor. "And done or not, you need to get naked, Lincoln. I'm not asking this time."

She got busy working my belt while my fingers circled her entrance, her hips rocked against my hands while she unzipped my pants, not bothering to pull them all the way down before freeing my cock.

"Jesus, Zara." She fisted my shaft, jerking me off as I tried to go back to what I was doing. "Just give me—"

Fuuuuuuuuuck.

Whatever I was going to say was lost as her hot mouth covered the tip of my cock. It felt so good, the heat of her tongue and the gentle scrape of her teeth teasing me while she pushed me farther down her throat.

My abs tensed, every muscle in my body going coil tight as she sucked me hard. Her hands moved up and down my length, working every inch while her mouth was kept busy.

"You first." The words pushed out through my gritted teeth, refusing to come even though I desperately wanted to. "I will not—"

"Won't what?" She pulled my dick out from between her lips with a wet pop. "Because I think you will."

Yeah, fuck that.

Not sure when I lost control of the situation, but I was regaining it as of that moment.

Not giving her a chance to get back the advantage, I pulled myself away and got the hell out of my clothes. Pants, boxer briefs, socks and shoes, were all torn from my lower half and discarded in a haphazard pile I'd happily burn. But not before I retrieved a condom, the little packet held between two fingers as I turned my attention back to Zara on the bed.

Oh.

Fuck.

Her back was arched, her thighs spread as her fingers had taken over where I'd left off. Bright red-tipped nails circled against her silky skin, her tits rising and falling as her hips gently bucked.

"That is the hottest thing I've ever seen." I dropped my mouth to her core, sucking, kissing and licking around her fingers while I tried to tear open the damn condom.

The sound of tearing foil was a welcome relief, blindly moving the latex to my cock while Zara's hands pushed my head closer to her heat.

I wasn't sure what I wanted more.

To fuck her with my tongue, or to let my cock take over.

And it was a motherfucking shame I wasn't a contortionist because if I could, I'd have bent myself in two and done both.

My dick throbbed, my balls ached, and every inch of my skin tingled. With the condom finally secured, my body made the decision for me and I lifted back up the bed.

"You're so ready for me." I fisted my length, the head of my hard rod circling her opening. She was slick, warm and welcoming, the tip slipping inside with only the smallest amount of effort.

"More." She bucked, trying to get me deeper while I held myself still. "Lincoln, please."

Hearing her beg was a bigger turn-on than it should've been, my abs tightening as I pushed in one more inch painfully slow.

"More like this?" I breathed in deep, my grasp on control fraying by the second. "Or like this?" I pushed in another inch, most of me still outside of her while my hand wrapped around her legs.

Her pelvis tilted, desperate thrusts trying to find purchase as her panting increased. I loved how wild her eyes got when she finally lost control, inky black pupils dominating those dark beautiful irises.

I could feel how close she was, the need vibrating through both our bodies that wouldn't be staved off much longer. And the minute her gaze connected with mine, I was done denying us. I drove into her hard, one swift, deep thrust burying myself into her, balls deep as heat jacked up my spine.

And then I couldn't stop.

Plunging into her again and again, each thrust getting deeper and harder and more desperate.

"Touch yourself," I ordered, watching as her hands moved to her tits and cupped them.

"Pinch your nipples for me, baby. Let me see you do it."

She didn't hesitate, not giving me so much as a blush as her fingers reached for the pale tips and squeezed. Moans escaped her lips, her pants more erratic as one of my hands moved back to her clit. She was so close that literally one sweep of my thumb was all it took.

"Yes, Lincoln, oh, my, God, yes."

I felt her tighten around me and then detonate, tiny pulses traveling down my shaft. Her body shook, waves of pleasure rolling through her as I pumped into her again and again until I exploded.

"Zara." Her name caught between a plea and a breath, her pussy milking me as I spilled my load. I couldn't stop, my hips continuing to piston, until we were both reduced to a panting mess.

I dropped my lips to hers, keeping us joined while I kissed her. She wiggled underneath me, freeing her arms from under my chest and then wrapping them around my neck.

"Sorry, baby, I'm crushing you." Words were spoken between kisses as I propped myself up on my elbows, easing my weight off her. I loved the feel of her skin against mine, the press of her body under me, and how well we fit together.

"I like being crushed." She laughed against my mouth, wrapping her legs around my hips and keeping me captive. "I think you should stay like this all night."

It was a challenge I was more than up for, not able to think of anything better than being buried inside her for eternity. That hadn't been the plan, but I could improvise like no other.

"Why don't I clean us up, get dinner, and then go back to crushing you?" I offered, rolling to the side as I eased out of her. "I've seen you hungry." I grimaced. "And it's not pretty."

"Jerk!" she scoffed, playfully jabbing me in the ribs. "But I'm not going to argue with food, especially if it means I get more of *that*." Her whole face animated with the spread of a sexy smile.

She looked so happy.

Relaxed.

Peaceful.

And if I could've frozen a moment in time, it would've been that one, seeing her exactly like that.

Naked, content, and beautiful.

"I'm in love with you." The words were effortless, coming out of my mouth before they'd even formulated properly in my head. And even though I hadn't meant to say it, I didn't regret it.

Her eyes widened, the surfaces getting glassy as her hand swept against the edge of my jaw. "I'm in love with you too."

I hadn't known how much I needed to hear it, until I did. My lips coming down on hers so fast to stop her from taking them back.

There was so much more to be said—things I needed to tell her—but I couldn't do any of it. Refusing to let anything seep in and ruin it.

There'd be time, I reasoned, whispering I loved her again and again against her lips.

There'd be time.

Chapter 24

Zara

It was the second time I'd woken up in Lincoln's bed, but the first time I'd woken up in his arms.

My eyes fluttered open, the gentle woosh of his breathing tickling my shoulders as I tried not to move. His arms were wrapped around me as he cradled my body, and I savored the way it felt. It was different to how it had been with other men, my happiness so deep, it had seeped into my bones. But there was also sadness too, because I had no idea how long it would all last.

He was leaving.

Ticket booked, clock ticking, and neither of us had discussed what would happen after last night. I'd been so sure I'd be able to say goodbye, to remain friends, to watch him walk away, and I'd been wrong on every single count.

I loved him.

As unexpected and ridiculous as it sounded, I'd fallen in love with a man who—if not for a case of mistaken identity—I never would have met.

My eyes closed again, just living in the moment where everything was fine. Where I remembered how he told me he loved me, and we were together. It was only a matter of time before he woke up and reality would sneak in whether I was ready or not.

"I can hear you thinking." The chuckle was low from behind me, his hand sweeping up and squeezing one of my breasts. "You debating your breakfast options? I'll go get you food, just give me a few minutes to enjoy my morning buzz."

My body rolled in his arms so I was facing him, his smile so big and bright it made my stomach flutter. "I love you." My lips moved to his, kissing him because while we were in that bed, he was still mine.

"Mmmmmmm," he mumbled, his grin getting wider as his fingers trailed down my back. "I love you too. Although the lack of obscenities and demands is throwing me off, how long have I got before you yell at me for coffee? I'm not complaining, your bitchy side is incredibly hot."

Usually his humor was one of the things I loved about him, except for currently where I didn't want to laugh. Truth was, I didn't even know what I wanted. To face his departure and talk about how it was going to work. Or ignore it completely and make love to him again. "What time is your flight?"

Well, guess a decision was made. *Thanks a lot, mouth.*

"Four." He kissed me, his mouth moving down the column of my throat. "And until I get on that plane, I'm all yours."

Until I get on that plane, no indication as to what would happen after.

But he loved me, right? He wouldn't just forget me.

"Lincoln." I arched into him, trying to fight what my body wanted and give my brain what it needed. "We should—"

I didn't get to finish, the rest of my sentence cut off by the phone.

It was the ringtone I'd assigned to Belle, which was unsurprising since she'd assume—after the long and impassioned speech I'd given her—I wasn't spending the night with Lincoln.

"It's Belle, it's easier if I just answer it." I sighed, giving him a quick kiss before shuffling out of his grasp.

I padded—naked—to where I'd dumped my bag on the floor, wriggling my ass a little while I retrieved my phone. Lincoln groaned from the bed. "Unless you want your sister to get more than what she bargained for, you should probably stop that."

I didn't doubt him for a second, still smiling when I put the phone against my ear and answered it. "Belle, I know I didn't come home last night but—"

"Zara, Mom's in the hospital."

The happy, bubbly voice I knew was gone, and in its place was a Belle I didn't recognize. She was panicked, desperate, almost hyperventilating on the phone. "Dad is with her and they're going to the hospital. Oh my God, Zara, one of the people she was trying to help, just freaked out. He beat her, Zara, hit her until she blacked out. I'm such a terrible daughter. She asked me to go visit, and I haven't seen either of them in weeks. And now," she sucked in a breath, "I just want her to be okay."

My heart fell, the blood feeling like it was draining from my veins and out of my body, the weight of gravity crushing me as I dropped to my knees. I hadn't seen my parents either, putting off stopping by my old childhood home because they were always there. It wasn't even far, the trip to Queens something I should've done at least once a week.

"Belle, where? Where are they taking her?" I tried my best not to sound frantic, knowing one of us had to be the strong one and Belle just didn't have it in her. "What did Dad say?"

"New York Presbyterian in Queens," she managed to get out in between sobs. "He kept saying she'll be fine, that she's strong, but. . . Zara, I don't know if he's telling the truth."

As a veteran criminal prosecutor, my dad had the ability to mask his feelings unlike anyone I'd ever seen. So when Belle said she wasn't sure if he was telling the truth, I knew what she meant. He wouldn't want us to worry, to be terrified of what kind of damage a man—who'd clearly lost his mind—could do to our mother.

"What is it?" Lincoln was beside me, pulling me to my feet. "Zara, what's happened?"

His eyes searched mine while I tried to formulate the words. I'd always been so levelheaded, so dependable but it was taking everything I could not to fall apart. "Our mom," I managed to wheeze out. "She's hurt."

Before I knew what was happening, the phone was out of my hand and into his. "Belle, I'm sending a car to come get you." He grabbed his phone and furiously started texting. "Terry will be there soon." He rattled off more details, letting her know they'd pick us up on the way to the hospital. He paused a few times and listened, deciphering whatever Belle was saying as he pulled an arm around me.

"She's going to be okay." It was only when I turned to face him that I realized he'd ended the call with Belle and was talking to me.

I shook my head, knowing there was no possible way he could promise that. "I just need to get there."

"I know, I figure by the time Terry gets Belle you will have time to get dressed. I also gave Nate a call. He should be getting off shift soon, figured he might know someone on staff at the hospital." He handed me my clothes, maneuvering me to the edge of the bed. "Do you need help?" he asked, looking at the clothes in my hand that I hadn't even attempted to put on.

"No, no I can do it," I assured him, begging my brain to kick into gear as I slid on my underwear. I didn't even care it was last night's clothes, too concerned about my mom to worry about the inappropriateness of my dress. "I'm fine. I can do this."

Not sure if it was for his benefit or mine, my hands shaking as I tried to pull up my zipper.

Belle and I had been spoiled as children, protected from any real trauma by two parents who were overprotective and loved us unconditionally. And for someone who had thought she'd been so strong, I hated that I wasn't living up to it.

"Here." He took over, having already pulled on fresh boxer briefs and a clean pair of pants. "You need anything, Zara? Anything I can do until the car gets here? I can run to a store, get you something else to wear? Coffee?"

"No, I just want to go wait for them downstairs." I turned around, doing my best not to cry. "Please don't take this the wrong way, Lincoln, but you can't come with me."

"Zara," he shook his head, resting his hands on my hips. "I know this is not an ideal way to meet your parents, but I'm not going to kiss you goodbye and send you to the hospital. I'll wait in the coffee shop or down in the ER waiting room, or even in the car if you don't want me around."

It was a sweet offer, and something I wasn't expecting. We hadn't even defined what we were, so meeting each other's parents wasn't even a consideration. But I couldn't have him there and use him as a crutch when in a few hours he was going to have to leave. As hard as it was to do alone, it was easier than the alternative.

"I won't be alone, I'll have Belle. And my dad. Lincoln, this isn't personal, but I just can't have you there." I couldn't have him see me fall apart, worried that was exactly what would happen.

It was bad enough our relationship had started unconventionally, add in a family emergency and a pending departure time and it was just too much drama for anyone to take. If we ended up together, it had to be because of us. Because we belonged together, because we couldn't stand to be apart. Not out of infatuation or obligation.

He opened his mouth to argue, but I stopped him. I knew he'd be able to convince me, but I didn't want to be convinced. I needed to know my own mind, and right now the only thoughts I could process were that of my mother.

"I love you." I pushed my mouth against his, holding him as tight as I could. "I love you, Lincoln, even though this doesn't make sense. But I need to go do this by myself."

"I love you too. Promise me you're going to call as soon as you get to the hospital. I want to know everything." He kissed me back, pulling me closer.

I nodded, promising to call and update him as I grabbed my bag and phone. I wasn't sure how much longer Belle and Terry were going to be, but I needed to go. It felt too claustrophobic in that room, like every one of my emotions was amplified. "Call Terry and tell him to take Belle straight to the hospital. I'm going to get a cab."

"Zara, please wait. Terry is one of the best driver's I've ever had. He'll be here shortly, NYC traffic is nothing for him."

"Lincoln." I took a breath, trying to stop myself from raising my voice. "I can do this. I know you are trying to help, but I need to get there now. I'm not waiting. So please call him or I'll call Belle and pass on the message myself."

He grabbed his phone and started to dial as I headed toward the door.

"Zara. Call me," he warned, his conflicted eyes watching me as I left.

I hated that he'd probably thought I was cold, or ungrateful, but I couldn't think about that. My body was on automatic as I took the elevator to the lobby, racing out the door and hailing a cab.

Please be okay, please be okay, I prayed silently as the taxi headed from Manhattan to Queens. *Please just let my mom be okay.*

Mom had thankfully regained consciousness in the ambulance but wasn't in a good way. She had a nasty concussion, her eye had swollen shut, and had a broken jaw. She also had multiple fractures in her arm where she'd tried to protect herself, surgery required to reset it.

I'd messaged Lincoln as soon as I'd gotten to the ER, letting him know I'd arrived safe. Then I sent a few more texts, telling him when she was going into surgery and not to worry. Each time he'd responded asking if I needed anything and whether he could come to the hospital, but I gave him the same answer I'd given him at his hotel. That I needed to do it on my own.

"You know." My dad wrapped one arm around me and the other around Belle. "Your mom might seem sweet and fragile, but she's stronger than she looks. This isn't the first time she's been in a hospital after an assault."

"What?" I choked back, the three of us sitting in her room around her bedside. She was so groggy from the pain meds after the surgery that she'd barely woken up. And even though I knew there was nothing I could do, I couldn't stand to leave. "What do you mean this isn't the first time?"

My parents had barely been sick when I'd grown up, my mom and dad having such strong work ethics they'd probably drag themselves to their jobs, half dead. Even cold and flus were met with little fuss, rarely had I seen either of my parents sleep in, let alone be laid up sick in bed.

"You were both young, your mom was working in a shelter. One of the women had an abusive ex-husband who found her and was trying to drag his wife home. Your mom wouldn't let it happen, even if it meant she ended up with fractured ribs and a broken leg."

I vaguely remembered my mom's broken leg, but had been told a different version of events. "So she *didn't* trip on a subway grate?" The excuse we were given for my mother in a cast and on crutches, never questioned. "What else has happened that we didn't know?"

"Zara, you were young, we didn't want you worrying about things you couldn't control." My father rubbed the back of his neck in frustration. "Both your mother and I had jobs that put us both in danger. We did our best to protect you."

My anger was irrational, understanding why they did it but still feeling betrayed. My parents had always been so careful to curate this perfect childhood for us. Insulating us from harm like it would somehow ensure we'd be saved from pain and suffering. And for the most part it worked, but I wished they'd trusted me and Belle enough to *know* we'd be okay. That we were strong enough to handle more.

"I need to go for a walk." I stood up, needing some fresh air and to get out of the room. Just because I understood his reasoning—believing they'd honestly just wanted the best for us—it didn't mean I was okay with it.

"Zara," my father warned. "Don't get emotional over this. You know better. Your mom is fine, and the past can't be changed. Between you and Belle, you are the one who should understand exactly why we made those decisions. I thought I taught you better than that."

"Whoa!" Belle joined me on her feet. "You think because she's always been so analytical, she doesn't get to have feelings. Newsflash, Dad, she's not a robot, no matter how hard you tried to make her one."

I grabbed her arm, trying to stop whatever she was going to say. "Belle—"

"No, let me say this, because obviously that's what is expected of *me*." Belle waved her hand dismissing my interjection. "Zara is brilliant. She's smart, and driven, and is destined for greatness. But she has a heart too, and has never ever let me down even though I know I sometimes drive her crazy. You should've told us, Dad. We're not little girls anymore and haven't been for a very long time."

And with that, she grabbed my hand and dragged me out of the room and into the hall.

I was so surprised, I didn't have time to react, following her out in what was the strangest role-reversal I'd ever expected. I was always the stronger one, the one who protected her—not the other way around.

"Are you okay?" Belle put her arms around me, her delicate lithe body curling around me once we were far enough away to stop.

"Yeah, thanks for getting me out of there. I was worried I was going to say something I might regret and now isn't the time." I hugged her back, grateful to have a moment just with my sister. "I understand why they did it, but it doesn't make it any easier to swallow."

Belle nodded, dropping her arms and leading us to some chairs. "Yeah, there will be time for all of that later. But who knows how long Mom's recovery is going to take, she needs us not angry. Besides, Dad is probably in shock right now." She laughed. "Did you see his face? Wasn't expecting that from his *little Tinker Belle*."

I laughed too. "Well, if he has a heart attack, at least he's in the right place."

My phone buzzed again, and I assumed it was Lincoln. He'd been sending messages all through the day and only been getting one-word responses. I wasn't intentionally blowing him off, just so caught up on what was happening with my mom to give him the attention he'd deserved.

I dug out my phone from my bag while Belle looked on, my fingers quickly lighting up the screen. But it wasn't Lincoln, it was Nate.

Hey, I'm here. Where are you?

My head whipped around, half-expecting him to be standing right there but he wasn't. Instead I responded.

Here? At the hospital?

My phone rang, quickly being answered as Belle looked on curiously. "Hey, Nate."

"Zara, can you talk?" His voice was calm and reassuring. "I can meet you, or you can come to me. Whichever works."

Lincoln had told me he'd called Nate, but that had been hours ago so I'd completely forgotten.

"Sure, Belle and I are just in the hallway. We needed some air." I gave Nate the details of where we were and said our goodbyes. I wasn't exactly sure what he was going to do, but it wouldn't hurt to get a doctor's opinion, especially since he was already here.

"Is Lincoln here?" Belle asked, wrongly assuming that was who I'd been on the phone with. Considering the amount of messages the man had sent me, it would've been a safe bet.

"No, Nate. He's here."

We didn't have to wait too long before he appeared, his warm smile greeting us as he approached the chairs Belle and I were camped out on.

"Ladies." He gave me a hug before turning to my sister. "I'm Nate, a friend of Zara's."

It was funny how he'd said he was my friend yet two weeks ago, we hadn't even met. But he was right, we were friends, and it was more than just because we had Lincoln in common.

"You're super cute." Belle grinned, elbowing me in the ribs. "Zara didn't tell me how hot you were. And yes, I know you're not into women, I'm not flirting."

Nate blushed, shaking his head. "Thanks. Anyway, I'm here to render my services. The staff here are great, but unless I get consent, I can't know anything about your mom's particular case because of HIPPA. But I'll be happy to talk to the doctors for you, or hold your hand? I'm a great coffee-getter too, but I think you already knew that about me." He shot me a cheeky wink.

"Thanks, she's out of surgery to reset her arm, but she's been mainly in and out. Lots of pain meds to keep her comfortable." I gave his hand a squeeze. "It was so sweet of you to stop by."

He grimaced, his face looking guilty. "Actually, Linc sent me. You've barely spoken to him and I'm supposed to be his inside man. But I'd have come even if I didn't still owe him for the prenup I bought at the auction."

"Is he . . ." The rest of the question got lost in my throat knowing it was already after four. He had a plane to catch, and I hadn't given him much of a reason to stay. Not that I was sure he'd have cancelled his flight if I'd asked, but considering I'd repeatedly told him I wanted to be alone, I couldn't really blame him for leaving.

Truth was, I didn't want him to leave.

I wanted, no *needed*, him to stay, but I'd been too afraid to ask. Too worried about our lack of definition, and whether letting him see me so vulnerable would be a good thing. We'd just confessed our feelings for each other, and the last thing I wanted was to become a needy, messy bag of emotions. I didn't even know what those I-love-yous meant. And when we were going to see each other.

"He's on his way back to Boston." Nate answered exactly how I'd expected. "But I really think you should give him a call when he lands."

It was obvious Nate knew more than what he was saying, but it was hard to decipher what that was exactly. Was Lincoln upset I hadn't spoken to him? Worried? Annoyed my family emergency had stolen what little time we had before he left? Angry we hadn't discussed what was happening next? There was no way to tell, my concern having been so focused on my mom, I hadn't really given it much thought.

"I've kinda got a lot going on here, Nate. I'll get to him when I can."

I hadn't meant to sound so defensive, but I had no idea what Nate would say when he reported back. I was sure I knew where his loyalties lay, and they wouldn't be with a woman he barely knew even if he was a really nice guy.

And part of me was angry.

Irrationally and stupidly angry that it was Nate standing there instead of Lincoln.

Even though it had been me who'd pushed him away.

Even though I'd demanded to be left alone.

Because how dare he actually respect my wishes and do what I asked him to do when really I'd wanted him to just stay.

To be there.

To comfort me.

To love me.

Gahhhhh, I wouldn't be one of those women. Who said one thing and meant another, who wanted to be chased by a guy.

And yet . . . I wished it had been him.

"Hey." Nate held his hands up. "I'm not telling you what to do. Just a suggestion. You can take my advice or not, lord knows it wouldn't be the first time someone hasn't listened to it."

There was a slight edge to his voice, almost like he was frustrated, which would make sense since he'd probably been guilted into a trip to Queens.

"I'm sorry. I'm just tired and cranky." I tried to apologize, knowing he was just trying to be a good friend. "We haven't eaten, and hospital coffee is the worst."

"Oh, you don't have to tell me." Nate nodded in sympathy. "But if you ladies want to get out of here for a while we can go get something to eat. My treat."

Belle looked hopeful, wrapping her arm around Nate's. "Yes, yes we will totally come. We need to check on our mom first, and then you can steal us away and feed us."

"Belle." I shook my head, wishing my sister had a little more of a filter. "I'm sure Nate has more important things to do with his time off. Thanks, but we'll be okay."

He probably had to work soon, or even if he didn't, could've found a more productive use of his time off other than babysitting us.

"Just tell Lincoln we're fine and I'll give him a call in a few days. Belle is right about needing to go back and check on our mom though. She might be awake, and I don't want to miss it."

"I can wait. I've got the day off and you know I hate eating alone," Nate offered, not so easily swayed by my refusal.

It was a tempting offer, and part of me desperately wanted to say yes. But I stuck to my guns, shaking my head and promising to feed Belle so she didn't waste away like she was threatening.

Nate paused, studying me like he wasn't sure he believed me. Which just proved how smart he was because I wasn't sure I believed me either. "Well, okay then. Guess I should leave you to it." He gave me a hug before turning to Belle. "But call me if you need anything."

"I will, I promise," I lied, knowing I needed something right then and couldn't ask for it, so I sure as hell wasn't going to call. "And thanks so much for stopping by. Even if it was under duress, it was still very sweet."

"Yeah, don't mention it." He lifted his hand in a wave. "We'll talk soon."

And as he walked away, I was so conflicted as to what I wanted him to tell Lincoln.

That I'd been strong, not needing any help, and was totally fine.

Or that he'd seen through my bullshit and I was a mess.

Chapter 25

Lincoln

"Talk," I barked, having just landed at Logan. "Because if I get one more *I'm fine* message from her, there's a very real possibility TSA is going to have to detain me."

There was no way Zara was fine. She'd barely been able to dress herself before she'd left the hotel, the pained expression in her eyes something I wasn't going to easily forget.

"She said she's—"

"Don't fucking say it." I cut Nate off, sparing us both from hearing what I knew was bullshit. "Did she look okay? Was her mom okay? Did she eat? She gets cranky when she's hungry."

"You know, Linc." Nate paused taking a breath. "These are all questions you'd know the answer to if you hadn't gotten on that plane. I told you to cancel your flight, or at least delay it by a day. She needed you with her."

A humorless laugh made it up my throat. "Yeah, needed me so badly she couldn't leave the hotel quick enough. Or make time to respond to one of those messages with more than three words. Not sure sticking around like some pathetic sap was the right call, especially since I'd already told the partners I wanted a meeting in the morning."

I'd been ready to drop everything, to blow off work even though the meeting had been one I specifically requested. But she hadn't given me shit. Not even the slightest indication that she wanted or even welcomed my concern. And while I understood her primary—and rightly so—focus should've been her mother, she could have thrown me a bone.

I'd waited hours in the hotel lobby. Waited for her to just pick up the goddamn phone and give me something. But nope, nothing. And considering I'd just told her how I'd felt about her, that spoke volumes.

Figures that the first woman I said I'd loved would find a reason to freeze me out. Yeah, well fuck that.

"Linc, women are complicated creatures. They don't always tell you what they need. Sometimes you have to read between the lines."

"Oh, and your wealth of knowledge has come from where, Nate? I forgot you were an expert." My tone had unintentionally been harsh, pulling my suitcase off the luggage carrousel and wanting to put my fist through a wall.

"Don't be a dick, Lincoln. You don't need to have had sex with a woman to know something about them." His tone matched mine, not willing to let it slide.

"Fuuuuck," I huffed under my breath, the older woman beside me tsk, tsking as she walked away. Like I gave a shit what she thought, or that I might have offended her delicate sensibilities. "I have no idea what I'm supposed to do. I was ready to throw this all in, to resign, move to New York, to be with her. But how the hell am I supposed to do that now? What if the only reason she admitted her feelings was because she knew I was leaving?"

It hadn't escaped my attention that the direction of our evening hadn't changed until *after* I'd told her I was leaving.

She'd been completely okay with dinner and *friendly*—seriously, who was she kidding—conversation when she thought I was sticking around. Then as soon as I mentioned I had a flight—which I had every intention of telling her about—she couldn't keep her hands off me. Like she needed one last roll in the sack before she kicked me to the curb.

"Why didn't you just tell her that you were thinking of moving to New York?" he asked, playing the fucking peacekeeper like he usually did.

"When?" I huffed out a laugh. "While she was on the phone to her sister, finding out her mother was in the hospital or while she was running out the door? Oh, I know, I should've told her when she avoided my calls, drip-feeding me one-line texts like I was an inconvenience. Yeah, that would have been the perfect time."

"You want to keep biting my head off, Linc, have at it. But we both know that you aren't that much of a bastard even if you'd have the world believe that you are."

He was right. Not only did he not deserve my shit, but he'd dropped everything when I'd called and asked him to go to the hospital to check on her. But fuck me, what the hell was I supposed to do? I'd been so convinced that Zara was the one, that I was making the right choice. But the first sign of shit not going to plan and she ran. It hadn't even been my fucking fault, and she was freezing me out.

"Look, I know it's not your fault. And I get that she's worried about her mom. But it's been hours, Nate. You mean to tell me she can't find two minutes to pick up the phone and just let me hear how fucking *fine* she is?" I was probably being unreasonable, oversensitive because when I'd told her I'd loved her, I honestly meant it. And those words didn't come easily for me. But it didn't make it sting any less, wondering whether I'd rushed into telling her. If maybe I should've waited.

I shook my head, making my way to the exit with the phone up against my ear like so many other assholes in the airport. Some of them were being greeted by loved ones, happy hugs exchanged and tearful reunions. Not for me though. Not only was there no one waiting for me but the one person I wanted to see was in another state.

"Hey, listen. I'm gonna catch a cab and go home, see if I can't clear my head." Not that it was going to be any different at home but at least I wouldn't be in public. And it would give me time to think. Maybe I was rushing into this whole thing with Zara, and quitting my job wasn't the smartest thing to do.

At least I hadn't sent that email, instead deciding to wait until I'd flown back to give my notice.

"Call her, Lincoln. I know you're all up in your own head right now and doubting yourself. But you love this woman. Don't throw it away because of your pride."

It was good advice, but I wasn't sure if it was valid. Love was a two way-street, and if she was having second thoughts, then I should probably rethink my strategy before I torched my life as I knew it.

I walked outside, hailing a cab. "Thanks for the advice, man."

"You going to take it?"

"I've got to go, Nate. I'll call you tomorrow."

"Linc—"

"Getting into the cab. Talk soon." And before he could argue, I ended the call.

I still was unsure of what I was going to do, but I had a few hours to work it out. Or at least try and work it out.

Fuck.

Never in my life had I agonized over a call.

Picking up my phone and scrolling to her name at least a dozen times before shaking my head and putting it back down.

I'd stopped texting too, figuring I'd told her to call me at least five times and I was starting to look pathetic. So much for her needing me like Nate said, maybe she really was "fine."

It was late when I finally went to bed, having showered and eaten the worst pizza ever, I grabbed my phone and got between the sheets like a loser. I wasn't into playing games, especially not with women, and I was more exhausted mentally than I'd been in a long time.

My phone buzzed with a message, and I just knew it was going to be her. But instead of being hopeful or excited—like I would've been earlier in the day—I glanced at it with caution.

> **Hey, sorry about today. It's been crazy. Mom is going to be fine. She has a concussion, lots of bruises and a few breaks, but we were able to talk to her and there doesn't seem to be any long-term brain damage. Anyway, she's going to be in hospital for a little bit and then rehab for her arm but we're so relieved. Hope your flight was okay and you're already asleep.**

Really? She hoped my flight was okay and that I was asleep? I shook my head wondering if she'd specifically waited until after midnight *hoping* she wouldn't have to talk to me. How hard was it to pick up the phone, call me, and tell me what was going on with her mom. I'd been concerned all day, drip fed the bare minimum like I was no one special. Guess it put things into perspective though, and got me thinking those emotions she said she felt were only because she knew I was leaving.

Not willing to let her completely off the hook, I fired back my response.

Good news about your mom, you all must be incredibly grateful. Let me know if there's anything you or Belle need.

It was a little frostier than I'd intended but given what I had to work with, it was as amicable as I could be. Maybe I was hoping she'd call me on my mood, give me some attitude right back. Or better yet, pick up the phone since it was obvious I was awake.

We're fine, thanks for asking.

Wow, and to think I was feeling slightly guilty for being an asshole, guess I shouldn't have been concerned. Deciding there was no real reason to respond—her last message hardly soliciting one—I left her on *read* and tossed my phone on the nightstand.

Annoyed, frustrated, and more confused than when I'd arrived home, I decided sleep was the sensible thing. Less chance of doing something stupid, like toss in my career and move to another city. Still wasn't sure what the hell I was going to do in the morning, but we'd always warned juries to weigh the evidence and take the emotion out of it when tendering a verdict. And if I knew what was good for me, I'd take my own damn advice.

While I'd been worried I wasn't going to get any sleep, my body shut down the minute my head hit the pillow. It was a welcome relief to be able to hit the reset button for a while, waking up just before my six-thirty alarm.

Then it was business as usual. I got up, ran on my treadmill, showered, drank my coffee and then got dressed in one of my many suits. There'd been no further messages from Zara through the night which wasn't all that unexpected.

When I was ready, I went down to the underground garage and got into my car. I didn't always drive into work, but today seemed like a good day to have my own set of wheels. Besides, I was hoping that dealing with traffic would help me keep my mind off Zara.

It was just before eight when I arrived at my office, and even though I hadn't been gone long, it felt like a lot had changed. *I'd* changed, the same buzz I used to get when I walked in, no longer there.

"Hey, Lincoln. Welcome back." Kerry—one of the partner's secretary—smiled warmly. "How was New York? Heard you were a *big* success." Her eyebrow lifted in suggestion as she slid her tongue across her cherry red lips.

We'd always flirted with each other, but it never went any further than that. Neither of us was stupid or willing to lose our jobs, but we liked to talk dirty when no one else was around. And considering both of us were single, there was no harm done.

Ordinarily I'd have quipped back with something about exactly how *big* I was or something else that alluded to my dick. But my heart just wasn't in it, even though Kerry was one of the prettiest women at the firm.

"New York went well, thanks. I'll be in my office." I barely managed a wave before closing my door, shaking my head at myself and wondering what the hell was wrong with me. There was no reason why I couldn't flirt with Kerry, especially since as far as I could tell, I was well and truly still single.

Reasoning I didn't need the distraction, I sat down at my desk and went over in my head the rehearsed speech I was going to give the partners. Deciding on a whim that a vacation was probably more than earned and less drastic than my original option, I figured other than grumbling about my lack of notice, I wouldn't get much pushback. They'd want to keep me happy, want to give their star player whatever he needed to keep him lining up at the plate and hitting home runs, so their approval was something I was counting on.

That, and technically I hadn't taken any personal time in a really long time, so I was more than due.

"Archer!" Adrian Locke walked through my door, his beaming smile almost as big as his bank account. "I heard you slayed it out there in New York. And on time too. Well done."

He sat opposite me without invitation, slapping his hand on his thigh. "Also heard you wanted a meeting this morning. If it's about a raise, consider it done. Your review is only a few months off anyway, and I know Collins won't fight me."

Ironically, it wasn't cash that was the problem, my salary having been more than fair considering how long I'd been with them.

"It wasn't about a raise. And I was hoping to talk to both of you, which is why I set the meeting."

Adrian Locke and Damien Collins appreciated that I always got to the point, leaving the theatrics for a courtroom or boardroom when needed. And regardless of my current feelings as to the work I was doing, they'd been exceptionally good to me.

His feathery-white brow rose, straightening in his chair. "They make you an offer? I assumed they would but didn't think it would be even close to something that you would consider. Besides, we both know you'd be bored within a week being an in-house attorney. You like the thrill of the hunt too much, you're not built to be someone's house pet."

He was right about that, and I'd rather hand back my license to practice than be shackled to a single client. It wasn't even about the money anymore, the zeros that once got me excited, not having the same appeal.

"They offered, I declined," I confirmed, assuming he'd find out the truth anyway. "Damien in? Or do you want us to wait until nine-thirty like we'd planned?"

Adrian stood up, his carefree smile all but disappearing. "You're worrying me, Archer. Something happen to your family while you were back?"

Ha! Little did he know I hadn't even seen my folks. They didn't even know I was in New York, and were probably going to be a little pissed I didn't at least call. But I'd deal with the wrath that was the Archer brood later, especially since I was planning on seeing a lot more of them in the next few days.

"Nope, family are all good."

Adrian nodded, tipping his head to the door. "Well, then let's go get this over with. Damien is already in his office and my instincts tell me you have something important to get off your chest. I'm not big on surprises, Archer, I hope you remembered that."

For once, since I'd joined the ranks of Locke and Collins, I really didn't much care what they thought. It wasn't that I was looking to disappoint anyone, but I was going to get what I wanted regardless of what their feelings were.

Wordlessly, I followed Adrian to the door and down the hall to where the partners had their offices. No point going through it all twice, which was why I waited until we were safely inside Damien's glass torture chamber—as the associates liked to call it—before I started.

"Archer." Damien stood; he was the less jovial of the pair but managed to crack a half-grin. "I thought our meeting wasn't until later."

"It wasn't, but if you've got the time, it's probably for the best we just get it done now." My assertiveness didn't surprise either of them, both used to my cocky, shoot-from-the-hip style.

"Sure, take a seat. I'm assuming it's about your upcoming appraisal and potential raise. Good work on New York. I don't have the patience to deal with those bastards anymore so glad you could get it taken care of so efficiently."

"Thanks, but this isn't about that. At least not directly." I took the seat Damien gestured to while Adrian took the other beside me. "But it is about my future here at Locke and Collins."

Not sure why I'd added the last part since all I'd been intending to do was ask for a vacation. A couple of weeks, three tops, to sort out what I wanted in life. And where my head was at since it was obvious my heart was having some kind of existential crisis.

"This can't be about making partner, Archer. I know you're ambitious, but that would be a ballsy move even for you." Adrian leaned forward, slightly excited by the prospect. "But you play your cards right, and that seat will open up soon enough."

"I don't want it." It was out of my mouth before I'd even processed the words, the two men just as stunned as I was. I laughed, realizing that regardless of what I'd intended to say, my mouth was going rogue, so I might as well just go with it.

Alrighty, then.

"I'm tendering my resignation. Happy to give you whatever notice you need, or if you'd prefer, I can terminate immediately. I'll let you decide." Honestly I didn't give a shit, knowing they didn't like attorneys hanging around once they'd decided they were on the way out. They'd rather be short staffed, cutting people loose and making it look like the change in personnel was their decision than risk showing any sign of weakness. And I was prepared for that, happy even to be told to go pack up my desk and clear out.

"What?" Adrian choked out, the old guy looking like he might have a heart attack. "I thought you said you declined their offer."

"I have. This isn't about New York." Well, that wasn't entirely true, but it wasn't about a job offer I'd received.

"I'll remind you about your non-compete, Archer," Damien warned, clearly not pleased with my morning news. "And if this is about leverage, I'm not going to be extorted."

"It's not about leverage or extortion, or a job offer that I've received. And the non-compete only pertains to the Commonwealth of Massachusetts, and I'm not planning on practicing here."

Huh, more interesting news I was learning about my apparent plans.

"You're making a mistake, Archer. Whatever you think you're doing, it's the wrong move. You've got your next five years mapped out here. The kind of opportunity most men would kill for." This time it was Adrian, the man who'd not only recruited me but had been my mentor.

"Yeah, but it's my mistake to make. And for better or worse, it's one I intend to." Not sure when I'd decided I was done, especially since as far as Zara was concerned, shit was in limbo. She hadn't given me any indication she wanted me to go back to New York or if she was even interested in pursuing a relationship. Not some bullshit one-to-two-week fling, but a *real* relationship, where we both stopped pretending like we weren't meant to be together.

"Who? Who's made the offer?" Damien asked, not buying that I didn't have something else waiting in the wings.

And to be fair, there weren't too many attorneys who'd pull the pin without a backup plan. Even if it were only a lead, you'd expect there to be something. Which is what I'd originally intended when I'd sent the email. Give them notice of my intention to resign, and look for something else. But instead I decided to go off-script, screwing common sense and logic, and doing it all without a safety net.

"No offer. And you should know me well enough to know I wouldn't lie to you. I respect you both too much. But my mind is made up. So, I can hang around for a week or two, while you find someone else, or I can leave now. There's no hard feelings, gentlemen, I know it's just business. I'll leave you two to discuss."

My ass lifted from the chair and for the first time in months, I felt lighter. There was a chance I was going be spending the next few weeks canvassing every law firm in New York just looking for an in while I drained my savings. Manhattan rent was going to be brutal. But I'd never been known for being cautious. And it was time I started playing by those rules in my personal life as well as my professional.

"Lincoln. Is there anything we can do to make you reconsider?" Adrien grabbed my arm, giving it one last effort to change my mind. "We're willing to work with you, find a happy medium to get you what you want and what is best for the firm."

I shook my head, knowing there was nothing they could offer me. The one thing that I wanted—even though I wasn't sure it was something I could have—was in New York. And if I ever wanted to give myself a chance of happiness, I was going to have to take it.

"Nope. Nothing. But I genuinely appreciate the opportunity. If things were different," *if I hadn't met her, if I hadn't seen how different it could be*, "I wouldn't be leaving."

And before either of them could say anything more, I left Damien's office.

There were a lot of calls I needed to make, and I wasn't sure which one was going to come first. My parents were the obvious choice, both of them probably elated they might get to see more of me soon. But as much as I loved them, they weren't who I wanted to talk to. What I didn't know was, did she want to talk to me.

Chapter 26

Zara

"**Z**ara, stop hovering."

I'd spent every spare moment at my mother's bedside, making sure she was taking her pain meds and her recovery was on course. Her attacker had already been apprehended, but I didn't feel any better about things.

"I'm positive you have better things to do than be my nurse."

Despite her protests, I wasn't leaving. I had asked for and received a few days of personal time from work and didn't have anywhere else to be. And while I hated hospitals and everything that went with them, I wasn't leaving until they pushed me out the door.

"Actually, my schedule is wide open. Don't have anything else to do, so guess you're stuck with me."

Belle and I were taking turns, even though both my mother and father assured us we didn't have to. Belle was between auditions and loved having a captive audience; the nurses and doctors utterly adored her and her quirky monologues. I wasn't as entertaining, my effort to liven things up consisting of reading her gossip from trashy magazines and playing her old school jazz. I wished my motives had been purely altruistic, but as much as I loved my mother, I was still avoiding the situation with Lincoln.

He'd left—as he was always going to do—but I'd slammed the door. Every attempt he'd made since I'd left the hotel had been met with what I'm sure he perceived as indifference. What it actually was, was fear. I had no idea how to try and make it work, worried we wouldn't survive a long-distance relationship and which one of us would ultimately need to make the sacrifice. I wanted to believe love would conquer all, but I knew different. And when our last interaction had been so cold—again, I completely shared blame in that—I felt that maybe it was better to just let things cool off. I didn't want to have feelings for him, didn't want for him to be the first and the last thoughts I had every morning and every night, but ultimately it's not always about what you want. I was a realist, I should've known that.

"Fine, then tell me who's dating who." She pointed to the stack of paparazzi-filled rags I'd collected from the gift shop on my way in. "I really hope Hanna is still with her co-star, Matt. I know their love affair is probably just from spending so much time on set together, but they have real chemistry. You can tell when he looks at her, he is totally smitten, and I don't believe for a second that the feeling isn't mutual."

"Uhhhhhh," I sighed, wishing we could be discussing something other than love and affection. Surely celebrities were doing things other than falling in love and dating. "Fine, let's see if she's confessed her undying love for Matt or if she's run off with the pool boy."

With as much enthusiasm as I could muster, I grabbed the first magazine off the stack. I hadn't told my parents about Lincoln and our short-lived romance, so Mom assumed my despondence was my usual lack of excitement when it came to fairy-tale love stories. It was too hard to admit the truth to her, that I'd finally found someone who was perfect in every way and it just hadn't worked out.

My fingers flicked through the glossy pages while I sipped my coffee. It was hospital cafeteria coffee and incredibly bad, but somehow I figured that was what I deserved. "Are we ready?" I asked, finding the page with the goods. "I feel like we should have some dramatic music to lead us in."

My mother chuckled, appreciating my effort to be more entertaining—Belle would've belted out a rendition of some showtune for sure—as my eyes floated to the page. It was there, looking at celebrities, that I spotted a photo of . . .well, me.

"Shiiiiiiit," I coughed, my eyes opening and closing to be sure I was seeing it correctly. Nope, it wasn't some secret twin or mysterious doppelgänger who was snapped chatting to Edwin Carlisle at the recent gala he attended, it was yours truly. I hadn't even seen anyone take our photo, our interaction barely long enough to classify as a conversation. But regardless of that, and the fact I'd gone home with Lincoln, I was listed as *the mystery date of Mr. Edwin Carlisle, one of the city's most eligible bachelors.*

Great.

Just, fucking great.

"What sweetie?" my mom asked, her head lifting to try and see the page. "Did they break up? Is it confirmed? If neither of them are the source, I won't believe it."

Yeah, my biggest problem was no longer Hanna and her co-star Matt, but being linked to someone who I'd spent maybe ten minutes with and who wasn't the guy I was in love with. And that right there was why I didn't read magazines, preferring the *Wall Street Journal* and *The Atlantic.*

"Mom, I just need to step out for a moment and make a call." I grabbed the magazine and shoved it under my arm. I had no idea if any of the others had similar incriminating evidence, but I needed to get some facts straight before I explained to my mother why *With You* magazine thought I was dating a millionaire.

She looked puzzled but thankfully didn't argue, letting me shuffle out to the hall with my phone, magazine and handbag like I was looking to make a quick escape. Once in the hall I dug through my purse for the business card I thought I'd never use, dialing the number for Edwin Carlisle, a man, who for some reason, had lately become the bane of my existence.

I wasn't sure if he'd seen the article or even cared, no doubt going to think I was being hysterical and ridiculous for even bringing it up. It was too late to change my mind, the call connecting after the third ring. "Carlisle," he answered, his tone bored and impersonal.

"Hi, Edwin. It's Zara Mathews. We met at the gala. Last weekend." I shook my head, disappointed by my staccato greeting.

"Ahhhh, Zara." His voice instantly warmed. "How lovely to hear from you. I'm so glad you called. I was really hoping you would. I haven't stopped thinking about you."

Great, because on top of our fictional relationship the press was trying to pedal, I had to worry about him getting the wrong idea.

"Yeah, about that. This is sort of awkward to mention but did you happen to notice any stories about us recently?" I hedged, hoping it made me sound less pathetic. "You know, that we were dating."

He laughed, my ear filled with the sound. "You mean that photo of us in *With You*? Yeah, I saw it, you looked gorgeous by the way, red is definitely your color."

Oh, so he knew?

"Well, I think we should issue a statement making it clear that we're not," I added, knowing how stupid that sounded. "I'm not sure how they're able to get away with publishing lies about people, but all we were doing was talking."

"Wow, not sure if I'm offended or surprised. Is it really such a terrible thing to be linked to me?" I could hear the smile in his voice, clearly enjoying it. "I knew I liked you, but I hadn't realized how entertaining you could be. Are you still with that other guy? Because if you're not, I'd really like the opportunity to have dinner with you since we were robbed of the chance."

Not only did he not care about the speculation of his love life, but he was asking me out on a date. I hadn't even confirmed if Lincoln and I were no longer together, Edwin going in for the kill regardless.

"I'm not sure dinner would be a good idea since it would probably just feed the tabloids," I reasoned, not willing to admit I was no longer with Lincoln.

"Oh, so you *aren't* together." Edwin read between the lines. "What if I can promise there will be no cameras or reporters? Then will you have dinner with me?"

I rolled my eyes, wondering if women thought his insistence was charming. I'm sure he wasn't turned down a lot, probably assuming I was playing hard to get so I didn't seem easy. But no, it wasn't an act, my desire to have dinner with him truly being low.

"That won't change my answer. I'm sure you're a nice guy, and most women probably love your attention, but I'm not one of them." I was careful not to be unnecessarily cruel. After all, he'd been a victim of the gossip too, and it wasn't like he'd clubbed me over the head and dragged me into a cave. He'd been mostly respectful.

He sighed loudly, blowing out a long breath. "To be honest, I sort of enjoy that you're not like one of them. You really captured my attention, Zara. That's the only reason why I went along with Delia's stupid idea."

"What?" I gasped, fairly sure I was going to dislike Madame Delia more than I already did. "What was her idea?"

"I casually mentioned that I'd been interested in you, and she may have hinted to one of the reporters we were dating. You know the old adage, visualize it and it will happen. Besides, they were going to link me to someone anyway, might as well be someone I liked."

It felt like my head was going to explode. Not only had his sister-in-law had me chasing fantasy predictions from when I was a teenager, but she also saw fit to play the puppeteer in real life as well. What the hell was wrong with her? And why was she constantly messing with my life.

"You know, Edwin, I'll agree to dinner on one condition."

"Name it."

"You invite Delia. Seems fitting since she's the one who orchestrated the article. And no photographers."

I was so mad but needed closure, once and for all, and to confront Delia for the mess she'd caused. Granted, it wasn't entirely her fault, but I was looking for someone to blame and I couldn't find it in my heart to be angry at Lincoln. I was already tired at beating myself up so could use a new target, and deep down I was curious to see her face when I confronted her with her bullshit.

"Done," he agreed without any further negotiations. "Friday night at six, suit you?"

"She'll be there?" I asked, reaffirming that our "dinner" came with stipulations. "And if I see one photographer, I bail."

"She will. And no press. I promise."

I still wasn't sure I was making the right call, but I was already committed. And while I was positive nothing good would come of dinner with Edwin, it would be one night where I wouldn't be sitting at home, agonizing over whether to call Lincoln.

"Fine, I'll see you then. Send me the details." I was already regretting it. "And just so there's no mistake, Edwin, this isn't a date."

"Understood. Not a date. Just two friends having dinner."

Funny how my last dinner with Lincoln was supposed to be exactly that, not that it had worked out that way. Not that I'd be making the same mistake twice, in no way interested in anything romantic with Edwin. Even if I couldn't have Lincoln.

"Goodbye, Edwin."

"See you Friday, Zara."

The call ended, the phone held up against my ear even though the line was dead. The magazine crinkled underneath my arm, reminding me I still had some explaining to do. Even if I assumed my mom hadn't seen the photo, it was only a matter of time before someone else did. And it was better if my parents heard the whole sorry tale from me, rather than gossip fodder and speculation, and that included telling them about the real man I'd been dating that night.

I cursed softly under my breath, wishing things were different. For someone who apparently had her life so together, it had sure turned into a big mess.

Chapter 27

Lincoln

It seemed that once I'd made my mind up, things went fairly quickly. Amazing what can be done if you're willing to spend a little cash. My entire apartment was packed, shoved into a moving truck and transported to a storage unit in Rochester. Since I wasn't sure what I wanted to keep or even where I was going to live, I figured I'd leave it stashed near my parents and deal with it later.

Locke and Collins did their best to convince me to stay, throwing unbelievable amounts of money at me. Me, turning it down, had me wondering about my own sanity. But as valiant as the effort was, there wasn't anything that was going to sway me. But since I'd already made the choice to bail, we came to an amical solution for my termination. I'd operate as an independent contractor, doing some freelance work for them in New York. Meant they didn't have to send anyone from the Boston office and lose an extra person and they could still conduct business in NYC. We negotiated six-months with an option to continue. It gave me the freedom to leave without sticking around with a terminal end date, and them time to retain someone else. It also meant I wasn't completely unemployed, and I could head to New York sooner than later. And if I got to New York and Zara had decided that we were really going to be just friends, then . . . well I wasn't sure what exactly I was going to do, but it wouldn't change that I no longer wanted to be in Boston.

My parents—as expected—had been thrilled their middle, wayward child was moving to Manhattan. While only slightly closer than Boston, I think they saw my lifestyle in New England as questionable. Not that they'd ever said anything, supporting my choices even if they didn't always agree with them. And since I promised to be around more—birthdays, holidays—they were planning on holding me to it.

Zara, well, I hadn't exactly told her.

Not the smartest idea.

But since our last exchange hadn't been the greatest, I wasn't sure exactly what I was going to say. I reasoned that doing it face-to-face was better, which was probably why I'd been avoiding her texts. She'd sent two, giving me updates on her mom, but neither were anything more than what you'd expect from a group message. I wasn't even sure it *wasn't* part of a group message, the info dump feeling completely impersonal. And yeah, that probably made me a dick, but part of me was still mad she'd iced me out to start with.

So while I was—possibly irrationally—holding a grudge, I wanted to grab that beautiful body of hers and shake it. Then kiss her, take her to bed, and hold her all night. Because as much as she drove me insane, I was positive I wasn't able to be without her. And she had to know it too, regardless of how we came to be.

"All that money you have, you think you'd be able to afford a hotel." Nate laughed, helping me carry in my stuff. I'd packed the essentials, clothes, shoes, home office—basically all the things I couldn't live without.

I rolled my eyes knowing he wasn't even close to being annoyed we were becoming roommates again. "Why would I spend cash on a hotel when I can get daily heckling from you? You think the concierge is gonna tell me I have my head up my ass? Someone's got to keep my ego in check."

Nate nodded, pretending to agree with my assessment. "I bet for the right price, you could get anything. But you're right, no one is going to heckle you better than me. And it might be nice to have someone to come home to. Was thinking of getting myself a dog, at least you already come house trained."

"Woof," I mock barked.

Nate's spare room wasn't much bigger than a closet. It was barely big enough to fit a bed, with most of my belongings needing to stay in the living room. But even though it was going to be a tight squeeze until I found my own place, there was nowhere else I'd rather be. Well, with the exception of Zara's of course, but while I was hopeful, I wasn't completely delusional either.

"Have you called her?" Nate asked, reading my mind as to who I was thinking about as we got the last of my shit inside his apartment. "Because if we're taking a vote, mine is on calling her, telling her you're back, and having a serious conversation."

I shook my head, still unsure what to actually say to her. It wasn't like we broke up, or had a fight, or even agreed we weren't together anymore. If anything, our conclusion had been rather anticlimactic. It was just done, I guess. Or it would be done had I'd stayed in Boston.

Maybe if she hadn't needed to rush off to be with her mom, we might have had that conversation. The one where we admitted that loving each other wasn't just where it ended. Those feelings were ones that weren't easy to come by for me, and I had a hunch it was the same for her. And I'd bet, if we'd given each other a chance, seeing a future together would've been a forgone conclusion. But we'd both handled it badly. Her, shutting me out, and me, not fighting harder. Because really, when have I ever let go of something I wanted so easily? Apart for Zara, fucking never.

But it was a lot to gamble on, and it wasn't until I was miles away in my shitty apartment in Boston that I realized, I didn't want the alternative. I didn't want to be relegated to her past, to be some guy she messaged from time-to-time. To be the idiot who let her walk away.

"I'm going to go see her." I collapsed on Nate's couch, accepting the beer he handed to me. "I can't do this over the phone, Nate. I want to see her face, have her looking at me and know this isn't just a flash in the pan. That I love her, that I'm here, that I want to go as fast or as slow as she needs as long as she's going there with me. I can't walk away, Nate. It feels like it would be the biggest mistake of my life if I do."

Nate sighed, taking a seat beside me as he took a swig of his beer. "Awesome, because nothing says I love you like showing up on a doorstep unannounced when you haven't even spoken the last few days. Could you at least send a text? Ask her how her mom is? Or how she's enjoying the weather? Because if you went radio silent on me and then showed up with declarations of undying love a week later, I'd probably call the cops."

I laughed, figuring I was definitely walking the line between incredibly romantic and just plain stupid. "I have to get familiar with the NYPD sooner or later, might as well be now. But if it makes you feel better, I'll text her and ask her something."

"Anyone else and I'd be comforted by your compliance, you not so much." Nate pointed his bottle at me accusingly as he barked out a laugh.

It was only after we ate dinner and I was in bed that I pulled out my phone. I needed to be alone when I sent it, flicking to my contacts and just staring at her name for a minute or two before I opened up our last message thread. She'd sent two messages I hadn't responded to, rationalizing neither had really warranted a response. The last one cut me deeper than it should, re-reading it and almost having second thoughts.

Thanks for all your concern for Mom, she is recovering nicely. We're hoping she'll be home soon, and life will return to normal for all of us. Talk soon.

What did that even mean? Normal as in, without me? Normal was relative and such a terrible word, so why she'd used it was beyond me. And *talk soon*? It had pissed me off so much that I wasn't sure I wanted to talk at all. So started our standoff, which was probably childish and unproductive.

It had been two days since she'd sent it, and my fingers hovered over the keys on my phone. What did I even say? And when did I start agonizing over sending a fucking message? Cursing myself to grow a fucking pair and just write anything, I typed out a quick message and sent it before I could change my mind.

Glad she's doing better. I stalled, wondering what to say next. **How's the weather?**

What the fuck, Linc! Of all the most ridiculous things to ask, the weather was at the top of the list. Firstly, because if I wanted to know, I could look out a goddamn window, and second, because I didn't give a fuck. I didn't care about the weather, or anything else other than how she was doing. Was she really okay? Did she need me? Did she want to see me? And of all the possibilities, I went with weather.

Well done, asshole, nice work.

The three jumping dots appeared almost a second after I'd sent it, my heart beating way faster than it should.

> After a high of 77 it has cooled to a moderate 63. Tomorrow we're looking for a warm 81 with a 50% chance of afternoon showers.

I laughed, because I'd half-expected her to tell me to fuck off. Which would've been valid considering she'd probably assumed I didn't care. But instead, she'd given me the weather, no extra subtext because she'd always liked to keep me guessing. It was more promising than I could've hoped, reinforcing that we were far from over. It was tempting to just tell her how much I missed her, and her smart, sarcastic mouth. But I wasn't going to break the bubble.

> 50% chance is hedging their bets. It's not even a real forecast. I've zero respect for Meteorologists.

> Wow, strong opinions. Sounds like you were traumatized by unscheduled rainfall. I hear there's therapy for that.

> Thanks, I'll take it under advisement.

I was so close to just calling her, wanting to hear the snark firsthand. But it had gone well, so I wasn't going to push my luck. I waited to see if she sent something else, but those three dots didn't move. So instead I put my phone down and tried to get some sleep. I'd see her tomorrow because there wasn't a chance I could wait longer than that.

━━━

Assuming she was working, I waited until six before I made my way to her Greenwich apartment. Not willing to deal with parking in the city, I left my car at Nate's and hailed a cab. Of course

I probably could've walked from Nate's pad on the Lower East Side faster than it took to get through traffic. With it seeming like every person in Manhattan was on the road and no one was in any hurry.

"Can't you go around them?" I gestured to the windshield, feeling my impatience growing.

The driver just grunted something about me being a tourist, turning up the tunes on his stereo and ignoring me completely. Man, I should've insisted that my retainer for consulting work with Locke and Collins include Terry.

"Just drop me off here." I grabbed some cash out of my pocket, checking the meter for the fare. "I'll walk the rest of the way."

I didn't bother waiting for the change, giving him a bigger tip than he probably deserved as my feet hit the sidewalk. It was only a block to Zara's apartment, and I had to physically stop myself from running. Just as well considering my dress shoes wouldn't have made it easy, and I didn't want to look like I'd slept in my suit when I finally got to her doorstep.

My pulse was racing by the time I hit the buzzer, a crazy mix of nervous and excitement pumping through my veins while I waited for her to answer.

"Hello?" Belle's sweet voice came barreling through the speaker.

"Belle, it's Lincoln. Can I—"

She'd pressed the door release before I'd even finished the question. I didn't waste a second, taking the stairs two at a time until I got to the open door, Belle standing there in a pair of yoga pants and a tank, blinking in surprise.

"What took you so long?" She grabbed my arm and pulled me inside. "I hope you're here to profess your love, marry her and have lots of babies or I'm going to be very disappointed."

"Whoa, Belle." I held up my hands, looking around to see if her sister was around. "Slow down, and I think I should be talking to Zara before I answer any of that."

I hadn't really given much thought to marriage and babies. But now that Belle had mentioned it, I guess it wasn't such an out there idea. Yeah, yeah I wanted those things. I wanted a future with Zara and everything that came with it, including rings, and forevers, and babies if that's what she wanted.

"Well, you can't talk to Zara because she's on a date."

"A date?" I barked out, my pulse rate rising by the second.

It hadn't been that long, surely she hadn't moved on. And even though I knew she had every right to see someone else, I wanted to find the asshole and beat him to death with his own arms. "Belle," I warned, hoping she was kidding.

"I'm not telling you anything else until you tell me your intentions." She folded her arms across her chest, narrowing her eyes in an attempt to be intimidating. It might've worked too, except she was five-two and maybe a hundred pounds, but she was getting an A for effort.

"What *date*, Belle?" I did my best to stay levelheaded even though the idea of Zara being with some other guy was making me crazy.

"Intentions!" Belle demanded, proving to be a worthy adversary in not backing down. "Unlike my sister, I've got no plans this evening. I can stay here eyeballing you all night, hot shot!"

I had no doubt she could especially since she shared DNA with one of the biggest hard-asses I knew. "I'm in love with her, Belle. I can't live without her," I confessed, knowing there was no point denying it. I wanted to be saying those words to Zara, but since I couldn't, I'd tell whoever would listen. "Please tell me where she is."

Belle's lips spread into a smile, curling her hands to her chest. "I knew it. And you're going to stick around, right?" She looked hopeful.

"I'm going to stick around."

"Fine." Belle grabbed my arm again. "But if I tell you, you need to promise not to freak out."

"Freak out? Why the hell would I freak out?"

Sure, the woman I loved was currently on a date with some other guy I wanted to dismember with my bare hands, but how serious could it be? I'd been gone a week? It wasn't like Zara was going to magically fall for some asshole she'd just met.

Fine, bad example.

She wasn't going to just fall for some asshole she'd just met, *again*. That was our thing.

"Just tell me, Belle." I shook off the uneasy feeling, needing to know. "Where is she and who is she with?"

Belle's smile thinned into a grimace. "Just remember you promised."

I hadn't but I wasn't going to admit that, instead nodding my head.

"She's with Edwin Carlisle and they're at his penthouse. You know, since you clearly didn't want to be with her."

What.

The.

Fuck.

Heat traveled up my spine as I tried to rationalize it meant nothing. She'd had her chance with him, and she'd gone home with me, *chosen me*. It didn't matter that the prick could buy her an island off the coast of Bermuda and apparently was her soulmate. Not to mention that technically we weren't even dating so she was free to see, date, fuck, or anything else she wanted to do with anyone else.

"You promised." Belle's finger pointed accusingly at me. "So put your scary face away."

"It's not scary," I argued back, not needing a mirror to know I looked far from pleased. "This is the face I always have when I'm thinking, you just haven't seen it."

"Ha! Because I belieeeeeeve that," she scoffed, jabbing me in the arm. "Now tell me what you are going to do before I call Zara and tip her off."

Her other hand was already on her phone, the threat not an idle one.

I didn't even need to think, the words coming out of my mouth automatically.

"I'm going to go get her back."

Chapter 28

Zara

"This wasn't a date." I was welcomed by Edwin at the elevator to his penthouse, my dress so conservative there wasn't any mistake it was a business meeting.

"Of course not." Edwin grinned, leading me into his loft residence, the interior so immaculate it was obvious the cleaners had just left. The aroma of lemon floor cleaner was still wafting in the air, competing with the freshly cut peonies in the large glass vase on the entrance room table.

"Zara." Delia walked toward me with a warm smile and clearly no clue. "Such a lovely pleasure to meet you. I'm sorry we didn't get the chance the other night at the gala." Her eyes roamed to Edwin in a telling glance. "But it seemed we were both occupied."

"Yes, clearly." I shook her hand, wondering what the hell her brother-in-law had said about me. "But actually, we've already met."

It was tempting to go have dinner—I could see the polished wooden dining table set up with starched white linens from the hall—and having the conversation like civilized people. But I wasn't sure I could sit through dinner, and possibly give Edwin the wrong idea.

I had zero interest in dating him or anything that would classify as close to dating. And it had nothing to do with Lincoln and how much I still loved him.

Yes, *loved* him, because I was stupid and was in love with a man who came with all kinds of complications. Namely, one who was in another state and I wasn't even sure I'd see again. Unless he needed a weather update on the greater city of New York, and then apparently, I was his girl!

"Oh?" Delia laughed, completely bewildered like she hadn't made bullshit promises about me, my love life and her then future brother-in-law all those years ago. "I'm sorry. I'm usually really good with names and faces. Where did we meet? The Met Gala? Oh, was it the Hanson Society benefit? I have to admit, I did have slightly more champagne than usual that night." The giggle that followed almost as fake as her stupid ass predictions.

"Why don't we sit down, and you ladies can reminisce," Edwin suggested, his hand pressing against my lower back. "My brother Hal will be joining us for dinner, and I'm sure he'd love to hear how you lovely ladies know each other."

Great, I'd unwittingly walked into some cute double date, not what I'd hoped for.

"Ah, that won't be necessary." I rested my hand on Edwin's chest as I moved my ass out of reach from his sliding palm. "This is only going to take a minute, and then I'm going to go."

"You're going to leave?" Edwin looked utterly incredulous as he laughed. "Come on, Zara, it's dinner. I'll even keep my hands to myself."

"Oooooo such a tempting offer." I tapped my chin, pretending to give it some thought. "But I'm going to have to pass. I like my men to withhold sexual advances because of lack of consent, and not as a bargaining chip." I turned, facing a bewildered Delia who clearly had no idea what to say. Maybe she'd already started on the champagne and it was one of 'those' nights, or maybe she'd lost the ability to think for herself when she married a pig with a large bank account.

Ouch, that was harsh. I wasn't sure Hal was a pig. I was being very unfair in my profiling.

"Delia." I ignored my bias, secretly promising to repent for being an assuming, judgmental bitch *after* I left the Carlisle penthouse. "Do you remember working as a—" I waved my hand around trying to find an accurate description of the con-artist she'd been. "A fortune teller at Coney Island? I'll give you a moment to remember since it was probably when you were either a senior in high school or had just started college."

Since I didn't know how old she was—or had been—I was guessing. But no one forgot the shitty part-time hustle they had to do before they became an adult, even if it felt like a hundred years ago.

"Ummm, yes." Delia laughed, her body relaxing. "It was my freshman year of college. It was this stupid carnival attraction. Easy money. All I had to do was sit there and pretend like I knew what these gullible morons wanted me to say. Occasionally I'd give them the opposite, which would just make them come back. Why? Did you work there too?"

It was the most anyone had said since I'd arrived, her trip down memory lane obviously a fond one. Pity it wasn't going to stay like that.

"No, I didn't work there." I pretended to laugh, annoyed she could be so flippant about playing with people's emotions. Sure, I knew it was fake, but I still remembered how upset my sister had been. "My sister Belle and I were customers. You told her she was going to never be happy in love, and me." My hand dramatically fluttered to my chest in a move that would've made

Belle proud. "And I was going to fall in love and marry Edwin Carlisle."

Edwin laughed nervously, looking between us and probably assuming I was crazy. "Hey, I just wanted to take you to dinner, maybe sleep with you. I didn't say anything about getting married."

"Really?" I pretended to look shocked as I rolled my eyes. "Here I was thinking that your sister-in-law was really a modern-day cupid, and we were destined for eternal happiness. Give me a break."

"Look, I don't remember what I said." Delia held out her hands, trying to put distance between us. "I was high a lot, Hal and I had just started dating and Eddie was a pain in the ass. I used his name a few times."

"How was I a pain in the ass?" Edwin shot back indignantly. "And why the hell did you drag me into it?"

"Because these girls would never have met you, stupid. They were riding the Ferris wheel and eating two-dollar cotton candy. Unless you hired them to be your maid, none of them were going to end up your wife."

"Wowwwww." It flew out of my mouth, wondering what kind of entitlement you needed to have to say something like that. And considering Delia had been a college student working a Coney Island sideshow, she probably hadn't been born with a trust fund, her elitist boyfriend/later husband affording her the audacity.

"A person's worth doesn't come from their social standing, and you have no idea what someone is destined to become." I was offended, not for myself, but for the other people who Madame Delia had not only duped but probably used as punchlines over the years. "Funnily enough, I came here annoyed at you." My eyes connected with Delia. "But now I just feel sorry for you. That the only way you could feel superior was to make others feel small. Seems like you should be spending more time working on your own self-esteem instead of attending charity galas."

"Hello, everyone! What did I miss?" Hal burst through the door, his smile a mile wide. "I hope dinner is soon though, because I'm famished." He moved to his wife's side dropping a kiss on her shocked-as-shit face.

"Well, Hal, you can have my share." I bowed dramatically—seriously Belle would be so proud. "I'll be leaving you all, figure I should go slum with the help." I turned, heading toward the door but not before tossing over my shoulder. "And for the record, Edwin, I'll be making a statement clarifying that we aren't and never were dating. It's nothing personal, but I wouldn't want my reputation sullied by the assumption that I dabble with *your kind*. And I'd be careful what blind items you suggest to tabloids as well. I've not lost a libel suit yet, and knowing your net worth would make this very attractive to a two-dollar-cotton-candy-eater like myself. See ya."

Then I flipped them off—completely childish but whatever—leaving them all stunned as I called the elevator and got inside. I was so done with them, the stupid prophecy, and any and all things that involved any Carlisle.

I couldn't wait to tell Belle, almost wishing she'd been there to see it. The smile was still on my face when I got to the lobby, my phone in my hand ready to call an Uber to take me home.

"Zara."

My name stopped me in my tracks, spoken by a voice I'd dreamt about all week. I was almost worried I was hearing things, until I turned around and saw him there.

Lincoln.

Here.

In front of me.

"Hey," he said softly moving closer, hesitating for only a moment before resting his hands on my hips. "I didn't trust the weather report, figured I should come see it for myself."

I couldn't breathe, wanting to be wrapped in his arms and kissed more than I wanted oxygen. "Yeah? Trust issues don't speak fondly of your character, you should work on that."

"I trust you." He brought me closer, our faces only inches apart. "So maybe you could help me with that."

My mouth opened to answer but before I could get any of the words out, his lips were on mine, kissing me. My moan was stolen by his inhale as my hands latched onto the front of his shirt. I knew I wasn't dreaming but couldn't be sure it was real, desperate to absorb every second with him in case it faded again. I just didn't want to be without him, the idea of saying goodbye to him a second time—like actually saying goodbye—something I wasn't sure I could face. Maybe that's why I'd avoided it in the first place, figuring it was better to live in the possibility of purgatory than a reality of hell.

His hands were everywhere, touching my body in a way I was sure was inappropriate for an upscale apartment building on the Upper East Side. But I didn't care, ignoring the clearing throat coming from the doorman who was probably three seconds from throwing us out. I needed to feel him, to feel his mouth on mine while I touched him, if only to convince myself that he was there and it was really happening.

"Lincoln." His name was the only coherent thing my mouth was able to utter.

Please don't stop, I didn't add, unwilling to waste the opportunity to say words.

"Fuck, I've missed you," he groaned out, his lips seeking mine so desperately you'd think it had been years since we last saw each other, not a week.

It might as well have been a lifetime.

"What are you doing here?" I gasped out between kisses, unwilling to stop to ask properly.

"Belle told me." *Kiss.* "Needed to see you." *Kiss.* "Don't date him."

I laughed, trying my best to pull myself away. "I meant in New York, and Belle played you. This wasn't a date."

"Your sister is diabolical." Lincoln chuckled against my mouth. "And I'm in New York because I couldn't live without you. Leaving you was a mistake, Zara. I should never have gotten on the plane."

My eyes got misty, tears pooling at the corners wondering why I'd needed to hear those words so much. I should've told him not to go. I should've fought for us too. "I didn't give you much choice. I'm sorry, Lincoln. I pushed you away and that wasn't fair. Letting you go was *my* mistake."

He wrapped his arms around me, bringing me closer and kissing the top of my head. "So can we agree that we're both at fault, because regardless of who is responsible, I just know I can't live without you. Not since that day at that hospital, and every single day since."

"Ahhh, well that mistake was most definitely mine." I laughed, finally seeing the funny side. "And Lincoln, it is by far my greatest mistake."

"That's a good thing, right? This isn't the part where you tell me you're shacking up with Moneybags and I was just a distraction." He grinned.

I elbowed him in the ribs, rolling my eyes. "Please, like I would. I'm dating a high-powered Boston attorney who makes CEOs cry."

"Yeah, about that." He grimaced, wrinkling his nose. "I no longer live in Boston and technically I no longer work at Locke and Collins."

"What?" I coughed out, not sure which part of his statement surprised me the most. "What are you saying, Lincoln?"

He took my hands, kissing each of my knuckles. "I no longer live in Boston, Zara. I broke the contract on my apartment, paid out my lease, and packed up a big truck. Oh, and I resigned."

"Why?" I squeaked, daring to hope it meant what I thought it did.

He smiled, the warmth of it lighting up his beautiful dark blue eyes. "Because I'm in love with this crazy woman in New York, and I was tired of breaking things apart instead of putting them together. I want to do more, Zara. I want a life that I'm proud of and not just because I make a lot of money. And that life has to include you."

It was one of the most beautiful things someone had ever said to me, the tears I'd desperately tried to stop overflowing and falling down my cheeks. "You wouldn't ask me to move?" I shook my head, realizing how unfair it seemed that he was making the sacrifice, taking that huge chance.

"Are you kidding?" He laughed. "My future wife is going to be a Supreme Court Justice. She's got important work to do right where she is."

"Future wife?" My heart skipped a beat, and not because I couldn't see myself marrying him, but because I could. I could see all of it. Marriage, kids—holy shit, where did that come from—and growing old together. And I'd never felt that way before.

Lincoln tucked me close to his body, whispering in my ear, "yeah, you are definitely my future wife. We'll both act surprised when I eventually ask and you say yes, and let's face it, you already started working on our prenup. Or if you want to be the one who asks, I'm fine with that too."

"Big of you." I coughed out a laugh between sobs, completely and utterly sure I wanted nothing more than to be his wife. "But let's try dating for a little while first."

Lincoln lifted his eyes to the ceiling, shaking his head. "Now she wants me. Now I'm unemployed and homeless. I have to tell you, Zara, you're taking this pro bono work waaaaay too seriously."

I shrugged, unwilling to let him go. "The heart wants what the heart wants."

And my heart wanted Lincoln.

Epilogue

Lincoln

"My god! My eyes!" Nate walked in dramatically, shielding his vision as he walked in. He'd been working the mid-shift at the ER and we hadn't expected him so soon. Guess we'd lost track of time, my habit of getting Zara naked the minute she walked in the door not a great one to have when you had a roommate. "You have a bedroom, Linc. It has a door." He shook his head while I pulled a blanket over Zara.

Since Zara had been lying on the couch with her legs wrapped around me, he hadn't seen much, unless you counted my bare ass. But I didn't want Nate catching a glimpse of anything more than he should, regardless of whether he wanted to or not.

Zara chuckled, adjusting the blanket so she was decent, my cock still hard and buried inside of her even though we'd been forced to stop.

Honestly, we weren't trying to be deviants or disrespectful. But with both of us working so much, we were taking advantage of all the spare moments. And being inside Zara was one of my favorite things.

"Sorry, Nate." I laughed, Zara playfully punching me in the chest. "I thought you weren't back until later."

"Sorry, Nate," she added. "It's Lincoln's fault. He's a bad influence but I promise it won't happen again."

"My fault?" I scoffed, knowing exactly who had started our latest naked escapade and it *hadn't* been me. Not to say that I wouldn't have if she hadn't, but in the current instance it was Zara's hands down the front of my pants which had stopped us from making it to my bedroom. "You want to rethink your position, counselor?"

"I don't care who started it." Nate stormed past, holding his hands up to his face. "But this is the third time in a month and I haven't seen this much heterosexual sex since college. Someone needs to pay for my therapy." He rushed into his room and slammed the door.

"I feel bad." Zara bit her lip, her eyes darting in the direction Nate had disappeared to. "He's been so good about letting you stay here, and it is *his* apartment."

"But it's my couch," I shot back indignantly. "And right now." I thrust in deeper, unable to stop despite our interruption. "I want to make love to my girlfriend on it. I'll pay for the therapy."

Zara's hand slapped against her mouth, trying to stop the moan. She'd been close right before Nate had gotten home, and I was hoping I could get her back there. I loved it when she was about to come, the way her body tensed, how her breathing changed, and the desperation in her sighs. It got me so worked up, it was sometimes an effort to make sure she came first.

"Come for me, baby." I leaned forward and whispered in her ear, "I need to feel you, Zara, to hear you. I need you so much."

"Linc-oln." My name breathed out as her chest rose and fell. "Oh, that feels so good."

Don't get me wrong, if she'd asked me to stop, I'd have done exactly that. I'd have either dealt with the painful hard-on, cursing Nate and my blue balls, or gone and jerked off in the bathroom. But Zara wasn't some little wallflower I'd corrupted, which was why—in case anyone had forgotten—we were having sex in the living room in the first place.

"Yeah, baby. I know it feels good." My hand dropped down between us, circling her clit. "You're so close."

Zara's eyes widened, two hands clamping her mouth as she suppressed the scream. She didn't need to tell me she was there, my cock feeling the pulsing against the shaft as she came undone. It was all I needed, following her over that cliff as I shoved my face into the back of the couch and rode it out. I wasn't a fan of being quiet, but I wasn't a total prick either. And Zara was right, it was still Nate's apartment and he'd been more than generous.

"We're so bad." Zara kissed my chest, my skin still tingling from the amazing high. "I hope he doesn't hate us."

"No one could ever hate you." I kissed the top of her head, slowly sliding out of her. "But if he's going to blame anyone for this, it will be me."

Once the impending orgasm had been taken care of, I'd agree it hadn't been my finest moment. But it was hard to be rational when you were making love to the most incredible woman you'd ever met. It was more surprising that I *hadn't* done more stupid shit.

Lifting my head to make sure Nate's door was still closed, I planted my feet on the ground and lifted her off the couch. Taking the blanket with us, I carried Zara to my closet/bedroom and laid her on my bed. "Better?" I asked, closing the door and switching on the light. "And I promise it won't happen again." *Well* . . . "Okay, I promise to try so it doesn't happen again."

Zara laughed, shuffling up the bed and kissing me. "I think I might have something that will help with that. Wait here a minute, okay?"

My eyes narrowed as she wrapped the blanket around her like a makeshift dress, cracking open my bedroom door and checking if the coast was clear. Satisfied that we'd traumatized Nate enough he might never leave his bedroom, she crept back out to the living room and returned shortly carrying something in her hand.

"What is that, Zara?" I stared at what looked to be a black velvet jewelry box. "Tell me it's not what I think it is."

I wasn't kidding when I said I wanted to marry Zara.

Marriage, kids, a dog, getting old and arguing over television channels—the whole fantasy. But as much as I said I was okay with her asking me, I really wasn't. And not because I was some old-fashioned asshole who didn't believe a woman could. That was shit I didn't and would never subscribe to. But because I wanted it to be special, with a ring that I'd had custom designed because nothing in a store window would be so uniquely her. There'd be dancing and wine—or arguing and coffee, I was a realist—and then I'd get down on my knees because that was the way I felt whenever I was not with her. It was because of her I was able to stand tall. Because of her that I was able to start over in a new city, and not worry about whether or not my career would suffer. And I wanted that for both of us.

So to see what I thought was a ring box, when I still hadn't even found a full-time job, was not how I'd wanted that moment to go.

"Wow, are you freaking out, Lincoln?" She shoved the box behind her back, grinning like she was enjoying my anxiety. Had I mentioned my girlfriend was a sadist?

I shook my head, planting my ass on the bed and refusing to look at her. She couldn't do it if I didn't make eye contact, right? Who the hell proposed to someone when they weren't looking? I'd wait her out, keeping my eyes nailed to the floor as two feet appeared in my field of vision.

"Lincoln," she purred, my name breathed out like aural sex. "Come on, baby, look at me."

There was a gentle thud, the blanket that had been wrapped around her pooling on the floor as her sexy bare legs got closer.

Fuck.

She was naked.

"Don't you want to see me?" She reached down, grabbing one of my hands and placing it on her ass, my hand staying put even after she'd pulled hers away. She took hold of the other one, my traitorous hand curling around her tit even though I'd threatened my own arm with amputation, neither of those bastards listening to me.

"Ooooo I like your hands on me."

See, sadist, her body shimmied, and I had no fucking choice but to look up. I was trying to fight it, promising myself all kinds of things if I just held strong, but at the end of the day, I could never say no to her.

"Ahhhh, there he is." She grinned, the black velvet box held out in front of her proudly, right below her tits. You know, so I couldn't miss it. "I have something very special to give you."

I swallowed, reassuring myself I could still do everything I had planned. I could still design the ring, have the moment, do all the things even after she asked me to marry her. And in the end, did any of it really matter? I wanted to be with her, and she wanted to be with me, so if asking me to marry her was so important, then I'd suck it up and let her do it her way.

"Okay." I nodded, reluctantly removing the hand on her tit and accepting the box. The other hand from her ass also had to forfeit its position seeing as opening it was a team effort.

"Lincoln Archer." She took a breath, waiting for me to crack open the lid. "Will you move in with me?"

Inside the box, nestled against the soft black material was a silver key.

"Jesus, Zara." I grabbed at my chest, holding the key tightly in my hand. "I thought you were going to—"

"Hey, slow down there, Lincoln. It's been a month. We still haven't even ironed out the prenup." She giggled, knowing exactly what I would've thought when I'd seen the box.

Absolute.

Sadist.

"Yes." I pulled her into a kiss. "Yes, I'll move in with you. I'm assuming you have cleared this with Belle?" I was pretty fond of her little sister, and while I didn't need anyone's blessing to be with Zara, I didn't want to be the thing that came between them.

"Who do you think got the key cut? It was my idea to put it in the box." She grinned, wrapping her arms around me.

"Good. Then that's a double yes." I kissed her, loving the feel of her naked skin on mine. "Wait, should we call her and let her know? I know how impatient she is waiting for news."

But before Zara could answer me there was a thundering of fists on the door.

"Don't come in," both Zara and I screamed out, cursing that my bedroom didn't have a lock. I tossed on a pair of sweatpants, giving Zara some basketball shorts and a T-shirt so we were at least semi-decent. And took a deep breath before opening the door.

"I told her 'stop, don't do it, no'," Nate chuckled standing behind a beaming Belle. "But she overpowered me."

"She overpowered you?" I raised a brow, Nate being over a foot taller than Zara's sister, and at least eighty pounds heavier.

"I'm stronger than I look." Belle flexed her non-existent bicep muscle, screaming when she saw the key in my hand. "Yay! He's moving in! OMG, I'm so excited. I finally get a big brother."

Belle flung her tiny body at me, hugging with all her might. "And don't forget, when you get married, I'm still the maid of honor."

"Belle!" Zara shook her head, pulling her free from my chest. "He just agreed to move in, can we chill on the wedding talk?"

Belle grinned at her sister. "Sure, sure. But I have a witness." She pointed to Nate. "And a verbal contract given in good faith is almost as good as a written one provided it is witnessed by someone impartial and in good standing."

"You sure she didn't go to law school?" I whispered, dropping my lips to Zara's ear. "Because she'd have made a killer trial lawyer."

"I know." Zara sighed.

"Okay!" Belle clapped, calling us to attention. "Both of you get properly dressed and then we're going out to celebrate."

"Belle," Zara started to protest. "Can't we just order take out and chill on the couch?"

"You mean the couch you both defiled and will require hospital-grade sanitizing before I sit on it again?" Nate smirked. "Yeah, I'm going to take a pass and go with Belle on this one."

I flipped him off, not bothering to hide my grin.

Belle waved her hand, overruling Zara's objection. "Pleaseeeeeeee. You know I require celebrations. Even Nate agrees. And since the last time I insisted, you both met, I figure you should be thanking me instead of complaining. Now hurry up, I'm hungry." Belle clapped again before turning to leave. "Oh, and Lincoln." She paused, standing just outside the doorway. "We need more creamer. Be a super big brother and see that we don't ever run out. Okay? Thanks." She blew a kiss and then disappeared.

"You want to change your mind?" Zara asked, shaking her head as she closed the door. "Unfortunately, you've done it once, and now she's going to expect it. It's not too late for you to find your own place."

"Nah." I pulled her in for a hug. "I've made up my mind. And I will make endless trips to the store for creamer, and take constant demands from Belle if it means I get to be with you. Think of it as *my* greatest mistake."

To keep up-to-date with all T Gephart's news,
appearances, and releases,
please subscribe to her mailing list
(http://eepurl.com/bws5Av).

Also please consider leaving a review
on your retailer of choice. They help the author
and future readers and we're all eternally grateful.

Acknowledgements

Thank you so much to my family who have loved me through one of the toughest times in my career. Gep, Jenna, Liam and Woodley, I know it hasn't been easy, but thanks for loving all my broken parts.

Thanks to my extended family and friends, who I haven't seen nearly enough. 2022? 20223? Whenever it is we come together, there are going to be so many hugs. Love you guys so much.

Thanks to Sally Thorne who told me I wasn't done. Who called me as often as I needed, reading chapters in parts, telling me she wanted more. I don't think I'd have finished without your constant encouraging—sometimes angry—emoji filled messages. #IfYouCan'tLoveYourselfHowTheHellYouGoingToLove SomeoneElse.

Special thanks to the beautiful Gayle Williams, who was going through her own hardship. No matter what was going on in your life, you always wanted to be in mine. Thanks for all your love and support, and most of all, your beautiful heart.

Thanks Kimberly, Aimee, and Caroline and everyone at Brower Literary and Management. Thanks so much for being so understanding and supportive, love you ladies!!!

Thanks so much, Nichole Strauss from Insight Editing. I blew through every single deadline, and you stayed with me. Thanks for believing in my work and working with my craziness.

MK! What can I possibly say about you? You read this one in record time, your insight invaluable as always. Thank you, thank you, a million thank yous.

Thank you Elaine York from Allusion Graphics LLC, Publishing and Book Formatting for making my pages look beautiful. And for working with my crazy schedule—what schedule?—and not telling me no. Lord, I'd have cried if you did!

And Hang Le, thank you seems like it's not enough. I've never been so horribly unorganized and just a general hot mess as I was this year. Every single date went out the window and you squeezed me in regardless. I will never forget your kindness and grace and your incredibly beautiful covers. Thank you, all the hugs xx

Thanks a million to Rebecca from Rebecca Fairest Reviews Editing Services for proofreading and final eyes. I know you had your own busy time, and yet you fit me in, I can never be thankful enough.

So much thanks, love, hugs, and lack of social distancing to all my author friends both near and far. I hate it's been so long since I've seen you guys, I miss you so goddamn much. Every connection, message, text, smoke signal—whatever—means the world to me. Can't wait until we're together again and I can give you all inappropriate hugs filled with gratitude. PS Keep those books coming, I love reading all your beautiful words.

Thank you, thank you, THANK YOU to all the bloggers, reviewers, bookstagrammers, group admins and promoters who read, promote, review, and share my work. I will never take any of it for granted and am so thankful for all your LOVE and SUPPORT.

Thanks so much to Mary Dubé from Grey's Promotions. It's been a pleasure to partner with you and share my work with the world with you guys at the helm.

Thank you, Liz, MJ, and Jillian at 1001 Dark Nights.

THANK YOU TO THE T GEPHART REVIEW CREW AND ENTOURAGE. Thanks for all your love, support, messages, and just for showing up. It means the world to me and I adore you.

Special thanks to Pole and Aerial Divas Richmond and Pole Divas Reservoir who helped me put myself together this year. Your love, support and encouragement made me feel so empowered and strong, and each and every one of you is a beautiful precious soul. Shannon, Casey, Franny, Lauren, Bec and ALL the DIVAS—I came looking for fitness and instead found a family.

And lastly, as always, thank YOU. To the person reading this book who could've easily been reading something else. I will never take the opportunity to entertain you for granted. It is—as always—an honor. YOU ARE BEAUTIFUL, STRONG AND BRAVE. And don't let anyone else tell you different. PS eat the cake, wear the dress, and dance like EVERYONE is looking but you no longer give a shit.

About the Author

T Gephart is a *USA Today* and International bestselling author from Melbourne, Australia.

With an approach to life that is somewhat unconventional, she prefers to fly by the seat of her pants rather than adhere to some rigid roadmap. Her lack of "plan" has resulted in a rather interesting and eclectic resume, which reads more like the fiction she writes than an actual employment history. She'd tell you all about it, but the statute of limitations hasn't expired yet. But all those crazy twists and turns have led her to a career she loves—writing romantic comedy.

When she isn't filling pages with sassy and sexy characters with attitude, she's living her own reality show in the 'burbs of Melbourne with her American husband, two teenage children, and her fur child—Woodley.

She loves adventure, to laugh, travel, and strives to live her life to the fullest.

Connect with T

tgephart.com
Facebook (https://www.facebook.com/tgephartauthor)
Goodreads
Twitter (https://twitter.com/tinagephart)

Other Books

The Lexi Series
Lexi
A Twist of Fate
Twisted Views: Fate's Companion
A Leap of Faith
A Time for Hope

The Power Station Series
High Strung
Crash Ride
Back Stage

The Black Addiction Series
Slide
Sticks
Stand

#1 Series
#1 Crush

#1 Player

#1 Rival

#1 Lie

#1 Muse

#1 Love

Collision Series
Train Wreck

Car Crash

Hot in the City Series
Send Me Crazy

One Click Love

Not Just Friends

Between The Lines

Crazy in Love Series
My Greatest Mistake

Crazy in Love #2 (Belle's Story- Coming soon!!!)

Crazy in Love #3

Crazy in Love #4? (I mean, it could happen, I suck at planning)

Standalones
The Fall

One-Night Stand-In

Viral

Made in United States
North Haven, CT
20 November 2022

26973859R00178